# Murder Is An Education

Randy L. Hilmer

Randy L. Hilmer

This book is a work of fiction. Names, characters, places and incidents are the product of the author's imagination or are used fictitiously. Any resemblance to actual events, locales or persons, living or dead, is coincidental. Actual race track names were utilized in writing this book of fiction, however, the races, lengths of races and the frequency of races are all fictitiously used.

Copyright © 2015 Randy L. Hilmer

All rights reserved

ISBN-13: 978-1502928986
ISBN-10: 1502928981

# DEDICATION

To my brother-in-law and sister, Gary and Sheri Albertson.

## ACKNOWLEDGMENTS

I would like to thank Frank Utley for his guidance and expertise in the field of law enforcement practices, procedures and investigation techniques.

Thanks to Joe Coe for giving me precise information concerning weaponry.

I would like to thank Jeff Hahn for sharing his knowledge of security procedures and equipment.

I could not have completed this book without the editing skills of Debbie Thomas. Your countless hours of editing, re-editing and re-editing again and the meticulous manner in which you spent time searching for just the right word to enhance my story is so much appreciated.

# Chapter 1
# The Detective
*December 2012*

The large second floor open air room was empty of all other life. Desks with computer terminals, scattered papers, over flowing in-baskets and an occasional photo of a loved one were his only company. The room was dark except for one overhead fluorescent fixture beaming above his desk graciously left on by the last person who had wished him a Merry Christmas and departed for the evening. The decorated pine tree standing in one corner had all of its lights off and its garland twinkled with the reflection from the sole light source.

He slumped in his chair with files upon files spread across his rather disorganized desk. He was the only one who knew where everything was. He shuffled between folders, opening one, thumbing through it, laying it down and opening another. The words, photos and timelines in the folders were becoming blurred by fatigue. He solemnly peered out of the window near his desk and watched the heavy snowflakes lazily but steadily drifting past as they were illuminated by the street lamp below. It had been snowing since early in the afternoon and had accumulated to almost eleven inches.

He was practically in a hypnotic state staring at the moving snow. It was mesmerizing and his eyelids were becoming heavy with fatigue and were slowly closing until he could see a picture of the snow moving past the window with his eyes closed. His head jerked as sleep nearly overcame him. He sat up in his chair, blinked his eyes back to the reality of the evening and continued his perusing of the files.

Detective Gilbert Clifton was a well-respected, down to earth, no fluff type of guy. He earned his reputation as a pit bull investigator; never relinquishing his hold on a case until it was firmly in the hands of a district attorney for prosecution. During his thirty-three year career with the Camden, New Jersey Police Department, he had spent twenty-seven in the homicide division. Gil was not about to retire, although he could have. He passed up chances for promotion because he was not the type to just sit around and make decisions. Decisions that seemed more based on politics than reality. That was not his style. He wanted the action of solving violent crimes. He was, after all, a victim's advocate.

However, because of his strong personality, he more frequently than not bumped heads with the suits one flight up. He envisioned his captain peeking through peep holes in the floor of the third level to keep an eye on the detectives who did the *'real'* work. The work that he loved and the work he was good at. But the files before him screamed in silence of his inability to solve these seven murder cases.

In August, three unrelated murders with no apparent connection brought him to a tenable conclusion that he may have to consider - there very well may be a serial killer in the area. He had alerted Joseph McCadry, the precinct captain and his boss, of his suspicions but because each victim had been murdered by different means it was unlikely the murders were committed by the same person as McCadry had concluded.

The suits were keenly aware of the elections coming up in November and the last thing the department needed was pandemonium because of a serial killer fanning the flames of public unrest and fear. That, in turn, would probably get that radical (as thought of by the inner sanctum of the police department working class) Carl Brisbane elected as sheriff. Brisbane vehemently advocated policy transparency of police procedures, open public hearings for officer involved shootings and overtime reduction for all officers on the force. Although McCadry never came right out and told him not to explore the possibility, Gil knew by his superior's nonverbal communication that the serial killer theory was the road which should be less traveled.

The public was uninformed about a possible serial killer. The modus operandi was different for each of the murders which were committed. The news media never picked up on the investigations as being linked. Nothing came out of the precinct in their weekly press conference sessions.

All that changed in September. The press was starting to ask questions. Somehow they found out that Detective Gil was working on a fourth murder case suspected as being linked to a serial killer. Newspapers ran headlines and Carl Brisbane could be heard on every radio talk show and all television news conferences espousing his platform of open investigations to the public. A torrential avalanche of advertising bytes proclaiming nondisclosure of information was detrimental to protecting the public welfare and was on the air more or less every hour. It didn't matter to Brisbane if that kind of information could actually hinder an investigation or not.

It had been speculated by the homicide department, and Detective Gil in particular, that someone had leaked the information; someone on the inside. Most likely because of that, Carl Brisbane was later elected sheriff and during the transition of power, was now coming down hard on Gil and his team to solve the murders. The new sheriff was, once again, using the news media for his own agenda. Gil felt contempt for Captain McCadry but had absolutely no proof his boss had leaked the information.

Detective Gil, as he liked to be called, would clear one to two homicides per month. The first forty-eight hours of each investigation was the most important. If there wasn't an arrest by then, the probability of an arrest started to dwindle dramatically. If that happened, they would need a big break to lead the way to solving it. He and his partner, Cornell Bush, had received no such break in the cases lying before him. So far they had no forensic evidence, no eyewitnesses, no pattern and no clues.

At age 54, Gilbert Clifton had balding gray hair atop his roundish head. He was slightly overweight but not out of shape. His deep-set inquisitive eyes showed a person who was always in deep thought and appeared never to really focus on what a person might be saying to him. That was not the case but it did make him seem aloof to his fellow officers. But, not to his partner as Cornell knew Gil better than any person alive. Even better than Gil's girlfriend, an attractive lady in her early forties who owned a successful advertising agency. Cassandra Marshall was twelve years his junior, at 42 and still a petite 5'6" to Gil's hefty 6'3" frame but she made up for it with a confidence of her abilities in business as well as in life. The age difference did not matter to either one. Cassandra was very passionate about everything she did. She put her heart and soul into every project and that carried over to her relationship with Gil.

They met at a fundraiser for children with Eisenmenger Syndrome, a charity for which Gil gave his wholehearted support because his sister died from the heart related disease. Gil had asked Cassandra if she had a sibling or child with the disease but she said only that she had heard about the disease and knew no one personally who had it. She expressed her desire to help in any way she could. That was two and a half years ago and the two had been keeping steady company ever since.

Together Gil and Cornell had solved over thirteen homicides within the last six months; a good record by anyone's account. But they had seven unsolved cases, now in folders, troubling Gil on this Christmas Eve. He looked at his watch: 9:37. He was supposed to have spent Christmas Eve with Cassandra. He picked up his phone and dialed her number.

She answered with only concern in her voice for his well-being. During their two and a half year relationship, she was now accustomed to his long hours sometimes lasting well into the night or early morning. She was relieved just to hear his voice.

"I'm sorry," he genuinely apologized. "Do you still want to spend the rest of the night with me? Am I still welcomed?"

"Of course, honey. Come over as soon as you can but be careful, the snow can be treacherous. Besides, we have the rest of the night to enjoy."

He put the receiver back and gently patted it as a small smile crept onto his face. She was wonderful. She understood. She understood him.

They hadn't moved in together but he spent many nights in her cozy one story, two-bedroom home nestled in a nice suburban neighborhood. He found solace there and once he heard her voice he was anxious to have her in his arms once again. Gil took one last look at the file covers, which to him now looked like tombstones, as if to indelibly etch in his mind each name.

*Allen Venter, white male, 42, divorced, shot at close range with a .45 caliber pistol in an alley in a rundown business district. Harold McDonald, white male, 65, married, victim of a sniper's bullet in the parking lot of a convenience store. Dorothy Coel, white female, 29, single, suffocated in her apartment near downtown. Roberta Waverly, black female, 31, married, strangled in an upscale park. Adin Williamson, black male, 23, single, stabbed in a gay bar. Yosef Rabinovich, white Jewish male, 34, married, bludgeoned in his own jewelry shop. Hikaru Yoshi, Asian American male, 25, single, poisoned in a sports club near Rutgers University where he was a graduate student.*

A pall cascaded over him as he laid the last file on his desk and realized one thing for sure that he certainly didn't like. Nevertheless, he owed his best efforts to these victims. Gil reluctantly concluded that it was time to talk to The Professor.

---

Cassandra kept a vigil through her front room window waiting for Gil to arrive and share their third Christmas together. The streets were not plowed and her driveway had over six inches of freshly fallen snow. It was warm enough outside to make the snow wet and heavy which also meant when cars drove over it the snow would compact and become very slippery. She was slightly concerned.

She busied herself puttering around the house, rearranging pillows on the couch which didn't need rearranging. She made sure the table was set perfectly by moving a spoon or fork ever so slightly and checked on their late night supper. It was almost 10:45 when she heard Gil's car race its engine to get further into the driveway. She turned the lights down low, adjusted the instrumental Christmas music and picked up the two glasses of pinot noire she had poured and placed them on a table next to the front entrance. She opened the door to greet him.

Gil came into the house stamping his feet on the throw rug to remove the snow from his shoes and lower pant legs. He handed a package to her and she set it aside so she could wrap her arms around his neck. They embraced and kissed. He finally shut the door and she helped him off with his coat. She hung it in the closet and retrieved the two glasses of wine and gave one to Gil.

"Merry Christmas, sweetheart," she toasted.

"Merry Christmas to you too, Cassandra."

They each took a sip and then both walked over to the couch. Cassandra picked up the oversized package Gil had given her and placed it under the Christmas tree. The fireplace was glowing and the warmth it generated felt comforting. The house was decorated, but not overly so.

As they sat close together on the couch Cassandra said, "I have a roast in the oven and I made the sweet potatoes just the way you like them, with marshmallows."

He looked at her, took another sip of wine and said, "A perfect Christmas Eve."

"Would you like to open your gift now?" she asked.

"Only if you open your gift first."

She giggled, "We're worse than children, aren't we?"

"Maybe, but do children do this?" Gil gently pulled her head towards his and their lips met. The loving kiss was passionate and caring.

"Whew. I love you Gil."

"I love you too."

Cassandra rose up from the couch and casually walked over to the tree and brought the two gifts and handed one to Gil. "Merry Christmas."

He took it and said, "Open yours first."

Cassandra sat down and carefully broke loose the tape from the pretty Christmas paper. She knew Gil did not wrap it because it was impeccably neat. "I wonder what it could be," she said as she slowly removed the paper and exposed a very large plain white box.

"I guess you'll just have to open the box to find out."

Gil's thoughts about the seven unsolved murders and his questioning of his ability as a detective temporarily left him as he watched the love of his life open the gift he had bought her. Cassandra carefully opened the box and pulled the thin paper to the side. She lifted out a beautiful full-length woman's soft black leather coat. She stood up and put it on. She pirouetted to model it for him.

She stopped in front of him, put her left hand on her extended left hip and held up her right arm in the air with her hand effortlessly posed. It looked stunning on her. Cassandra's face was beaming with delight. She truly liked her gift.

She didn't remove the coat as she handed him a small gift wrapped package and said, "Now it's your turn."

He looked at the small gift, jiggled it and looked at her. "I hope I don't have to model it," he quipped.

She chuckled, "Maybe."

Gil tore off the wrapping paper and opened the box inside. He pulled out what looked like a billfold. He was surprised when he opened it and there was note paper on one side.

Cassandra took it from him to demonstrate. "See, on this side you put your badge and it will always be visible when you're writing notes so the person will understand you are the law."

"How unique. I have never seen one like this."

"I want them to know just who they're dealing with," she proudly proclaimed.

Gil instantly saw the seven tombstone folders in his mind's eye and thought to himself, *yes, they'll see a failure*. He quickly erased the image and said, "It's a wonderful gift. Thank you."

"So, baby, you sit and relax and enjoy your wine. I'll get supper put together. It will only take a few minutes."

"Do you need help?"

"No. Just relax. I have everything under control."

Gil couldn't argue with that. She always had everything under control. She was organized, beautiful and successful. Gil felt himself to be a very lucky man.

"You might want to take off your coat," he warned her.

"I might want to take off more than that," she playfully shot back.

The candle lit supper was terrific. Gil complimented her several times on how good everything was. He got up and poured each another glass of wine and returned to his seat.

"There is something troubling you, isn't there?" she asked.

"A little."

"Is it about those cases you have been working on? The serial killer cases?"

"I'm sorry if I am ruining your Christmas. I just can't seem to get a handle on them."

Cassandra slowly got up from her chair and glided in behind him and started rubbing his temples. "I know how hard you work and you're not ruining anything. You will solve them, I have faith in you." She continued to massage his temples.

Gil reached up with his right hand and gently clutched her wrist and pulled her around. She sat in his lap and they embraced.

"I think I have to see The Professor," he finally said.

Cassandra looked startled. He had told her many times about the person everyone called The Professor and she knew Gil didn't like stooping to that level. "Are you sure?" was all she could say.

"Yes."

"So then tonight I'm going to try to make you forget about your caseload and The Professor." Cassandra wrapped her arms around Gil's neck and kissed him passionately. She looked deeply into his eyes as she started unbuttoning his shirt and said, "I'm going to teach you something The Professor can't."

***

Randy L. Hilmer

# Chapter 2
# Allen Venter
## *June 2012*

Thunder was booming loudly as if right overhead and could be felt throughout Detective Gil Clifton's body. It had been raining all day but started to intensify as the afternoon progressed towards evening. It was nearly 10:00 p.m. on this first Saturday in June. Four patrol cars were flashing their lights making the light refracted in the rain appear as if coming from disco lamps. Officers had cordoned off the area with yellow 'Do Not Cross' police tape. A make-shift tent was protecting the officers and a body lying in an alley of a rather seedy and rundown business section of Camden, New Jersey.

A spotlight from one patrol car was focused on the body, now covered with a tarp. A body bag was lying on the ground for when it would be needed to transport the victim to the morgue. The crime scene had none of the curious onlookers usually surrounding the area mainly due to the weather conditions. That was just fine as far as Detective Gil was concerned.

"What's the story?" Gil asked his partner, who had already been on the scene for about twenty minutes.

Gil Clifton and Cornell Bush had been partners for the last four years. At that time Cornell had just been promoted to detective. Gil had been in the detective bureau twenty-three years when they were put together as partners. Cornell had been warned by Captain Joseph McCadry that his new partner had some idiosyncrasies and did not always follow the rules of police investigative policies to the letter. McCadry also said he had an open door if things didn't work out between the two newly assigned partners.

Cornell took an instant liking to his new partner and never used that open door to file any complaints, although there were ample situations which would have warranted a discussion. Cornell had been on the police force for seven years and knew how important it was to trust your partner. While he was only 29 years old, Cornell had the looks of a teenager sans the acne. His baby-face belied his legitimacy as a seasoned officer albeit a rookie detective at the time. But to this day he still looked up to Gil as his mentor and knew his place in the partnership.

"Appears to be a gunshot wound to the chest," Cornell answered and then continued, "No shell casings have been found yet. This weather is slowing us down a little bit."

"Yeah, washing any possible evidence down the gutter," Gil responded as he surveyed the area around where the body fell. The body was close to the side of a hardware store and a river of water with floating debris from the alley was flowing towards the main street. He observed the water was gushing into a sewer drain in the street at a pretty high rate causing a cascading effect around the drain entrance. It reminded him of river rapids where he used to go kayaking in his younger days.

"Have someone check the bottom of the drain over there," Gil stated, pointing toward the rapids. "Check every inch from the body to the drain. Maybe we will find a bullet casing."

Cornell went and gave those instructions to two officers standing nearby. Gil noticed the two officers reacting as if they had just been given the worst job in history but then they nodded in compliance. Cornell had a way about him which most often got the results he wanted. He wasn't demanding. He probably told them he agreed that it was a stupid idea and added his own doubts about the outcome. He was persuasive.

Cornell informed Gil that a worker from Jersey Waste Disposal had been emptying garbage containers from the week and had driven into the alley to get the two dumpsters shared by the surrounding businesses using the alley when he discovered the body at approximately 8:15 p.m. A police officer had arrived at the scene shortly after the call was received from the Jersey Waste Disposal's dispatcher. Cornell had interviewed the driver and released him.

The forensic officers came on the scene and strolled over to Detective Gil. "Any chance of us finding anything in this downpour?"

Both officers looked miserable and were not happy about their assignment. Gil wondered to himself why they were acting that way as this was not the first time terrible weather conditions had interfered with an investigation. Gil shrugged his shoulders and answered with a rather sarcastic tone, "Depends on how hard you look."

Cornell returned to stand next to his partner under the tent and Gil asked, "What have you found out so far?"

"The victim had a billfold and we found everything intact including fifty-seven dollars in cash. The driver's license identifies him as Allen Venter, 42, from 14147 Circus Drive, Camden. We also found some business cards indicating he was a car salesman over at Cooper River Auto Sales. We found two credit cards, a medical insurance card, a customer card from Computerland and a grocery store club card. Normal stuff. Everything's in the evidence bag."

"You searched the body before the coroner got here?" Gil asked incredulously.

"Just took out his billfold. Figured it was in his back pants pocket. Wanted to get some ID before the rain got to it and turned it into mush."

"Next time wait for the coroner."

"Yes, sir."

"Run a credit check."

"Will do."

"Get all of the license plate numbers from cars sitting in the street and run them. See what you come up with."

"I've got someone on that already. Not too many cars in this area tonight. Nothing residential that we can find. There may be a couple of apartments above one of the business places down the street. Everything else says this place is deserted on a Saturday night. No night clubs or bars."

"Then I wonder what this guy was doing in this area on a Saturday night?" Gil asked rhetorically.

Gil had been on the scene for approximately thirty minutes when the coroner arrived. He recognized Gil and quickly strode over to him under the tent. "Nasty weather."

"Nasty homicide," Gil shot back.

Dr. Carl Ingersoll had known Gil for many years. The coroner had been in his job for the last fifteen years and had seen about everything there was to see. He was hardened by the cruelty of man and wouldn't be afraid to bend the rules when asked by Gil. Over the years the detective had been harsh with the good doctor when the evidence he wanted just wasn't there. The doctor would bend the rules but would never fabricate. Although Gil never once asked to him fabricate evidence, he just didn't understand why sometimes the coroner couldn't find something that just simply didn't exist.

Carl shook his head in affirmation to Gil's comment and bent down to do a preliminary on-site examination of the deceased. "Okay to start a little look see?"

"Yeah, we got everything we need. The photog guy is still here if you need him," said Cornell.

The coroner glanced over at Gil and Gil nodded his head in agreement. Carl slowly unbuttoned the victim's shirt where a bullet appeared to have had entered. He leaned in closer, spread the shirt open and turned to Gil. "Close range would be my guess."

Gil had presumed that because of the surrounding location. He speculated that someone lured the victim to this desolate site in an otherwise very busy city. Gil already had people looking at the buildings encompassing the alley for a bullet lodged in its structure.

Dr. Ingersoll rolled the body over gently and lifted the shirt up around the victim's neck. "Exit wound. Bullet is probably in one of these walls."

"Doctor, you're going to make a good detective someday," Gil mused.

The police photographer took pictures of the entrance and exit wounds placing a ruler in the picture to identify the size relationship of the wounds. Dr. Ingersoll finished up his preliminary examination and went over to Gil and whispered, "Even if you find the bullet, it probably won't do you any good. This was a large caliber weapon, maybe a .44 or .45. Small entrance wound but a very large exit wound. The casing should be around here someplace if the perp didn't pick it up." Dr. Carl Ingersoll thought of himself as a detective, using language and giving advice as if he were.

"Time of death?"

"Well, the weather isn't helping but it's not too cold. Rigor mortis has started in his limbs. I would say he been dead for about five to six hours." Dr. Ingersoll looked at his watch, "I'd say he died somewhere between 4 and 7 p.m. I'll know better when I do the autopsy."

Gil shook his hand and said, "Get me what you can as soon as possible."

"I'll do my best."

"It doesn't look like we have a lot of evidence to start with on this one." Gil was always pessimistic at the beginning of an investigation; always complaining about not having enough evidence to steer him in the right direction. But the bulldog kept pursuing the perpetrator on behalf of the victim until the bad guy was behind bars for good.

---

Gil was sitting at his desk at 1:30 a.m. on Sunday morning while his partner was seated across from him as the desks were butted up and facing one another. They had been on the scene of the Venter murder until almost midnight. They found a bullet in the wall behind the victim. It was not of much forensic value.

The best discovery was the bullet casing. One of the officers assigned to search the sewer drain had found the casing caught in debris at the entrance. The torrential rain had been reduced to a slight drizzle by midnight when the casing was recovered. The police photographer had already left the scene when the coroner departed. Gil took pictures of the casing's location and adjacent areas with his phone camera.

The partners were preparing their sequence of steps to solve this case. Gil hated murders that happened on Saturday night, especially with no witnesses. This case was even worse because there were no employers or nearby businesses to interview until Monday, no nearby residences to talk to and no forensic evidence to investigate. This case stalled immediately and wouldn't restart until Monday morning, almost 36 hours of void from the magical 48 hours to solve the crime.

---

Gil and his partner arrived at the precinct early Monday morning and prepared to go interview the victim's employer. Cornell had already run a check on Venter and found out that he was divorced for eleven years, had only one DUI on his record from nineteen years ago, and had fairly good credit. He had served in the Navy for four years immediately after graduating from high school and received an honorable discharge.

The casing they had found would have come from a .45 caliber pistol. The projectile found in the wall could not be positively connected to the casing because it was so damaged by going through the victim's body and entering the brick wall; however, it was consistent with belonging to that caliber.

Mail was delivered to both partners before they left by Nathan Bowen, an 18 year old lad hired to do odd jobs required of a homicide bureau such as getting coffee, running errands, sweeping the squad room and receiving, sorting and delivering the mail to the detectives three times per day. He replaced the very likable Jonathon Gilcrest, who entered the police academy and was now a uniformed officer for Camden, New Jersey. Nathan was more introspective and did not interact too often with the detectives. He just did his job quietly and efficiently. The envelope he handed Gil had been addressed to Detective Gilbert Clifton and had <u>URGENT</u> typed in capital letters and underlined. There was no return address listed and he was skeptical about opening it at first, but felt the contents with his fingers and he thought it would be safe to open. Gil carefully unsealed it with a letter opener and slipped out the one page document inside. It read:

> **'*Doubt thou the stars are fire,***
> ***doubt that the sun doth move,***
> ***doubt truth to be a liar,***
> ***but never doubt I love'***

Gil's face got flushed as he reread the poem. Cornell looked up from opening his usual mail and asked, "Something wrong?"

"No. Nothing at all." He put the unsigned letter back into the envelope, opened a bottom desk drawer and filed away the poem he had received, obviously from Cassandra. He thought it was a sweet sentiment but would ask her not to send love notes to his office. He would have to consider how to broach the subject without hurting her feelings. This was the first time she had ever done anything like this so he secretly hoped it would be just a one-time indiscretion on her part.

The detective's interview with the president of Cooper River Auto Sales turned up nothing. Allen Venter had been an employee for seventeen years, had no known enemies, was never late and was a good salesman who always went the extra mile for his customers which was why he was one of the top salesmen in the company. The other salesmen were interviewed and the detectives only came away with the fact that Venter was a little depressed when he first got a divorce but nothing unusual.

They interviewed Venter's ex-wife who was working as a beauty consultant in a fashionable department store. She was in her middle thirties, still very attractive and had nothing bad to say about Allen Venter except they just grew apart and so they divorced. She had remarried a real estate broker about four years ago and lived in a nice suburban area. She hadn't seen Allen after the divorce. There was no alimony payment and they had no children together. It was an amicable split.

Cornell slipped into the driver's seat as Gil slid into the passenger's seat of their unmarked car. Cornell said, "Do you believe her? This guy Venter sounds like an all-around good guy. Nice paying job, good credit, no enemies that we know of. Too good to be true?"

The seasoned veteran answered, "I tend to believe her. Why? I'm not sure. Let's just say it's just a hunch."

"Those hunches of yours are pretty much a truth serum, but I think this guy is too squeaky clean for my book. I'll put money on bad blood between Venter and his ex's new husband."

"Of course we'll check him out, but I think I would be taking your money. There's something else at work here."

Cornell shrugged it off and drove back to the precinct as it was near the end of their shift. When they arrived Gil called the new husband and found out that he and Venter never met. He knew his wife was married to Allen, but all he knew was his name and nothing else. There was no animosity between them and he and his wife rarely mentioned Venter. The case was not developing at all.

When they reached the precinct Gil called the coroner's office but there was no update yet from Dr. Ingersoll. Gil asked the coroner to put this in top priority as there was far too little information to go on at this point. The doctor agreed.

A 2011 Toyota Corolla registered to Allen Venter was discovered abandoned in a shopping center near downtown after hours on Tuesday, June 5. The car was taken to the police impound yard and was thoroughly inspected for trace evidence. None was found because someone had completely wiped down the car. Gil made a presumption that the victim had been abducted and taken to the desolate alley where he was murdered. It was only a presumption and not fact at this point.

This wasn't the first case that could go cold on Detective Gil but this is how they started out and if there was no new forensic evidence or if somebody didn't come forward it would probably end up in the cold case files. But Gil was in no way prepared to give up just yet. He needed to find the something else that was at work here. His gut told him so.

***

# Chapter 3
# Harold McDonald
## *July 2012*

The coroner's report added little to help with the investigation of Allen Venter. Gil had struck out and the case was headed for the cold case files if something didn't break for them soon. The only thing the coroner could add was that the victim had probably eaten a pepperoni pizza about 2-3 hours before he died. Detectives Gil and Cornell had solved two other murders during the month of June but the Venter murder still haunted Gil. There was something about it that just didn't add up but it kept itself hidden. Hidden from Gil but not forgotten.

Gil took the Fourth of July as a paid holiday. He hadn't taken a vacation day since New Year's Day. Cassandra had dragged him to a New Year's Eve party the night before and wanted nothing to prevent them from dancing the night away. They spent New Year's Day relaxing at Cassandra's house, watching the parades on television in the morning, fixing a large meal together in the afternoon and listening to music as they soothed the pangs from eating far too much. Cassandra was happy that Gil didn't just want to sit around all day and watch football.

As of yet Gil had not brought up the subject of the love note she had sent him early in June. She was uncharacteristically quiet about it also. Gil wrote it off as a one-time thing and had decided not to mention anything about it to her.

They had spent the holiday on Cooper River. Gil had rented a two-seated paddle boat and they paddled their way up and down the river for several hours. Cassandra had brought a picnic lunch and they stopped at the Cooper River Park where they ate their lunch, played a game of miniature golf, and watched as a group of teens engaged in a lively game of volleyball.

They paddled their way back to the boat rental dock completely exhausted but in a wonderful mood. Gil had forgotten he was a police detective. He put all thoughts of Allen Venter out of his mind. They drove home to Cassandra's place and flopped on the couch. As they curled up on the couch together Cassandra wrapped her arms around his neck and whispered, "I love you, Gil."

"I love you too, Cassandra. This has been a wonderful of day. The best I have had in a very long time. Thanks for everything."

"No thanks needed. It's been great for me too." She laid her head on his lap and looked up at him with adoring eyes. "What would you think about taking a fall cruise to the Bahamas or Mexico or someplace exotic?"

Gil looked at her in inquisitively. They had been together for a long time and she was the best thing in his life. He wondered if they should take their relationship to the next level. Should he propose? He quickly decided this was neither the time nor the place. Instead he answered her, "Maybe we should look into that."

She reached up with her right arm and gently pulled his head towards hers as she lifted her head towards his and they kissed. A kiss that signified their relationship was leading somewhere more permanent. Cassandra returned her head to his lap and they both rested in silence, each with their own private thoughts, listening to the soft jazz music emanating from the stereo, the dim lights casting gentle shadows as the sunlight slowly gave way to the summer darkness and serenity captured the mood.

Suddenly there was a tremendously loud noise that immediately startled the two lovers. Gil's reaction was to stand up, which dumped Cassandra on the floor. He ran over towards his coat to grab his gun but before he could get there Cassandra yelled, "It's just the fireworks, Gil!"

Gil stopped dead in his tracks and sheepishly turned around. "Guess I got a little jumpy. I forgot it was the Fourth. Sorry."

He went back and helped her to her feet. She grabbed his hand and stood up, brushed herself off and straightened her hair.

"Living with a police detective sure has its moments!"

There she said it. *Living with a police detective.* He heard her loud and clear. She already had them married in her mind.

"I'm sorry. I was so relaxed that it startled me."

Another loud boom could be heard. They looked at each other and laughed.

"Let's go outside and watch."

Gil agreed, "I'll get the ladder from the garage and we can go up on the roof for a better view."

"Sounds good. While you do that, I'll get our tennis shoes."

As Gil was walking to get the ladder he thought of how many of his belongings were already over here. He had shoes, socks, underwear, a suit and a couple of sport jackets, shirts and pants. They had accumulated over time. She washed them and put things on hangers in her closet or in a dresser drawer she designated for him. He confirmed his previous thoughts and would find the appropriate time to ask her to marry him.

---

Cornell had placed a call to Gil saying that he was following up a lead on the Venter case and would be late for roll call. Gil said he would cover for him and arrived at the precinct around 3:30 p.m. for his swing shift following the fireworks from the previous night. Thursday's roll call would be at 4:00 p.m. so Gil went through his mail which Nathan always laid neatly on the corner of his desk. Nothing unusual in the mail today. Gil received the court date scheduled for one of the murders they investigated for which he needed to testify. He turned on his computer and recorded the date on his calendar.

The detectives had a separate roll call from the uniformed officers. Captain McCadry briefly went over bulletins that he would share with the detectives. The captain was a small man in stature and everyone thought he had the 'little man's syndrome' as he always tried to appear strong and domineering.

As McCadry was reading from one of the last bulletins the captain's secretary rushed into the room and handed him a note. McCadry read the note, looked up and motioned to Gil to come up to the podium where he was standing. "You're up on this one. Shooting over on Park Street. Where's Cornell?"

"He's following up on a lead on the Venter case."

He handed the note to Gil and said, "You're dismissed so you can go now."

Gil read the brief note and replied, "I'm on my way."

He proceeded to his desk, got his sport jacket, notepad, pen and radio and promptly left the precinct and headed to 5511 W. Park Street. He called Cornell on his cell phone and told him to meet him at the scene. The location was only about two miles from the precinct so he would be on this case almost immediately. Cornell told him he was only a couple of blocks away as he was on his way back to the precinct.

The address turned out to be a Qwik-E-Stop convenience store. The body was lying in a pool of blood in the parking lot next to a dented and rusted 1986 Ford F150 pickup truck with New Jersey plates. The driver's door to the vehicle was open; a plastic bag was dropped near the body, as was a large soft drink container which had spilled its contents onto the ground.

Cornell was already on the scene and instructing two uniformed police officers to start surrounding the area with the police tape. Onlookers were gathering and muttering amongst themselves. Gil approached the body and looked at the small crowd and asked, "Did anyone see anything or hear anything?"

People shook their heads no. Some stayed while others departed as if they didn't want to get involved. Cornell went into the convenience store to start questioning the clerk. Gil waited as the crime photographer was working the scene. One forensic officer arrived and began surveying the area. He gently draped a sheet over the body and laid a body bag next to it.

One uniformed officer sauntered over and informed Gil that a search of the area came up empty as far as a bullet casing was concerned.

"How do you know that man was shot?" Gil asked.

"The dispatcher told us there was a shooting at this address so we started looking for evidence."

"Good job. Thanks. Did you come up with anything at all?"

"We asked a lot of people standing around if they saw or heard anything but we got nada."

"Figures. Do you know who called it in?"

"It was the store clerk. She is very upset. One of your guys is with her now," he reported as he turned and walked away.

Gil took in the surrounding area and began to stare at a small wooded area across the street.

"Officer!"

The uniformed officer pivoted around and came back over to Gil. "Yes?"

"Take someone with you and search that area across the street." He pointed to the woods. "See if you can find anything."

"Sniper?"

"Who knows at this point? It's just a hunch."

The officer waved to his partner and they hurried across the street and started searching the area.

Cornell exited the store and headed over to Gil.

"What did she have to say?" Gil asked.

"Her name is Bonita Rodriquez, 22, single mother of a three year old daughter. Has worked the day shift here for about a year and a half. The guy bought some cookies, hand towels, large lemonade and a package of double-A batteries. She happened to look out the window as the victim was hit. She didn't see anyone near him but saw him fall down. She ran out from behind the counter to see what had happened and saw blood pouring out of the man so she ran back into the store and called the police. I got her home address and phone number."

"Did she hear a gunshot?"

"No. She just saw him fall. At first she thought he had a heart attack or something but then saw the blood." Cornell looked up and saw two police officers searching across the road. "Do you think it might have been a sniper?"

"Don't know. Just a hunch. We'll have to see if this guy had any enemies."

"I hate it when you have hunches like that. I hope we don't have a sniper on our hands like they did up in DC a few years back."

Gil didn't answer and walked over and met the coroner who had just arrived.

"Right in your own back yard? Not good PR, Gil," Dr. Ingersoll said.

"No, I don't suppose so. Shooting, no witnesses, broad daylight. It doesn't pass the smell test. I need you to get on this one right away."

The doctor grinned, "Naturally. You know something, Detective Gil? One of these days the killer is going to leave his business card on the body so you have some evidence to start with and you won't have to ask me to hurry-hurry-hurry."

"They do leave a calling card, Carl, but it is up to you to find it for me."

The doctor slipped back the sheet and took his first look at the victim. "Pretty good size fella." He then started his on-scene investigation. After a couple of minutes he asked Cornell to help him turn the body over on its stomach. The doctor lifted the man's shirt then lowered it back over him. He stood up and said to Gil, "Gunshot wound to the lower chest. No exit wound that I could see. We might get lucky and retrieve the bullet. He's big enough that it may still be lodged somewhere in his back."

"Good start, Doc," Gil said and then turned to his partner, "Have them burn you a DVD from those two security cameras on the corner of the store. Maybe Big Brother saw something."

Gil left the immediate scene and entered the convenience store. The clerk was being consoled by a middle aged man. He walked up to them and asked the sobbing woman, "Are you the clerk?"

She looked up at him with tears in her eyes and in a trembling voice replied, "Yes."

"I'm the store manager. Josh Knutson," interjected the man consoling her. "I came over as soon as she called me," he said to Gil. He then said to Bonita, "I have someone coming in to cover for you. You go home and get some rest and try to get this off your mind."

"First let me ask you," Gil interrupted, "did you hear anything when you saw the victim drop? A popping noise, maybe like a car back firing? Anything at all?"

"No, the doors to the store were shut. I just happened to look out the window and I saw him drop. I thought he had a heart attack."

"Okay. Thanks for your help." Gil started to depart and quickly turned around and addressed the manager. "Josh, get with my partner, we need a DVD copy from your security cameras."

"Sure thing."

Gil went outside and saw the two police officers coming back across the street. They went directly to Gil.

"Nothing there we could find."

"What's behind that wooded area?"

"Just an old dried up river bed. There are some businesses on the other side. Looked like a lumber yard, a warehouse of some kind and the back entrances to shops. No cars."

"I want you to take a team and canvas the area. Go a half mile west and east of this mid-point. Look for footprints in the river bed and interview all of the business people available. They may have seen something. Find out if they saw a man carrying a long object or running from the area or heard or seen anything peculiar."

Cornell had reached Gil as he was instructing the officers. Gil turned to him and said, "Head up this search. You know what to look for."

"Okay."

"I'll get an ID on the deceased and start running a check. I'll meet you back at the precinct."

Cornell took off with five officers in tow. They crossed the street and Cornell started pointing in directions and the men scattered off to their assignments.

"The body is all yours, Gil," Dr. Ingersoll said when he had completed his on-scene investigation.

"Anything else you can tell me at this point?"

"Only that he was overweight. Probably dead before he hit the ground. I think the bullet may have clipped his heart."

"Thanks, doc. I will talk to you later."

Gil reached in and took out a wallet from the man's back pocket. A New Jersey driver's license showed his name as Harold McDonald of 23137 W. Halverson Drive, Camden, born April 18, 1947, 323-lbs., license expired. The picture matched that of the deceased. There was nothing unusual or suspicious in the wallet. Gil wrote down the pertinent information in his notebook and slid the wallet into an evidence bag.

A reporter standing near Gil on the other side of the tape barricade called out to Gil, "Can you give me a statement?"

Gil looked up and shook his head no.

"Was it a drive-by shooting?"

"Don't know."

"Is there anything you can say about the dead man?"

"We are starting an investigation into the man's death. We will make an announcement as soon as we can. That's all I have to say."

Several reporters quickly gathered around like piranhas that had discovered fresh meat in the water. They were all shouting questions over one another trying to get some small tidbit of information. None of the officers or Gil responded any further to their frenzy.

Gil got into his car and drove to 23137 W. Halverson Drive and parked on the street in front of the small two-story framed house in an older working class neighborhood. He appraised the immediate surrounding homes and found broken or torn screens, curtains in the windows in disarray, lawns overgrown with weeds or large patches of dried dirt and houses badly in need of paint.

The sun was low in the sky. He looked at his watch, 8:18.

He walked to the front door and pushed the doorbell. He didn't hear anything so he knocked on the screen door. The door rattled as the top hinge was missing and the middle and bottom hinges were working loose from the door frame. After a second series of knocks the inner door opened. A heavyset woman wearing a well-worn flowered house dress appeared.

"Yes?" She looked curiously at the man standing outside her door.

"Good evening, ma'am. My name is Detective Gil Clifton of the Camden Homicide Division." He flashed his badge for her. "May I come in?"

"Sure, officer." She pushed the screen door open with her right hand. The middle and bottom hinges squeaked and a spring dangled on the interior. Gil opened the door further and entered the dimly lit home.

"What's this all about? Has something happened to Harry? Did he have a heart attack?"

"Like I said, ma'am . . . ."

"You can call me Arlene."

"Thank you. Like I said, Arlene, I am from the homicide division and your husband has been shot...."

"Oh my God!"

Gil reached out and grabbed her hand as she looked like she was about to faint. "Would you like to sit down?"

"Yes." She walked over to the couch and plopped down into a sagging cushion. Tears were streaming down her cheeks.

"I need you to come down to the morgue and make a positive identification. Can you do that?"

"He's dead!?"

"I'm afraid so, Arlene.

"How did it happen? Did Stefan kill him?"

"Stefan who?"

"Our son."

\*\*\*

Randy L. Hilmer

# Chapter 4
# Dorothy Coel
*August 2012*

Detective Gil was interested as to why she would think her son would murder his father but thought better to wait and probe deeper into that subject a little later. He took Arlene McDonald to the county morgue where Dr. Ingersoll was preparing to leave. Gil told the doctor that he had the wife of the deceased with him to make a positive identification. Although it was nearing 9:00 p.m. the doctor escorted the two into the vault room and pulled out the body picked up earlier outside of the Qwik-E-Stop convenience store. When he pulled the sheet down to reveal the face of the man on the gurney, Arlene let out a screech, held her hand over her mouth and turned away.

"Is that your husband?" Gil asked.

She nodded her head, "Yes, that's him."

Gil put his arm around her shoulders and said, "Thank you. I know how hard this is on you."

"Thank you," she sobbed, dabbing at her eyes with a handkerchief.

"I would like to ask you a few questions before you go. It's quite important."

"Right now?"

"It would be most helpful. It won't take too long and I will have somebody drive you home."

She accompanied Gil to a nearby room fitted with a table along one wall, three chairs pushed in, an old couch and two overstuffed chairs. Gil pulled out one of the chairs at the table and had her sit down. He sat in the other chair at the end of the table.

Gil began gently. "I know how difficult this can be but please believe me when I say that I need to ask you some very important questions so we can apprehend your husband's killer." He reached across and gingerly patted the top of her hand.

"Do you need anything? A cup of coffee or a glass of water?"

"No. I'm fine."

"Okay. Now, you mentioned something about your son and that he may have been involved. What made you think he might have killed your husband?"

"He and Harold had a fight a few nights ago. My son is on drugs and needed money. We don't have a lot of money because Harold was wounded in Viet Nam and has been on disability ever since. I work at the Camden Inn. I do all the laundry. It doesn't pay much but we get by. Stefan has been hitting us hard lately. He even stole some money from us about a month ago. That's when Harold put the stop on it. Stefan was plenty angry and threatened to kill him. I know he didn't mean it but it just came out. I didn't really mean to say he had anything to do with it."

"Do you know where Stefan is now?"

"No. He usually hangs out down by the river with the homeless but I don't know where."

"How old is Stefan?"

"He just turned 25. I had him when I was almost 40. He has just wasted his life. Never held a steady job. He was in prison for six years on an assault and battery charge. He's been nothing but trouble for us."

"I see. Do you know if he had a street name? You know, something his friends called him other than Stefan."

"Yeah. They called him Lil' Mac."

"Do you know of anyone else who would want to harm or kill your husband?"

"Naw. Harold mainly just drank beer over at the VFW Club or at Rotterdam's Tavern. He didn't have a backbone to stand up to anybody.

He was pretty much a good for nothing. I guess that's where Stefan got it from. Two of a kind, they are."

"One last question, Arlene. Did Harold have any insurance policies?"

"Are you kidding? He drank his money away and most of mine too. Like I told you, he was a good for nothing but I stayed with him, God only knows why."

"Thank you very much for your time, Arlene. I'll have someone take you home now. If you think of anything that might help, please give me a call."

"Sure. But you know something? It'll be kind of lonely not hearing the big baboon come stumbling in at night."

---

On Friday, July 6th Gil got to the precinct early. He thought he could get the McDonald case wrapped up fairly quickly even with no real leads. He only hoped that Cornell would find out something that would help break the case. Gil sat at his desk re-reading the file reports. It was only 9:18 a.m. but he didn't have a good night's rest because he kept thinking about Arlene McDonald and what she would do now.

He had a hunch that Stefan McDonald would not be a good suspect. If the shooting was from across the street as he suspected, a drug addict probably wouldn't have that good of aim. Besides, how would he have tracked his father, gotten around the block, across the dry riverbed, set up and shoot? No. This was a random sniper shot.

He sorted through his mail while he waited for Cornell to show up. He came across another letter marked <u>URGENT</u>. He opened it.

### *'Then must you speak of one that loved not wisely, but too well'*

*What was she thinking? Sending him love notes at the office. Once was bad enough! Does this one mean she wants to get married? Or that she was sorry that he hadn't asked her yet?* Gil put the letter back in its envelope and slid it into his coat pocket. He opened the bottom drawer of his desk and grabbed the previous letter from Cassandra and put that in his coat pocket too. He would definitely confront her about these. This was not the proper place to do such things. He knew she meant well, but after all, he was in the middle of a murder investigation.

Cornell entered the squad room and went directly to his desk and sat down. "Nothing.

Absolutely nothing. No footprints, no disturbed brush, no casings. Nothing. Nobody saw or heard a thing. No suspicious cars, no suspicious man, no sounds, no nothing. Can you believe it?"

"You canvassed all of the businesses on both sides of the riverbed?"

"A half mile up and a half mile down. That street is W. Valley Street and we hit stores on both sides of the street. Nothing. Nothing!" His voice got louder.

"The deceased is Harold McDonald." Gil tossed the file folder over to his partner. "Positive ID by his wife. They have a druggie for a son by the name of Stefan, goes by Lil' Mac on the street. I don't think there is much there, but I issued a warrant for his arrest on suspicion. Get down to the VFW. The victim hung out there. I'll go over to Rotterdam's Tavern. Seems like they were his two favorite haunts."

"Okay. I'm on my way." Cornell got up and started walking towards the door.

"Hey, Cornell!"

Cornell looked back at his partner, "Yeah?"

"Anything with that lead yesterday on Venter?"

"Nope. I thought I had something but turned out to be nothing." With that Cornell walked out the door.

---

Cassandra was late getting home. She was surprised to see Gil already in the kitchen. All she heard from him yesterday was that he was working on a new case.

"How did your case go yesterday?" She yelled as she went to her bedroom to change clothes not waiting for a response. "Just a minute, I'll be right in."

Gil pondered about how he was going to approach the subject of the love letters. The last thing he wanted was to get into an argument when she meant well. He had thoughts that perhaps he was taking it wrong and should just let it go. He hadn't decided what to do. He would have to play it by ear. When it came to matters of the heart, Gilbert Clifton wasn't the smoothest sailor on the lake.

Cassandra waltzed into the kitchen with a happy glow on her face. She had quickly changed into her comfy jogging suit she liked so well. "What I really need is a long hot bubble bath but what I really want is a long hot kiss. Anyone available here in the kitchen?" She threw her arms around Gil and kissed him. His return kiss was a little less passionate as he struggled with his thoughts.

"Something on your mind, baby?" she asked. Before he could answer she said, "I almost forgot, I got the Pilgrim's Insurance account today. I've been after them for months. I worked right through lunch so I am starving. I am so glad you started supper. What are you making?" She got behind him as he was stirring the pasta noodles and put her arms around his waist. She squeezed him and said, "My personal chef's delight."

"Just making spaghetti. Nothing special."

"Let me set the table. It will be wonderful. Oh, Gil, I am so happy. I needed that account and got it. What a perfect day. And to top it off, the man I love is making supper. It just doesn't get any better than this. Can you go for a red wine before supper, honey?" Her words were spewing out of her mouth like an onrushing avalanche.

"Sure. That would be great." Gil decided that he didn't want to upset her. She needed to celebrate and his concerns about two silly love letters could wait.

Cassandra opened a bottle of Merlot, poured out two glasses and gave one to Gil. They toasted their glasses together. "To us, my dear!"

"To us and to your new account!"

---

The following three weeks flew by. Cassandra was extremely busy at her advertising agency presenting different campaigns to her new account. Gil had two unsolved murders that plagued him. No breaks in either case. The interview with Stefan McDonald was a dead end. He was actually in jail from July 4th to the 6th on a drunk and disorderly charge and didn't know any of his father's acquaintances. They're all drunks from the bars, he told Gil. That was a strange comment, Gil thought, coming from a person whose only friends were drug addicts.

There was seldom a case where no forensic evidence was found whatsoever. Both of these cases had nothing. Nothing to go on. No leads. Even though Gil and Cornell solved a grisly murder over by the piers rather quickly this month, these two cases weighed heavily on Gil's mind and soul. It was the last day of July and Cornell, as junior partner, was tasked with writing the required monthly reports.

They were working the second twelve hour shift from 4:00 p.m. to 4:00 a.m. so they had pretty much all night to finish up their reports.

After the roll call meeting Captain McCadry was standing by Gil's desk waiting for him to return from the restroom. Gil spotted him standing there and had half a notion to turn around but he saw that McCadry had seen him so he went to his desk.

"What's up, Captain?"

"Any breaks on the Venter or McDonald cases?"

"No, sir. Not yet."

"Make sure you include them in your reports."

"Of course. Why wouldn't we?"

"Just make sure you include them, that's all." The captain made an abrupt turn and left the squad room.

"What was that all about, Gil?" asked Cornell.

"I have no idea."

Gil and Cornell settled in and started finalizing their month-end reports. Around 10:30 p.m. Cornell asked Gil if he could leave for a couple hours.

"Why, what's up?"

"I met this girl the other night and I promised her I'd pick her up after her swing shift at the plastics factory. She is a sectional leader there but her car is in the shop so I told her I'd pick her up. I forgot we had the four to four night shift tonight. Gil, she's got dynamite good looks. You know how it is. I'll just pick her up, take her home and come back."

"You'll do all of the reports for August?"

"All of the reports?"

"All. If she's that important."

"Okay, you got yourself a deal. And yes, she's worth it." Cornell jumped up and got his coat. "I'll be back by 1:30 or so."

They usually didn't wait until the last minute to finalize but July was a busy month so they had to cram everything in before they left. Gil hated to do the reports. He would much rather be investigating a crime scene than sitting at a desk doing what he considered to be busy work. But he didn't want the captain on his tail so he buckled down with getting the July reports done.

Surprisingly the night went by quickly and he saw Cornell come into the squad room. It was 1:25 a.m. Gil noticed.

"Cut that pretty close, partner."

"I told you I'd be back. But, man, she is worth it. Can I help out with the reports?"

"Here, you can look them over. I'm through but it won't hurt for you to double check them. I don't know what's going on with the captain but I sure as hell don't want to get stepped on because of some lousy reports."

Cornell took the reports and started looking them over. Gil got up to get another cup of coffee. "Want a cup?"

"No, I'm fine."

A call came in at 2:18 a.m. saying there had been a murder at the Silent Arms Apartments over on East 22nd Street. Gil and Cornell were assigned. Having completed their reports, they put them in the captain's in-basket and left to drive over to the scene.

"I wonder if the captain wants this on July's reports." Cornell laughingly said.

"Nope. It's 2:30; this goes on August."

The Silent Arms Apartments were located near the downtown section of the city. Normally it would have taken them about 40 minutes to make the drive from the precinct to the apartment complex, but because of the hour and light traffic they were there in less than 20.

The Silent Arms Apartments had been the scene of at least two murders in the last five years, and numerous battery and domestic calls. Three squad cars with lights flashing were in the parking lot. Gil told one officer to cut the lights. Cornell was talking to an officer while Gil looked at the outside perimeter of the building before going to the actual scene. Security cameras were focused on the parking lot and the main entrance. He made a note to get the DVD from management.

Cornell caught up with Gil and said, "Apartment 2D, second floor. White female. Her roommate found her in the bedroom. That's all I got from the first responder."

"Let's go have a look. You get the photog guy busy and I'll talk to the roommate."

They proceeded up the stairs. No elevator so the perp would have had to use the stairs. They would have to conduct a door to door canvas and he knew that wouldn't set well with the occupants who were sleeping through all of the commotion.

They walked in to apartment 2D. Several uniformed officers were milling about looking in drawers and cabinets. The photographer was snapping pictures. Gil and Cornell passed everyone without a word and went directly to the bedroom. The victim was on the bed with a pillow over her head. Nothing was disturbed before the coroner arrived.

Dr. Ingersoll greeted Gil and grumpily said to him, "If they're going to commit murder couldn't they, at least once, do it during normal business hours?"

"This is normal business hours for them."

The doctor shot Gil a nasty look and went to the body. When he pulled the pillow off of the victim's head they all saw for the first time that a gag had been placed in her mouth. Her feet were tied at the ankles with cable ties and her hands were underneath her body. When the coroner finally turned the body to the side they could see her hands were also bound with cable ties.

Gil left the bedroom and went into the small kitchen where a pretty young girl in her mid-twenties was sitting at a table and crying. Gil took a seat across from her as her eyes met his.

"I know this is difficult but I need to ask you some questions, okay?"

She nodded, tried to compose herself and her crying reduced to just a constant sniffling.

"What is your name?"

"Amanda Samuels"

"How do you know the victim?"

"We are roommates."

"What's her name?"

"Dorothy. Dorothy Coel. We work together over at IBM. We work as parts inspectors."

"Can you tell me what happened tonight?"

"Dorothy has this boyfriend, Richard Sawyer; anyways he and a bunch of his buddies took the week off to go on some fishing cruise so Dorothy and I decided to go out tonight. It's Ladies Night over at the Redbird Lounge just a few blocks away." She started crying again.

"You're doing fine. So you and her went to the Redbird, then what?"

She struggled to regain her composure. "We stayed there until about 11:45 and we came back here. I dropped Dorothy off at the front door because I realized that I was out of cigarettes so I went to buy a pack. I had to drive back to the Redbird because there aren't too many other places open around here. When I was leaving this guy offered to buy me a drink. I had seen him there before so I said yes. I only had one drink and then came back here and. . . ." she started to cry uncontrollably.

"It's okay. So you came back here and found her, is that right?"

She nodded yes.

"What time was that?"

"About 2 o'clock."

"So you had one drink from about midnight to 2?"

"Well, I actually had a couple more and then we went to his van and made out and stuff."

"What's his name?"

"Darryl. I don't know his last name. We've danced together quite a lot in the past but I was always with Dorothy so this is the first time we got together. I thought he was really cute. To be perfectly honest, I went back to see if he was still there."

"It's important you tell me truth about everything."

"I'm sorry. I will."

Gil kept jotting notes on his pad. "Did you see anyone around the building either before you left or when you returned?"

She shook her head no. She was losing control but Gil had more questions.

"Do you know of anyone who wanted to harm Dorothy?"

Amanda shook her head no.

"Was there any trouble in the relationship between Dorothy and. . . ." he flipped the page of his notes, "and Richard Sawyer?"

"No. Dorothy really loves him and he thinks the world of her," Amanda sobbed.

"Thank you, Amanda. You've been a great help. Do you have anybody who can be with you tonight?"

"Yes, I called my mother. She's on her way."

Gil left the kitchen and found Cornell, "What do you have?"

"Dorothy Coel, age 28, works at IBM. Don't know what she does there...."

"Parts inspector," Gil said.

"Okay. According to the lease they found in the desk the two girls have lived here for about two years. Not much else. The coroner left but only said it looked like she was gagged and then smothered. We snipped the cable ties off and are dusting the place for fingerprints. The gag was a hand towel that looks like it came from the bathroom. Could indicate she surprised a robbery or something."

"Was anything missing?"

"Not that we can tell."

"I think we can rule out robbery because the perp brought cable ties. He must have thought he was going to need them," Gil concluded. "We'll get a security camera DVD made from the manager and hopefully that will show us something. Also, get a couple uniforms to knock on doors."

Cornell looked at him oddly

"Tonight!" Gil emphasized.

"Okay. By the way, doc Ingersoll told me to tell you that he would hurry-hurry-hurry on this one."

\*\*\*

# Chapter 5
# The Mystery Letters
*August 2012*

Detective Gil arrived at the precinct at 8:15 a.m. on Wednesday, August 1. He afforded himself less than four hours of sleep after last night's investigation. He needed to get to work as soon as possible. Cornell hadn't shown up yet and Gil didn't expect him until at least noon. Gil busied himself transcribing his notes into the file when he saw Nathan delivering the mail. Gil waited for the young man who had a familiarity about him - maybe because of his shyness - but Gil took a liking to the lad even though Nathan had said but only a few words since he started in May.

Nathan dropped mail at each desk as he passed by and was about to hand Gil his mail when Gil said, "You're Nathan, right?"

"Yes, sir."

"How long have you worked here?"

"Since May sixth."

"Are you considering a career in law enforcement?"

"I'm not sure."

"This is a good place to learn. But let me ask you, do you run errands like the others did?"

"Yes."

"Would you mind going to commissary and getting me an egg sandwich?"

"No, sir, I wouldn't mind."

Gil reached for his billfold and pulled out a five dollar bill and handed it to Nathan. "Get yourself something, too."

"I have to deliver the rest of this mail first but then I'll get it for you. Thanks. Here's your mail, sir."

"Thanks, Nathan."

The young lad of few words hurried along his way dropping mail at each desk and then left for the commissary. Gil shuffled through his mail. He stopped suddenly and looked with amazement at the word <u>URGENT</u> on one envelope. He hastily opened the envelope and took out the letter.

### *'Take her or leave her'*

*What?* His thoughts were confusing. He picked up the phone and called Cassandra at home. There was no answer. He didn't want to call her on her cell phone when she was in traffic so he called her office and left a message for her to call him immediately. It was urgent, he said.

He took out the other two letters he had put in his bottom drawer after not finding the courage or the right time to confront Cassandra previously. He opened them, laid them side-by-side and studied them. All had the same type font, were the same size, and no return address.

Nathan returned with Gil's sandwich and change, and brought it over to him. Gil finally noticed the young man standing next to his desk with his hand extended to give Gil his sandwich.

"Sorry. I didn't see you there."

"That's okay, sir. Here's your change." He offered Gil the $1.53 left over.

"No, that's for you."

"Thank you, sir. Are you working on a big case?"

Gil observed Nathan trying to read the letters he had sprawled on his desk. Gil nonchalantly laid other papers over them and said, "Kind of a mystery of sorts."

"Well, okay," Nathan said bashfully, "I've got to get going now. Thanks for the sandwich."

"You're welcome. Hey, Nathan, come talk to me any time if you have any questions. See you later."

"I will. Thank you, sir."

Nathan turned and started walking away when Gil called out to him, "Nathan, just a minute."

Nathan returned to his spot next to Gil's desk. "Yes, sir?"

"What time does this first batch of mail arrive?"

"Seven o'clock."

"Thanks."

Nathan left and went back to the mail room. Gil made a mental note to talk to Nathan and help him climb out of his shell. All of the previous mailroom kids, except one, had entered the academy and were now members of the force. Gil knew that Nathan was part of a new program to help troubled teens. With Nathan being so introverted, he would have a hard time as a police officer. But Gil didn't have time for that right now; he had a mystery on his hands.

Just then his phone rang. It was Cassandra. "Gil, is everything alright? They told me it was urgent."

"Does that mean anything to you?"

"Does what mean anything to me?"

"Does the word urgent mean anything to you?"

"Of course it does. It means right away, without delay. I called the second I received the message. What's going on, Gil?" Her voice filled with inquisitive anxiousness.

"Let me ask you one thing without you getting upset, okay?"

"What in the world are you talking about?"

"Have you sent three letters to the precinct here for me?"

"What?"

"Just answer my question!"

"I don't like your tone, Gil. Now, what's this all about?"

Gil calmed his voice and repeated slowly but sternly, "Have you sent three letters to the precinct for me?"

"No."

"You're positive?"

"Yes I am positive. Now, what the hell is going on?" Anger crept into her voice.

"I'm sorry. I got three letters with no return address and cryptic notes inside. I thought they may have come from you. I'll explain the rest later." There was silence. "Cassandra, I'm sorry if I came on like a stupid detective. I love you."

"You're all right, correct?"

"Yes, I'm fine. I'll talk to you later." Gil paused but there was only silence on the other end. "Goodbye," he said softly but all he heard now was a dial tone. He had made her mad by the way he had spoken to her. He would have to explain and hope she would understand.

Gil sat back in his chair and didn't know if he was relieved or not. Now he had three letters that meant . . . . what? He looked at the postmarks and tried to think what he was doing when he got them. There had to be some kind of connection. He started thumbing through his desk calendar starting in June, then through July and August. He flipped the pages from June 2nd to July 5th then to August 1st then back again, and then forward once again. That's it! All the letters came one day after a murder. But what did he have? Two of the letters were mailed before the murders took place.

He read and re-read them to try to find a pattern. They were all about love. *What did love have to do with the murders?* The first letter spoke of not doubting love. The second seemed to say that the reader picked the wrong person and the third was telling the reader to either love her or leave her. *Did someone know about his private life with Cassandra and how he was vacillating on how and when to ask her to marry him?* He never spoke much about their relationship, not even to Cornell.

*But if they're about love, then is it only coincidence that they came the day after a murder he was investigating? If they are tied to the murder, then why talk about love? Besides, if they are tied to a murder, how would the person know he would be assigned to the case? But the murders are not tied together, so how could the letters be? Were the murders tied together after all? But the letter he had just received was postmarked yesterday afternoon - <u>before</u> this morning's murder.* Thoughts kept darting in and out of his head like pinballs, bouncing from one subject to the next.

He put the letters back in the bottom drawer. He was functioning on too little sleep to give them rational thought. If there was an answer, he would find it. He hated that he couldn't think straight.

Cornell came storming into the squad room and slammed down the paper on his desk. "Did you see where that son-of-a-bitch Brisbane is now calling for all overtime to be cut? Is he completely nuts?"

Gil asked, "You mean Carl Brisbane? Isn't he the captain over at the 17th precinct running for sheriff?"

"Yeah, I know. He's been running his campaign on police reform but now he wants to cut all overtime! He's supposed to be one of us! God damned suits anyway. If they just kept their noses out of our business maybe we could put some bad guys away instead of filling out ignoramus reports. Plus, he wants to reduce the size of the force? Just how the hell are we supposed to win? Let's just give up and let the bad guys take over this God forsaken town and let the suits try doing some real work! Then see what happens!"

Applause erupted throughout the squad room in support of Cornell's rant. Cornell turned a complete circle in confusion and embarrassment of what was happening and slumped down in his chair. "I'm just saying."

A broad smile took over Gil's face. "Well said, partner."

"Well, God dammit, Gil. It just makes me mad."

"Okay. Now just simmer down. We have three unsolved murders on our hands and the suits aren't going to catch them, so it's still up to us."

"I know. I know. So what's on the agenda for today?"

Gil reached into his bottom drawer, pulled out the three letters, and held them out for Cornell. Cornell stood up slightly, reached across the desk, took them and sat back down. He opened one, then the second, and finally, the last one.

"What's this all about?"

"I don't know. I'm too tired to think. At first I thought it was Cassandra messing around. But, when I got this last one, I don't know. They all came the day after a murder."

Cornell studied the letters and the envelopes more closely. "If they are tied to the murders, then what about this one? It's postmarked May 31st, a full day before the Venter murder"

"I know. So is the one I got today."

"Why do you think they are tied to the murders? Granted, they're a little creepy; but how do you make the leap to connect them to the murders? If you can make that leap, are you saying we have a serial killer on our hands?"

"All I'm saying right now is that it seems to be too much of a coincidence. I don't really know right now."

Cornell tossed the letters back to Gil and he put them in his desk drawer. "I'm going to see how the uniforms did with the knock-knocks last night and check out the boyfriend. You head over to the Silent Arms and get the DVD from the manager. We'll take a good look at both the McDonald and Coel DVDs."

"Okay, I'll meet you back here."

"Good." Gil started to leave and then said to his partner, "By the way, what brings you in so early? I thought you wouldn't be in until at least noon."

"I guess some of your bad habits are rubbing off on me."

The uniforms had submitted their reports before they got off duty. Gil signed them out from the duty sergeant and returned to his desk. He was disappointed when he got through, as not one person had witnessed or even heard a thing. Then again, the people who live at the Silent Arms Apartments aren't very cop-friendly in the first place, and most wouldn't want to get involved.

Gil called the coroner's office but he hadn't arrived yet. Then, he went to the evidence locker, retrieved the DVD obtained from the McDonald murder and started going over it for the fourth time. All he could see was that the victim had arrived, went directly into the Qwik-E-Stop store, spent about six minutes there picking up items, paid for them, and returned to his vehicle. As soon as he opened the door, he fell slightly back and to the ground. There was nobody within ten yards of him. From this video, forensics had determined the flight path of the bullet; it would have been consistent with being shot from across the street or possibly from a passing car.

Cornell returned with a DVD in hand from the Silent Arms. Gil inserted it into his player and they both watched intently, looking for a killer. The images on the screen were quite grainy. They were focused on the parking and front entrance to the apartment building. As the DVD played, they could see the residents coming and going. Nothing unusual. At 11:52 p.m., a car pulled up and let out a female passenger at the front door.

"The time checks out to what Amanda Samuels told us."

As the DVD moved forward in jerky steps, they noticed the car pull away. The female entered the building and a figure dressed in dark clothing and wearing a hoodie gathered tightly around his face followed behind her. They backed up the DVD and watched it over and over again.

"Looks like he appeared right out of nowhere," Gil commented.

"I wonder if he was waiting for her. Have you tracked down her boyfriend - what's his name?"

"Richard Sawyer," Gil said. "All I have is an address for him that was found in Dorothy's purse and a business card with his name on it. He's part of the Fixit Squad for Computerland."

The detectives tried to bring the image of the figure into focus, but failed. The camera was of cheap quality so the images were of little use for identification. They were even lucky that images were captured as so many times these types of complexes installed them only for insurance reasons but never had them activated.

They kept watching. The time on the DVD said 12:14 a.m., and showed an image of a figure dressed in dark clothing and a hoodie running out of the building and off the screen.

"Was this a robbery gone bad or was he there just to kill her? Twenty-two minutes and one beautiful girl dead. We have to get this guy," Gil sighed.

They took out the DVD and then headed over to the Computerland store to interview the store manager where Richard Sawyer worked. They were told that Richard was still on vacation and wasn't scheduled to return to work until

Monday. The manager said he was a great employee, worked there for two and a half years and had no disciplinary action on his record.

"He's an all-around nice kid," the store manager said. "I hope he's not in any trouble."

"Not at all. We just wanted a little background on him. Nothing serious. His name came up in a routine investigation and we have to check him out. What time does he start work on Monday?"

"Let me find out." The manager turned to his computer and after a few key strokes said, "He'll be in at two."

"Thanks. We'll be back then. Please don't mention anything to him. He's not in any trouble and we don't want to worry him."

The detectives returned to the precinct. Gil got out the letters from his bottom drawer and spread them out on top of his desk.

Cornell pulled his chair around so they both could see the letters and said, "Are you okay to start this?"

"Yeah. Maybe I'll get my second wind."

Gil started, "Saturday, June 2nd Allen Venter, white male, 42, shot at close range with a .45 caliber pistol between the hours of 4 and 7 p.m. Received this letter on Monday, June 4th, postmarked May 31st - two days before the murder - saying *'Doubt thou the stars are fire, doubt that the sun doth move, doubt truth to be a liar, but never doubt I love.'* Then, on Wednesday, July 5th, Harold McDonald, white male, 65, was killed from what we think was a sniper from across the street in the early afternoon in broad daylight with a. . . . Let me look at the coroner's report."

Cornell got up, reached across to his desk, pulled a file, and handed it to Gil. Gil thumbed through it and continued, "With a Remington .223 caliber bullet most likely shot from a Bushmaster XM15-E2S according to Ingersoll's findings. On July 6th I get this note postmarked July 5th - the day of the murder - that says *'Then must you speak of one that loved not wisely, but too well.'* Two separate methods with no apparent connection except these two letters."

Gil stopped and pondered the situation for a minute then continued. "Now, I can accept the coincidence of the letters arriving after the murders, and the letters could be about something else we're not seeing. But, then we have this," Gil pointed to the third letter. "This morning between midnight and two, Dorothy Coel, white female, 28, was gagged and suffocated. I would bet she was not sexually molested, but we'll wait for the doc to tell us. But for now, we have a boyfriend on a fishing trip; I get this letter postmarked yesterday afternoon, almost twelve hours before the murder simply saying *'love her or leave her.'* Now, I don't think that coincidence has anything to do with it. But most important, there is no physical evidence. No hair fibers, fingerprints, transfer evidence. How can there be no physical evidence? The letters are the only thing tying everything together."

"Why can't they be tied to something else? They seem to talk about love and relationships, not murder."

"I'm not sure at this point."

"But the methods of murder are all so different. If you are saying they are connected, don't serial killers, - if that is what you're suggesting - use the same method to commit their crimes? Isn't that how you caught The Professor?"

\*\*\*

Randy L. Hilmer

# Chapter 6
# Roberta Waverly
*September 2012*

Gilbert Clifton joined the Camden, NJ police department on February 4, 1979. He had graduated from the academy at the top of his class. After six years of uniformed service, he was promoted to detective, which is a job he worked hard to earn. He was assigned a partner in the homicide division by the name of Mason Dierikson. Gil learned a lot from his partner, but it was apparent that Gil had the superior capabilities for being a detective. They had solved three murders in Gil's first four months.

During the first three weeks in June, 1985, seven murders had taken place. The victims were all white women in their twenties, medium height; each had long brunette hair and a slender build. They all worked the streets as prostitutes within a five block area in the downtown district. Gil was assigned to a task force specially created to catch the killer. Gil quickly became instrumental on the force and set up a sting operation. An FBI profiler said that the killer would be a male of average looks, single or divorced, and most likely employed in a professional capacity. Because little forensic evidence was left behind, the profiler added to the description that the perpetrator would be of high intelligence and detail oriented.

On Tuesday, June 25, 1985, Gil and his partner were staking out a location in the center of the district and closely following a female police officer posing as a prostitute and fitting the description of the victims. She was wired for sound so the detectives could hear any conversation between the officer and any possible suspect. At 10:16 p.m., a white Cadillac with New Jersey plates stopped where the decoy was standing and lowered the passenger window.

When the decoy bent over to look into the window she asked, "Need a date for the evening?"

"I do not usually partake in this sort of frivolity, so I am not sure of the exact procedure," said a man from inside the car.

"Well, it's easy. First I need to know if you're a cop. You looked so well dressed."

"I am truly not a man of the law. I am a professor over at the university. I teach classical English literature. Are you interested in the classics?"

"Sure, honey. You want to teach me?"

"As I said, I know not of the correct procedure. However, if I were to speculate, I would imagine I should offer you some monetary compensation. Am I not correct, Miss?"

"Are you going to be my sugar daddy?"

"Oh, this sounds most exciting already. Yes, I shall most assuredly be your, as you call it, sugar daddy if fifty dollars is recompense enough. Please come in."

"Oh, daddy, that's not how it's done out here. You know the cops are looking for some sleazebag and if I get in your car right here in public, they might think a well-educated man like you could be a bad man." She took off a neckerchief that was tied around her neck and gave it to the driver. That was the signal to the surveillance team that she had a good suspect on the hook and to start the plan for the takedown.

With that, the surveillance team had enough to arrest him on a soliciting charge. However, the takedown would be too difficult on the main street so they waited for him to drive into the parking lot. If not, they would have to take him on the street as a last resort.

"Here, honey, do you like my perfume?"

The driver took the neckerchief and brought it up to his nose. "My, you sure have a delightful and wonderful fragrance about you."

"Well, if you like that, I have it all over my body so why don't you just drive around the corner into that parking lot. Nobody will see us there and we can leave and go someplace real nice and private to have some real fun. Okay, handsome?"

He handed the neckerchief back to the decoy but she refused to take it. "You can keep it for a few minutes. That way you know I'll be there to get it back. Okay, baby?"

"Your sweet fragrance shall guide my every thought. I shall see you very shortly, my dear." He drove off and turned into the parking lot one-half block away.

Gil had the entire meeting on camera and the handkerchief would tie the suspect to the soliciting charge. Two patrol cars screeched to a stop, one in front and one behind the white Cadillac. The suspect had been caught. He gave his name as James Edward Macklevy. He was divorced and employed as a professor of English literature at the University of New Jersey-Camden. He matched the profile to a tee.

A search warrant was issued for his residence and police found two rings allegedly belonging to two of the murder victims. They also found hair fibers in his vehicle matching three of the victims. The audio and video tapes, along with the handkerchief used as the signal for the takedown, were used by the prosecution. Gil had presented the prosecutor a very solid case.

The press dubbed Macklevy as 'The Professor' not only because of where he was employed, but because they thought he spoke like a professor of English literature. He seemed snobbish, arrogant and full of self-righteousness. He had one child, a girl, who was fifteen years old when he was convicted. She was placed in a foster home and was forbidden to make contact with her father.

During the trial it was apparent to the judge, jury, press and even the upper echelon of the police force that it was Gil who had put the case together with meticulous detail in which the capture was executed so that all of the evidence was admissible in court.

When the judge asked The Professor if he had anything to say before sentencing it was widely reported that The Professor rendered a soliloquy, as it were, stating his profound innocence. The most reported quote had him saying, *'I shan't be swayed nor shall I be intimidated by the provincialism and insularity of this bodacious encounter with the unreasonableness of accounts pertaining to activities allegedly perpetrated by a lowly scholar and interpreted so prejudicially as to afford not one scintilla of contemplation for a dispassionate exhibition of mortal benevolence.'*

James 'The Professor' Macklevy was convicted on five counts of murder and sentenced to life in prison without the possibility of parole The morning after the conviction the headlines read 'TEACHER RECEIVES DETENTION BY STUDENT' - 'ROOKIE DETECTIVE OUTWITS THE PROFESSOR' and 'THE PROFESSOR LEARNS LESSON FROM STUDENT.'

The Professor was housed at Rahway State Prison in 1985, which had just changed its name to East Jersey Prison. Gil interviewed him after his conviction with the hope of closing the cases on the other six open murders. The Professor refused to oblige.

"I shall be most enthusiastic to teach you the ways of a serial executioner but shall not be able to assist you with your inquisition to establish other criminal wrong doings upon my person as I sit before you an innocent man," The Professor had declared to Gil.

From 1990 to 2012 The Professor had been used to help the police in two cases from the viewpoint of a serial killer. This was completely against all that Gil stood for.

"He's a sanctimonious cold blooded killer and to inflate his ego by asking him to help the police is utterly ridiculous," Gil had exclaimed on both occasions. However, he was not involved in the investigation of either case but would tell anyone who would listen how he felt about The Professor.

Gil glared at his partner when Cornell brought up the name of The Professor. "It was the task force as a whole who captured that dirt bag and I don't want to hear his name brought up again. Do you understand? He is a self-serving egotist and I will not tolerate using him as a profiler."

Cornell slouched in his chair like a scolded child and answered, "Yes, sir."

Gil could see how his berating affected his partner and added, "I didn't mean to be so harsh but every time I hear that name by blood boils. I'm sorry if I offended you."

"That's alright. I wasn't suggesting that you use him for information; I was just saying that these patterns don't fit the crimes being linked like in his case."

The matter was quickly dropped with silence.

The rest of August was routine for the detectives. They were assigned a case on August 16th and had the murderer arrested and charged two days later. Cornell and Gil spent the rest of the month making sure the evidence in that case was formalized and sent to the District Attorney.

They also would take out the three unsolved cases almost every day, but there was nothing new with any of them that would lead to a suspect, never mind an arrest.

Gil could be found most nights viewing the footage from the security cameras, re-reading all of the reports, trying to find something that he may have overlooked. There was just no forensic evidence. That in and of itself convinced Gil that the crimes were connected and the letters solidified his reasoning.

Gil and Cornell were off duty for the Labor Day weekend. Gil spent the three day holiday with Cassandra. They drove sixty miles to Atlantic City and stayed in one of the hotel/casinos on the boardwalk. Although neither gambled very much, they did enjoy playing the slot machines and Baccarat. Cassandra would drag Gil through the shops or they would lounge in a poolside cabana during the day and take in a show at night. Gil had a wonderful time despite having three unsolved murders waiting for him back in Camden.

Tuesday morning, September 4th Gil was just sitting down at his desk at 9:30 a.m. in the squad room when Cornell came over to him. "Just got word we're assigned a case. Let's roll. I'll fill you in on the way."

They passed Nathan as they were leaving and he said to Gil, "Would you like me to put the mail on your desk, sir?"

"Sure, as long as there is nothing urgent."

"I believe there is, sir."

"What!?"

Nathan handed Gil an envelope with the word <u>URGENT</u> emblazoned on the outside. Gil tore open and read the contents.

### *'She had all the makings of a queen'*

Cornell stopped and returned to where Gil stood dead in his tracks staring at a piece of paper.

"What is it, Gil?"

He handed the paper to his partner. As Cornell read the verse Gil asked, "What is the assignment?"

"A woman was found dead over at Garden State Park," Cornell replied as his eyes widened in amazement.

"Let's go."

Garden State Park was a popular place for joggers, cyclists, tennis players and chess players. It was a densely wooded area with a walking/running/bicycling track encircling the entire park. In the middle was an open area where the tennis courts were located. Cement bench chairs were on either side of the permanent cement tables scattered around the courts where players would engage in games of chess or checkers. Pavilions with picnic tables were on both ends of the courts.

The wide track was divided in thirds by white lines and an occasional stencil indicating which lane was for walkers, joggers and cyclists. Affluent people with a propensity for keeping in shape and students most often used the track, while the idle rich would play tennis. The intellectuals and retirees would compete in impromptu chess or checker matches. The park was located in a very exclusive part of Camden and was patrolled regularly by an outside security firm called ProTect.

It was just past ten o'clock in the morning when the partners reached the park and saw a good size crowd gathering near a bend in the jogging path. The woods extended nearly to the path along its right side. Cornell started interviewing the uniforms on scene while Gil stepped under the yellow police tape and into the woods about thirty feet from the path. A beautiful fully clothed black female lay over the underbrush between two large pine trees. The coroner was already examining the body and a forensic officer was searching around the body extending his search ever wider.

Dr. Ingersoll came up to Gil, "Strangled. She's been dead for about three to four hours. Doesn't look like any other traumatic markings, but we'll know during the autopsy."

Gil asked, "She was strangled between 6 and 7 this morning?"

"Unofficially, yes. I want to do a thorough examination but it sure looks like strangulation to me."

"Would you say by hands, with a rope or some kind of ligature?"

"By the markings on her neck it looks like hands. Several bruised areas indicate she was strangled from behind."

"What else can you tell me?"

"Mr. Hurry-hurry-hurry, please let me conduct an autopsy and I will gladly answer your questions professionally and with an educated certainty rather than my guessing to satisfy your impatient nature."

"Doc. . . ."

"Yes, I will perform the autopsy later today and give you my findings as always."

"Doc, you are terrific."

"Yeah, sure. I got your Christmas card last year."

The ambulance attendants were ready to transport the body to the morgue. Gil left the crime scene and sought out Cornell who was now speaking to someone in the crowd. Gil waited for him to finish and then approached his partner.

"What do you have?"

"The victim's name is Roberta Waverly. I just interviewed one of her neighbors, an elderly lady named Phyllis Fullerton, who saw the victim leave her house alone this morning in her jogging suit. She said Roberta jogged in this park almost every day around six. Most of the time she was alone unless her husband joined her. The husband's name is Brandt Waverly. He is some kind of contractor or something."

"Brandt Waverly?"

"Yes."

"He's one of the biggest contractors in the state. Worth millions."

"Great. Anyway, Fullerton told me that Roberta and Brandt were having some marriage difficulties but didn't think it was too serious. The Waverly couple have no children and Mrs. Waverly did charity work for what Phyllis said was her 'cause of the week'. She also said that Roberta is a gold digger because her husband is so much older than her."

"What was the old lady doing in the park?"

"She saw a lot of commotion over here and was curious."

"Any witnesses to the crime?"

"None have come forward, yet."

"Who found the body?"

"A security guard from ProTect. His name is Anton Jackson and he has been part of their canine unit for the last two years. He said when he passed this location his dog reacted and led him to the body. I've got him coming down to the precinct later to give a full statement."

Gil looked around, his eyes stopping on every person in the crowd, searching to see if someone was acting suspiciously. Sometimes the perp likes to hide in plain sight. No unusual reaction that Gil could discern.

"Anything wrong, Gil?

"No. Find out where Brandt Waverly's office building is located. We'd better get over there before the press locks onto this story."

"A uniform is running that information on the computer in his car. I'll get it and meet you at the car. Anything else before we go?"

"Call in and have someone write up a search warrant for the Waverly's house. Make it generic enough just in case Brandt doesn't want to cooperate."

"Okay." Cornell was off. Gil reached inside his sports jacket and pulled out the letter he had received that morning. It was postmarked Saturday, September 1st. He read it again, 'She had all the makings of a queen.' From what he had learned so far, Gil thought to himself, *she practically lived like a queen.*

Gil and Cornell drove to the address where Brandt Waverly had his office. It was located in a huge corporate complex built by Waverly Building and Contracting. They parked and went into the fourteen story building and asked the receptionist to see Brandt Waverly.

"Do you have an appointment?"

"No." Gil pulled out his badge and showed the good looking young girl. "Camden police, Miss. Please tell Mr. Waverly it is very important that we speak to him immediately."

She made a call and whispered into the receiver and then hung it up. "Mr. Waverly will see you. Please take the elevator to the fourteenth floor. You will be greeted by his secretary."

The building was ornate with marble floors, art work scattered around and paintings on every wall. The elevator doors opened on the fourteenth floor and Gil and Cornell were met by a man in his twenties.

"Please follow me. Whom shall I say is calling?"

Gil pulled out one of his business cards and handed it to him. "Detective Gil Clifton, Camden Police Department, Homicide Division."

"Homicide? Is there anything wrong?"

"We need to talk to Mr. Waverly."

"Yes, right in here." He opened one side of the ten foot wooden French doors. Sitting in front of a window and behind an extremely large desk sat Mr. Brandt Waverly. Brandt immediately stood up and indicated for them to be seated in two chairs facing his desk.

Brandt took his seat and said, "That is all, Franklin. Thank you." The young secretary left and closed the door behind him.

"What's this all about?"

"I am Detective Gil Clifton and this is my partner, Detective Cornell Bush."

"Pleased to meet you. Now, how can I help you?" Brandt said cordially.

"We're here on some unpleasant business." Gil didn't say anything else for a moment and studied Brandt carefully for any reaction which was about to follow. Brandt's eyes turned questioning as the two never lost eye contact.

Gil broke the brief silence and said, "I regret to inform you, sir, but your wife has been murdered."

\*\*\*

# Chapter 7
# Adin Williamson
## *2012*

Brandt Waverly took the news of his wife's murder very hard. Gil thought it was a genuine and sincere reaction; not some staged and pretentious theatrical performance. But that was only a gut feeling and Gil would still have to investigate him as a prime suspect until such time he could be eliminated. Once the initial shock of the news had subsided, Gil wanted to question Brandt on a few details. The information obtained from a neighbor indicated that the couple were having marital problems and that Mrs. Waverly was a gold digger.

"My wife and I are not having any problems at all. The only person who would say anything like that would have to be that busybody Fullerton woman."

Cornell looked quickly at his notes and asked, "Phyllis Fullerton?"

"Yes. She's the neighborhood pain-in-the-ass. Always in the midst of rumors which turn out to be just that, rumors and nothing else."

"Your wife is quite a bit younger than you, is that correct?"

"Yeah. She's thirty-one and I'm fifty-eight. We have been married for eight years. The first marriage for both of us. I love her and she loves me. Sure, we might have a disagreement now and again, but nothing out of the normal. They're more misunderstandings than anything else, usually about a charity or something to do with a charity. Never one concerning us not getting along."

Brandt confided to the detectives that Roberta was dedicated to keeping herself fit and would jog twice around the 1.2 mile track at the Garden State Park every day. She generally started her run around six in the morning. He left for the office at about 6:45 and wouldn't see her until he returned home around seven in the evening or sometimes they would meet for lunch.

The officers asked about her charity work and Brandt replied that she was very much dedicated to several different organizations and fundraisers. She felt good about herself, not in an egotistical way, but was sincerely happy that she had the opportunity to help others. Gil asked him to accompany them to the morgue for a positive identification of the body. The grief-stricken Brandt agreed and the questioning ceased.

Brandt made a positive identification and broke down in tears at seeing his wife lying on a gurney. Franklin helped his boss from the room and into his car. Gil followed and asked Brandt if he could get his permission to search their home. Brandt said yes but he would like to be there when they did. Later that day Gil, Cornell and two uniformed officers searched the 5,600 square foot home of Brandt and Roberta Waverly and came away with only a letter typed and printed on their home computer.

When the two detectives returned to the precinct, the crime scene photos were laying on Gil's desk. The only thing they saw were two drag marks starting at the edge of the path leading back to where the body was found. No other footprints were seen. The autopsy report came in later that day and Dr. Ingersoll reported the death by 'asphyxiation due to manual strangulation'. There were no fingerprints or skin oil transfers on the neck which indicated that the perp had used gloves.

Hair fibers were found on the jogging suit worn by the victim, but were later identified as being from her and her husband, which would be very normal. A check of the husband's past showed no criminal history. He was active in charities along with his wife and was a current supporter of Carl Brisbane.

"That can't be good," said Gil.

"Why's that?" Cornell asked.

"We're going to get heat from Brisbane on this one, you can count on it."

---

Carl Brisbane had resigned his position as captain of the robbery division at the 17th precinct to run for sheriff. His promotion to captain in 2007 was more of a political move than a deserved position. He had been campaigning since April 2012 when he officially registered his candidacy at the county clerk's office. It came as no surprise as there had been rumblings throughout the entire police force of his desire to run for sheriff.

Captain Brisbane had risen through the ranks and his career was dotted with political undertones, backroom dealings and favoritism. He had started his campaign as the peoples' candidate and espoused a platform of policy transparency and public information of ongoing investigations as well as updates in a timely manner. In late July, he started turning up the heat by calling for fiscal responsibility across the whole department and campaigning for reduction in staff and the elimination of overtime for all hourly law enforcement personnel.

The current sheriff, Richard Winston, had been sheriff for six consecutive terms but had some bad publicity befall him over the last year and a half because of the high overtime paid and budgetary increases he had deemed as 'necessary'. Carl Brisbane was attacking those policies and had public support because a weak economy was plaguing the city of Camden.

Captain McCadry and Carl Brisbane were sitting in the living room at the home of Brandt Waverly. Carl and Brandt had many opportunities to cross paths, not only socially, but Brandt was a huge contributor to Carl's election effort. Both were members of the prestigious Camden Country Club where they would often play golf, enjoy a game of tennis or have an occasional dinner with their wives. Every so often Captain McCadry and his wife would join them for dinner.

"I am so sorry for your loss, Brandt. You know I thought the world of Roberta," Carl said.

"Thank you. It's been a hard few days."

"If there is anything we can do...."

"God damn right there is something you can do. Catch the son-of-a-bitch who killed my wife!"

"We're trying everything we can. Please believe me," said McCadry.

Carl was standing near the unlit fireplace with his arm resting on the mantel. "I'm on Brandt's side on this. Just what in the hell are you doing? It's been three days and not a peep out of police except for a two minute briefing. Meanwhile, the press is having a heyday with this!"

"We have one of our best detectives on this case...."

"And just the who hell is that?" screamed Carl.

"Detective Gil Clifton."

"Hasn't he failed recently on some other murders, if my memory serves me right, on your lousy briefings?" Carl said.

"Yes, there have been some challenges."

"For Christ sakes, man, challenges are what the job is all about! He's a detective and that demands that he overcome your so-called challenges. I want full accountability and disclosure on this case!" Carl was livid.

"Carl, you know we can't give full disclosure on a...."

Carl interrupted again, "I mean full disclosure about his record of solving murders, you idiot!"

"That wouldn't be quite fair at this point."

"Fair? You're talking about fair when we have a man of Mr. Waverly's stature sitting here with absolutely no knowledge as to why his beautiful wife was murdered. A woman who, by the way, supported the cancer research foundation that you love so dearly." Carl was now standing in front of the seated McCadry in an intimidating manner. "My friend is grief-stricken and all you give me is 'fair'? You had better do better than that."

"Carl, you're not sheriff yet...."

"When I do become sheriff in two months and if you don't have this case wrapped up and the killer behind bars then heads will roll. I'll start with yours! Do I make myself perfectly clear?"

"Yes." McCadry tried to stand up but Brisbane did not move a muscle and blocked his attempt.

"May I get up, please?"

Carl moved to one side and McCadry rose from his chair. He went over and spoke to Brandt. "I will put every effort at my disposal to solve this case as quickly as possible, Mr. Waverly. You can depend on me."

Brandt glared at him and said nothing. McCadry turned to Brisbane and said, "I'll get right on this." He left the house without any further discussion.

McCadry summoned Gil to his office. Gil gently knocked on the door and was told to enter and be seated.

"This won't take long. I want to know the status of the cases you have been assigned."

"Assigned since when?"

"Since June!"

"We've had seven assignments and solved four. There are still the Venter, McDonald and Coel cases pending."

"How about Roberta Waverly?"

"We just got that case."

"So you're telling me you have been assigned eight cases and solved only half of them, is that correct?"

"I guess you could put it that way. Not every case unfolds the way you want it to and sometimes it takes longer."

"Do you know what our closed case percentage is in this department?"

"No, sir."

"Eighty-four percent! The highest rate in the state of New Jersey! And you're sitting at fifty percent. Do I have to assign your cases to real detectives and you can go play crossing guard at some elementary school?"

"Sir, the cases you are referring to have had no...."

"I don't want any damn excuses. Now get out of my office and get these cases solved and I want top priority on the Waverly murder. Do you hear me? Top priority!"

"Yes, sir." Gil was mad but held his temper.

He left the captain's office and went down one flight of stairs to his desk. Cornell was there and looked up. He could tell Gil was upset and knew he had just been to see the captain. All of this told Cornell that Gil didn't have any good news.

"Doesn't look like it went too well."

"You got that right. Waverly is now top priority."

Gil and Cornell were planning their strategy when Carl Brisbane entered the squad room.

"What the hell is he doing here?" asked Cornell.

"Probably he thinks he's the goddamn sheriff already," Gil replied under his breath.

"Where is Detective Gil Clifton?" Carl barked.

"That would be me."

Carl walked swiftly towards Gil and stopped almost on top of Gil as he was seated in his chair.

"I want to know the status on the Waverly case." His voice was loud and demanding.

"First, with all due respect, you have no authority to be here." Gil pushed back his chair, stood up, and was now nose-to-nose with the candidate. "Secondly, we do not give out reports to civilians about ongoing investigations. Lastly - and this is the most important - I personally don't like the way you came barging in here demanding shit. Now, get out before I have you arrested on a trespassing charge."

"You'll regret this, detective."

Carl abruptly left the office, headed for the third floor and went directly to Captain McCadry's office. Carl threw open the door and stood in front of McCadry's desk, leaned forward toward the stunned captain, put his hands on top of the desk and shouted, "Who the hell does this Gil Clifton think he is?"

"Why, what happened?"

"I asked for an update on Waverly and he told me he would have me arrested for trespassing!" Carl stood erect and put his hands on his hips.

"Carl, if you went down there and started demanding information, naturally he would be upset. You resigned your position and...."

"Then you give me an update. And what's this I hear about a serial killer running loose in the city?"

"That has to be a rumor. We have no substantiated evidence of a serial killer. Who told you that?"

"A goddamn reporter outside the Waverly home. What's going on in this department?"

Captain McCadry rose from his desk, walked over and shut his door and invited Carl to have a seat.

---

All of the local newspapers were reporting on the story about a serial killer. Headlines read: BRISBANE UNCOVERS COVERUP OF SERIAL KILLER – BRISBANE TAKES LID OFF COVERUP and BRISBANE PROMISES TO CATCH SERIAL KILLER. All the papers were running front page stories. Carl Brisbane capitalized on his new found notoriety and started airing radio and television commercials condemning the inefficiency of the current sheriff and his staff while promising to do everything in his power to catch the killer.

*'This wouldn't happen on my watch'* was the tag line he was using in all of his ads and promotions. The campaign was heating up. Sheriff Winston could do little to stem the strength Brisbane was generating. The month of September found the Waverly case no closer to finding a suspect than the day it happened. Carl Brisbane was relentless in his attack of the current administration.

Brandt Waverly gave up his daily calls to Detective Gil. No news was not good news in this case. Captain McCadry had Gil in his office almost every other day but all Gil could do was tell his boss that they were still working on it. In reality this case had stalled, just like the other three cases had come to a complete stop.

The media stories spread throughout the state and spilled over into Connecticut, New York, Pennsylvania, Delaware and Maryland. Camden, New Jersey was receiving unwanted publicity. The Mayor was going to the press denying claims of a serial killer, while behind the scenes he would scream at the top of his lungs at Jacob Feinstein, the Chief of Police. In turn, Jacob would have words with McCadry, and on down the line it went. At the bottom, of course, was Detective Gil.

The homicide department was in turmoil, and to top it off, one detective suffered a heart attack while at home and a second detective was off on workman's compensation after being injured. The homicide squad was down to only four and Gil and Cornell were the only team still intact. This made assigning new cases that much more difficult and cut down McCadry's options. He put the two lone detectives together and decided not to break up Gil and Cornell. Now, the entire Camden homicide squad was made up of only two teams.

September was a difficult month for Gil and Cassandra, also. Gil was on the hot seat at work and Cassandra was extremely busy at her advertising agency. They spent only a day or two a week sleeping in the same bed. Most of the time, Gil would go to his apartment because of the late hours he was keeping.

One evening when they were together Cassandra asked, "Do you really think there is a serial killer in Camden?"

"I think there is but it is hard to convince McCadry to set up a task force because all of the murders I think are tied together are so dissimilar in nature. That doesn't follow the pattern of serial killers."

Gil sounded dejected. Cassandra would try to cheer him up, but because she was so tired her efforts fell short. The two would climb into bed and immediately fall asleep.

---

The night of October 3rd Gil was spending a rare night at Cassandra's when his cell phone rang at 4:58 a.m. Cornell told him to meet him at the Rainbow Lounge downtown. Gil got up, dressed and whispered goodbye to Cassandra. She told him to be careful and fell back to sleep.

Gil arrived at the Rainbow Lounge at 5:30 and saw Cornell, once again, the first on the scene. The Rainbow Lounge was a gay men's club open from 11:00 p.m. to 6:00 a.m., seven days per week. The club was dark even with the lights on. There was a body lying in the middle of the dance floor. Uniformed police officers were milling around the club looking for evidence.

A sergeant approached Cornell and asked, "Are you the detective in charge?"

"My partner and I are, yes. What do you have?"

"Young gay guy stabbed in the stomach and landed in the middle of the floor. By the time we got here the place was almost deserted. Everybody fled when someone said this guy was dead."

"Why does he have a mask on?"

"It was masquerade night. Everyone was wearing a mask. The owner and club manager are still here. You'll find them in an office next to the bar."

Detectives Gil and Cornell were not going to wait for Dr. Ingersoll to show up at the Rainbow Lounge. The only additional information he could provide would be other possible injuries but the cause of death was plain to see. The victim was lying on his side and the handle of the knife was protruding from the stomach area. And even though the lounge was dimly lit, they could see blood had soaked the victim's shirt and was pooling on the floor around him.

Jarad Avery was the owner of the Rainbow Lounge and was sitting behind an undersized desk in a small room off the main bar of the club. He had a large plume of feathers cascading around his shoulders and sitting on the desk was a mask of some sort of bird. Seated in front was Tony Ulric, the club manager dressed up in a penguin's costume without a mask. The two stood up, introduced themselves to the detectives and returned to their seats.

Detective Gil started the inquiry, "Can you tell me what happened here tonight?"

Tony spoke up first. "I was behind the bar. We had a pretty good crowd. Everyone was dressed up in costume because it was our semi-annual masquerade ball. I was going to take a break at about 4:15 when all of a sudden all hell broke loose. People were screaming, yelling and running for the front door. All I could hear is people repeating 'he's dead, he's dead'. When people vacated the dance floor, Adin was lying there motionless. I went over to see what the matter was and I saw the knife sticking out of him and the blood on his shirt. I called the police right away."

"You said Adin. Do you know him?"

"Yes. Adin Williamson. He's a regular."

"How did you know it was Adin with his mask on?"

"When he was ordering some drinks and I could tell by his voice. Most people hand me a note when they want a drink."

"If I may ask," continued Gil, "was this some kind of pre-Halloween party far in advance?"

"No our Halloween party is on Halloween Night and that is a completely different kind of party."

"How so?"

"For our Masquerade Ball everyone gets a score sheet, and at the end of the night each person will get up on stage. Everyone else would write the person's name on their sheet along with identifying the costume. The fun is trying to conceal your identity while trying to guess everyone else's. Once everyone was seen on stage, the sheets would be handed in and the person with the most correct answers would win $500.00. Second place $250.00 and third place $125.00. We do it twice a year. Our Halloween party is judged on the customer's costume in different categories."

"Was there anyone in attendance that you didn't know?"

"I can't really say. Most of them kept their masks on and, like I said, would hand me a note when they ordered drinks because they were playing the Masquerade Game."

"What do you know about Adin Williamson?"

"Not too much. He is a nice kid, probably in his early twenties. Comes in most weekends. Has a few drinks, parties a little and never causes any trouble."

"Did he have a special person?"

"You mean partner?"

"I guess."

"Naw. He was pretty much by himself. He had lots of friends and liked to socialize but I can't remember him being hooked up with anyone in particular."

The questioning went on for another half hour. Gil then asked if the security cameras worked inside the club area. Jarad handed him VCR tapes from the two cameras.

"We are a little behind in the digital age. This is all we have."

"How long do you keep the tapes?"

"If nothing happens we reuse the tapes. These may be a little scratchy because we have used them for about eight months now."

They left the small office and returned to the club room. Dr. Ingersoll was examining the body. Gil walked over and greeted the doctor.

"Stab wound as you might have guessed. I put the knife in the evidence bag. Here's his billfold, I thought you might want to go through it before I put it in the bag."

"Thanks, doc."

When they got back to the precinct Cornell ran a check on the victim. Adin Williams, black male, 23 years old, no apparent relationships, worked as freelance photographer. He lives over at the Silent Arms Apartments."

"Coincidence?" Gil asked as more of a statement than a question.

\*\*\*

# Chapter 8
# Yosef Rabinovich
*November 2012*

It was getting more frustrating every day for the two detectives who now have four unsolved murders, one pending investigation on their plates and no clues. No evidence. No solid witnesses. They arrived at the precinct at approximately 10:45 a.m. as Nathan was passing out the second round of mail.

"Good morning detective," Nathan said.

"Good morning, Nathan. Are you off to a good start?"

"Yes, sir. Thank you. Here is your mail. I left the first round on your desk earlier."

"Thanks." Gil took his mail and sorted through it.

"Oh, shit!"

Cornell looked up from his computer and asked, "Not another one?"

Gil held up the envelope so Cornell could see the URGENT on the front side. Gil opened it and saw the contents:

***'He that dies pays all debts'***

He handed the letter to Cornell. Cornell examined it. "Post marked yesterday?"

Gil took a closer look at the envelope and said, "You got it."

McCadry came storming into the squad room and proceeded directly to Gil's desk.

"Have you heard the news this morning?"

"No, we've been on a case since 5:30. We just got back here."

"Where were you?"

"A kid got knifed over at the Rainbow Lounge. I got the call around five this morning."

"All the local channels are reporting that this is tied to the serial killer. How the hell did they get that information?"

"I haven't a clue, captain. I just received another letter about two minutes ago." He handed the letter to his boss.

"You better get on this; Brisbane will have a field day."

"I think it's tied to the other cases."

"With what evidence do you make that conclusion?"

"I've told you about the letters. I think they're connected."

"What have you got on the Waverly murder?"

"No new evidence or leads. We're at a standstill."

"I told you top priority! Weren't you listening?"

Gil was getting a little aggravated. "With nothing new there's no place to go. I can't just make up shit."

"Well, you'd better start doing something. You can answer to Brisbane this time." He pointed at Gil, threw the letter on the desk and left in a huff.

"Forget about him, Gil. What do these letters mean?"

"I have no idea but they have to be connected to these cases somehow."

"Give me the letters. I have an idea."

Gil reached into his desk and gave all the letters to his partner. "What are you going to do?"

"It may be a stretch but I'm going to do a little research. I'll let you know in a few minutes. Could you get me a cup of coffee?" Cornell realized what he said and looked up at his partner with an awkward grin. "Sorry."

"No, that's alright. You work on your idea and I'll get us some coffee." Gil got up and then said, "Black, right?"

"Yeah, thanks."

Cornell turned on his computer and logged on the internet. He took the letters and one by one he typed in the message in the search engine. Gil returned with his coffee and set it on Cornell's desk.

"What's your idea?"

Cornell continued his searching of the internet, "I think you might be right. These letters may be connected to the murders. I'm just about through and if my hunch is right we may have something. I'll be done in a second."

---

The election was only a month away and Carl Brisbane was increasing his demands as if he were already elected. Captain McCadry was the buffer between Gil and Carl but he was clearly on the side of Carl. McCadry, however, would argue with Carl about speaking so openly to the press.

"Can you taper down your speeches about a serial killer, Carl? It's not helping us in the least," McCadry begged.

"If you get the Waverly killer, I'll back off, but until you do you're no better than the rest of these flunkies you call detectives. Have you formed a task force? No. Have you given briefing updates? No. Have you made any arrests? No!"

"Carl, you've been on this side of. . . ."

"I don't want excuses. This will not happen on my watch!" Carl Brisbane slammed the captain's door and proceeded down the stairs and out the door to the front steps of the precinct. He was beginning to believe his own hype. A throng of reporters were lurking around and hurriedly gathered as soon as they spotted the candidate. Each reporter was yelling above the next in order to get Brisbane's attention.

Carl held up both hands to silence the crowd and once they calmed down he said, "There are reports of a murder that took place earlier this morning has been linked to other unsolved murder cases over the last several months. First of all let me assure you that when I am elected sheriff this will not happen on my watch. But for now, I will tell you that Captain McCadry and his team are working to solve these cases and bringing to justice the person or persons involved. But, this makes an excellent point to what I have been advocating all along - that an open dialogue with the community and transparency in police procedures may have aided in the efforts of capturing this killer. But, the current sheriff refuses to put a task force together even while the public is asking - no, I should say begging for - a conclusion to these heinous crimes. When I am elected, if this administration has not brought these cases to a conclusion, I positively assure you that I will immediately form a task force and have open communications with the press. Thank you."

The press started their incessant overlapping questions as Carl stated he had nothing more to say. He inched his way through the crowd, got into his waiting limousine and drove off. McCadry was watching the event from his third story window and muttered to himself, *opportunist.*

---

Gil was reviewing the tapes from the Rainbow Lounge and saw something that unnerved him. There was a person in a hooded sweatshirt who had approached the victim. After reviewing that portion of the tape over and over again, he concluded that a stabbing motion could be detected, albeit, the tape was very scratchy. He showed his discovery to his partner.

"It looks like the same figure from the Dorothy Coel case" Cornell said.

"Yeah. I think we have another connection."

"Well, we might have another one." Cornell was explaining his discovery to Gil his search of the internet. "You see, every letter contains a solitary line. I typed each into a search engine and every time it came up, it was from a play written by Shakespeare."

"What?"

"Look at this. June's letter from Hamlet, July's from Othello, August was from King Lear." As Cornell was naming the plays he would throw the letter on the desk in front of Gil. "And it goes on. Look. September from Henry VIII and today's was from The Tempest. All plays written by Shakespeare."

"Okay. That ties everything closer but what do we have?"

"That's not all. We are so used to trying to link serial killers to a singular M.O. but look at the Gary Taylor case. His methods were all over the map. I am now convinced that there is a serial killer at work here."

Gil slammed his fist on his desk, "I knew it!"

"Now hear me out," Cornell was motioning for Gil to take a seat and he sat across from him at his own desk.

"What?" Gil was bracing himself for some bad news.

"Just hear me out before you start yelling. Now," he paused and took a deep breath, "maybe we should have a talk with The Professor and. . ."

"Never!" shouted Gil.

---

It was the weekend before the November 6th elections and Carl Brisbane's campaign was at its peak. All local radio and television stations were carrying the *'not on my watch'* slogan. Carl would have a media presentation in the morning and another one near the dinner hour that would be broadcast live by the evening news programs. The incumbent Richard Winston was barely putting on any campaign at all. The bad publicity he received about the budgets, the relentless public berating leveled by Carl and the anxiousness of a possible serial killer at large were all factoring into his defeat and he resigned himself to that fact. There was one other set of circumstances that kept Sheriff Winston from participating in a more vigorous campaign but he kept that to himself.

Jacob Feinstein, the Camden Police Chief, was not above being a target of Carl Brisbane. However, Carl's attacks on the well-liked police chief were tempered and far and few between. Carl and Jacob had a history together and both were allies of Brandt Waverly. Carl kept McCadry at arm's length, but out of public view, Carl would tell him that it was more for show than substance. McCadry bought-in to that philosophy and fed Carl inside information that would later wind up in the local newspapers.

Monday morning, Gil was at his desk looking at the files. Cornell came in late and took his seat at his desk. Gil sat and looked for his mail, but Nathan had not been around to deliver it yet. So, he took out the Adin Williamson file and began paging through the documents.

Cornell answered his phone at 9:37 a.m., "Camden Homicide, Detective Bush. . . . Yes he is. . . . You've got to be kidding. . . . Yes. . . . Give me that address again. . . . Thanks."

Gil looked over at Cornell, "For us?"

"Yes. Jewelry shop over on East Washington Boulevard. There's a note on the body addressed to you."

The two detectives left immediately and arrived at the Rabinovich & Son Jewelers in the Jewish business district at 10:06 a.m. The sidewalks were crowded with curious onlookers trying to peek into the shop. Yellow police barrier tape had already been put across the front entrance. Inside, Gil found a woman crying with two uniformed police officers. Gil looked behind the counter and saw the bloody face of a man lying on the floor. There was a note prominently affixed to the man's shirt. It was addressed to Detective Gil with the word <u>URGENT</u> typed on the envelope. Gil shuttered and glanced at Cornell who shook his head ever so slightly as if to say he could hardly believe it.

They would not touch the note until the coroner arrived, so Gil walked over to the police officers standing by a woman who was seated on a stool in front of one of the display counters. The officer told Gil her name was Shoshana Stein. She was the one who ran next door and had the owner of Abramson's Deli call the police. Calev Abramson was standing just inside the door with another police officer and Cornell went to interview him.

Gil would question the lady on the stool. "Is it Miss or Mrs. Stein?"

"Mrs."

"I know you are upset but I would like to ask you a few questions. It's very important."

"Yes," she sobbed.

Shoshana Stein stated that the store opened at nine and she was to pick up two rings and a bracelet Yosef had cleaned and polished for her.

"Is Yosef the owner or clerk?"

"Yosef Rabinovich and his son, Menashe, own the store."

"Do you know them very well?"

"Oh, yes indeed. I've known Yosef and his wife for many years. I have seen Menashe grow up to be a fine man."

Gil was told how she came in at nine and was surprised not to see Yosef behind the counter. She called out his name but there was no answer. She thought he may not hear her if he was in the back room. When she came around the corner, she discovered the body and fled next door for help. Shoshana was distraught, but kept answering Gil's questions as best she could. Gil thanked her and gave her his card.

Gil then went to talk to Dr. Ingersoll's assistant, Dr. Thomas Sutherland. The newest member of the coroner's office was examining the body and writing notes.

"I'm Gil Clifton, Camden Homicide."

"Pleased to meet you. I'm Dr. Thomas Sutherland. This is only my third case."

"Welcome to Camden, doctor. What have you got for me so far?"

"Am I supposed to render an opinion before the autopsy, sir?"

"Just general information. We know that it is only supposition until the official findings, but it is important to get some idea if it is not easily seen. Looks like this guy was beaten to death."

"He was bludgeoned with a blunt object. I am thinking along the lines of a hammer or pry bar."

Gil asked, "Any idea about the time of death."

"By the way it looks right now, I would say between 6:30 and 8:30 this morning.

"Thanks. May I take a look at the note?"

"Please put on these gloves first." He handed Gil a pair of blue surgical gloves.

Gil carefully opened the unsealed envelope and took out the letter. It read;

### *'The fool doth think he is wise, but the wise man knows himself to be a fool'*

Cornell was standing next to Gil and Gil showed him the letter. "Sounds like Shakespeare."

Cornell replied, "I'll check it out."

"Get a copy of this letter and envelope when we get back to the precinct. This is the only letter that will be held as evidence so far."

A very plump lady in her early sixties was being restrained at the door by a police officer.

"I must get to my Yosef! Please let me in!"

Detective Gil went to the woman's aid and told the officer that he would talk to the woman. Her name was Gabriella Rabinovich, wife of the deceased.

"Mrs. Rabinovich, it is much better that you don't see your husband right now." Gil guided her to a seat over by Mrs. Stein, who was still in tears sitting by the display. Once Gabriella noticed her friend they embraced and the crying started more intensely. Calev walked over and put his arms around both women to console them as best he could.

Cornell noted, "Seems like a close knit community."

"Maybe we'll get a cooperative witness or two. Go around and knock on a few doors." Meaning that he should go interview stores in the neighborhood block. Cornell left with notepad in hand while Gil went to talk to Gabriella.

"My name is Detective Gil Clifton. I know this is a difficult time for you but I must ask you a few question."

Gabriella Rabinovich was crying into her friends shoulder. She looked up at the detective and said she wanted to know what happened to her husband.

"That's what we're going to find out. It looks like your husband was beaten to death but I need to know a few more details. I understand you have a son, is that correct?"

"Yes. Menashe. He is in Israel now buying diamonds."

"How long has he been there?"

"He left last week and wasn't scheduled to be back until next Thursday." She burst into a crying spell at the mention of her son.

"Was he on good terms with his father?"

"If you think for one moment that my Menashe had anything to do with this then you can just forget it. He is a wonderful boy and loves his father very much. They ran this business together." Gabriella was indignant.

"I don't mean to suggest that he had anything to do with the murder, I just need to know all of the circumstances. I hope you understand."

"I don't understand if you think my Menashe is a bad boy."

"Did your husband have any enemies or people who he may have had trouble with?"

"Never. My Yosef and Menashe were loved by everybody. They had no enemies."

"That's right, sir," Calev Abramson added, "That is very true. Yosef was very well liked in this community and gave back so much to anyone who needed help. He was always helping out where he could. Menashe, too. Both are very well respected, detective."

"Yes, that's true," said Shoshana.

Gil looked at all corners of the small shop and did not see any surveillance cameras. "Did you husband not have security cameras?"

"No. He didn't believe in them. Menashe had asked to put them in several times but Yosef never wanted them. Menashe did as his father requested at this store."

Gil found out that Yosef and his son owned three other jewelry stores in the greater Camden metropolitan area. Menashe controlled the other two; one of which was located in a shopping mall and the other in the downtown district. They did have security cameras, but that didn't help Gil at this scene.

Gil thanked everyone, said he would be in touch and would work very hard at catching the person who killed Yosef Rabinovich.

"Is this one of the serial killer's doings?" asked Calev.

"I don't know, but we will find out who killed Yosef." Gil left the shop and found Cornell coming across the street back to the shop.

"Nothing. They all said Rabinovich and his kid were great people but they didn't see anything out of the ordinary. Seems kind of suspicious that no one noticed a person probably covered in blood walking out of the store. This could be a hard neighborhood to penetrate and get information."

"I don't get it. Why don't people want to cooperate with the police? We're here for them, not against them."

Gil's cell phone rang and he looked at the screen, "Captain McCadry's calling. Shit."

He answered it and a few seconds later told Cornell, "McCadry wants to see us. He's got Brisbane in his office."

"Oh, that's just great."

\*\*\*

# Chapter 9
# Carl Brisbane
*November 2012*

Gil and Cornell went straight back to the precinct to meet with Captain Joseph McCadry and Carl Brisbane. When the two detectives entered the captain's office, Brisbane slammed the door shut. Both McCadry and Brisbane had scowls etched on their faces and the atmosphere in the small office immediately turned adversarial without a word being spoken. Brisbane started by yelling at Gil and Cornell so the captain had to intervene.

"Carl, let's discuss this rationally. You have not been elected sheriff yet and therefore you have no right to demand anything from my detectives."

That sounded optimistic to Gil. Maybe the captain had changed his tune. But it was quickly confirmed that it was not to be the case.

"Tomorrow is the election. It's going to look pretty bad for Carl if the murder at the jewelry store can be connected to this serial killer. So, I want to know right now is it connected?"

Gil was very defensive, "I don't give a rat's behind if an unsolved crime makes some ungrateful candidate...."

"I'm warning you Gil, answer my question," said McCadry.

"Who said there was a connection?"

The captain yelled at the top of his voice and banged the table with his fist, "Is there a connection?"

"There...." Cornell was about to speak but Gil put his hand in front of him.

"The only thing we have is a letter left on the deceased similar to those that I've received previously. We are not ruling out any possibility or anyone. Captain, you know yourself it would put the department in a terrible position if we tried to guess what had happened in a murder case. We are detectives, experienced detectives, and I do not speculate. I deal in facts and logic - not politics!"

"I am asking...."

"I know what you are asking, captain. I'm telling you we are following all leads and we may have a serial killer. I am leaning towards that theory based on facts and not some ill-advised campaign...."

"Watch yourself, Gil!"

"I think I've answered your question." Gil stood up. "If there is nothing else we would like to get back to work."

"Sit down."

Gil obeyed and returned to his chair.

"Where are you on the Waverly case?"

Brisbane interrupted, "It's been almost two months and we haven't heard any new reports. Brandt is becoming rather irate about being left in the dark."

Gil replied, "There are no new leads at this time. However, the case is still open and we are certain it will be solved."

"I told you that case was top priority," McCadry said.

"I know. We are giving it top priority but there is nothing new at the present time to investigate."

"I don't want six unsolved murders on my watch," said Brisbane.

"Screw your watch," Gil responded bitterly. "If there is nothing else, we're out of here."

Gil and Cornell left the office together without any more conversation.

After the two detectives left the captain's office, Brisbane turned his attention to Captain McCadry and said, "Those two are worthless. How many homicides are going to be committed before this thing ends?"

"I was thinking about putting together a task force but we are so low on manpower that I just can't do it right now."

Brisbane asked, "What are these letters he is talking about?"

McCadry answered, "Gil has received a letter after each murder. The problem is that the letter only contains some short sentence and nothing relating to the murder. Besides, since the M.O. for each case is entirely different, it tends to lead me to the conclusion this is not a serial killer at work. However, the letter found on the body and Detective Gil saying it was similar to the others puts a new wrinkle on things."

"Don't you think the public should be informed?"

"Of course. I just don't want to start a panic. Besides, it has been pretty good fodder for your campaign at the expense of this department, I might add."

"My problem, Joe, is that you aren't close to capturing this killer and more may happen on my watch when I am elected. Then what are you going to do?"

"We'll catch him, believe me. He will make a mistake and that's all it will take to bring him down."

"Catch him before the end of this year or I'll be investigating this department."

---

When they reached their squad room on the second floor Cornell asked Gil, "How do you think they knew about the jewelry store?"

"Somebody is feeding them information."

They reached their desks and started working. It was nearly lunch time and Nathan was making his deliveries. The stack of mail he gave to Gil and Cornell was unusually large.

"Is this your first delivery today?"

"Yes. I was sick to my stomach this morning and just got in."

"Why didn't you take the whole day as a sick day?"

"I haven't earned any sick days yet and I need the money."

"How are you feeling now," Gill asked.

"Better. I took a couple antacids." Nathan didn't say anything else and proceeded to deliver the rest of his mail.

"Man of few words," Cornell observed.

"I'm trying to get him to open up a little bit. We have had a couple of conversations but it's slow. The kid is very introverted and shy."

"Well, good luck with that."

Gil was trying to work with the young intern and was mad at himself for not putting in a better effort to help Nathan gain more self-confidence. He felt a connection to Nathan because he himself struggled with being around people and knew the pain Nathan must feel. Gil resolved to have a longer conversation, but for now he would have to concentrate on his unsolved cases.

The detectives planned their day then each left the precinct. Gil was headed to talk with Calev Abramson and Shoshana Stein again. Cornell was going to do another canvas of the stores surrounding Rabinovich and Son Jewelry.

Brisbane left and went back to his campaign headquarters. Once there he made several phone calls to the local television networks saying he would be holding a press conference at 6:00 p.m. in the pavilion at Garden State Park. He chose that location as it is the same park where Roberta Waverly was murdered. The timing of the press conference conveniently corresponded to the evening broadcasts for the local stations. He instructed his staff to have a podium brought to the main pavilion draped with his campaign picture and slogan. He also called his friend Brandt Waverly and asked him to join him for the press conference, to which Brandt readily accepted. Carl said they should meet before going to the park.

---

Gil found Calev at his deli and talked to him for another forty-five minutes but came away with nothing new. He then went to the address Shoshana Stein had given him and was able to talk to her in her home. That, too, produced no new leads.

Gil headed to the coroner's office and spoke with both Dr. Ingersoll and Dr. Sutherland. It was confirmed by Dr. Sutherland that Yosef Rabinovich was killed by blunt force trauma to the head. Other injuries on the upper arm, chest and rib areas were consistent with blows from a weapon. The evidence ruled out a baseball bat because of some the bruising was too narrow. The injuries were most likely caused by a crowbar, metal pipe or a similar instrument.

"There appears to be 47 different blows, but that is just a guesstimate due to the close proximity of the injuries. The blows were a combination of abraded contusions, abraded lacerations, and lacerated contusions. The most likely injury causing death was a blow to the temporal region. It could be concluded that several of the blows were postmortem," Dr. Sutherland ended.

The time of death was established as between 8:00 a.m. and 9:00 a.m. If it were closer to nine then that would be around the time Rabinovich was opening up his shop

Gil called Cornell on his cell and told him about the autopsy findings and the perp would have most likely left the shop with a crowbar or metal pipe. Cornell said that he was asking everyone if they had noticed anyone leave the shop just before nine carrying anything unusual. Cornell found a store owner from down the street who stated that he had seen a man walking rapidly down the street with a large flower box tucked under his arm. The store owner couldn't identify the man because he had a black hoodie pulled around his head.

---

Carl Brisbane and Brandt Waverly met at Brandt's home at 5:15 p.m. so that Carl could brief Brandt on the strategy of the press conference. Carl was coaching Brandt for his role.

"Now listen, Brandt," Carl was saying, "I know how grief stricken you are, but we need to capitalize on that feeling, so when I call you up to the podium, walk slowly with your head down. Tell them how the police have not informed you about the progress of your wife's murder and that you are deeply concerned about this serial killer who might do to others what he did to your wife."

"I get it. It won't be too much of a stretch because I haven't heard anything for weeks."

"Now," Carl continued, "when you have said your piece the reporters will be yelling questions at you. Just say something to the effect that you are going to leave it in more capable hands."

"You got it," Brandt assured him.

---

Gil and Cornell met back at the precinct nearing 5:00 p.m. They gave each other a briefing of their findings and departed for the day. Gil went to Cassandra's with hopes of finding solace and comfort. When he got there Cassandra was not at home yet so he let himself in and started preparations for supper.

Cassandra arrived home about thirty minutes later and saw Gil's car parked along the curb. She parked in the driveway and went in the front door calling out his name.

"In the kitchen" he answered.

She entered the kitchen and said, "Is my private chef hard at work?" She went to him and gave him a hug. They kissed lightly and she said, "I will go change and be right back. What are you making?"

"A meatball casserole. I'm just putting it in the oven now. Should be about thirty minutes."

He had set the oven temperature to 350 degrees and when the alarm went off indicating the temperature had been reached, he stuck the casserole into the oven. He then went and opened a bottle of wine, poured two glasses and took them to the living room. He set one glass down on the coffee table in front of the couch. He sank down into the couch and took a sip of wine. His mind, however, couldn't relax. The day's events kept replaying over and over again until his heart started beating faster as he was becoming more upset with Captain McCadry's attitude. He took a deep breath and a sip of wine and then set the glass on the table. He leaned back on the couch and closed his eyes, desperately trying to clear his mind.

Cassandra came in, picked up her glass of wine and scooted down beside him. "Thanks honey. Did you have a rough day?"

Gil opened his eyes and smiled at her. "Yes, but now that you are here beside me it will get better." He picked up his glass and they toasted, "To a better evening."

"Gil, I have been meaning to ask you about your cases, but if this is a bad time, then we don't have to talk about them."

"I guess I'm alright to talk. What do you want to know?"

"Well, baby, the news is saying that we have a serial killer on the loose and nothing is being done about it. Now, I know that is not true, but where are you in the investigation? Are you close to getting this guy?"

"There are just no clues to sink my teeth into. We are no closer today than we were back in June."

"I wish there was something I could do to help you. But I know you don't like to talk about work so I'll go get the table set and you just relax." She kissed him and sauntered off to the kitchen.

Gil got up from the couch and turned on the television. There was Brisbane, talking about the murder that had happened at the jewelry store that morning while tying it to the serial killer. He was using the murders to bolster his own campaign.

"Damn him," was all Gil could say.

---

A crowd of reporters, cameramen and sound men had started to gather in front of the podium which was draped prominently with a red, white and blue cloth and an image of a smiling Carl Brisbane in the center. The local television and radio stations, along with the newspapers, had teams covering the impromptu press conference.

A small assembly of curious citizens from the surrounding affluent neighborhood was also milling about waiting for Carl Brisbane. A procession of five cars headed slowly into the well maintained park and drove to the area of the press conference. Out of the center car came Carl Brisbane and Brandt Waverly. Carl was waving to the crowd and Brandt walked beside him with his head hung low so as not to make eye contact with anyone. Precisely at 6 p.m. Carl mounted the stage and stood behind the podium.

"Ladies and gentlemen of the press and concerned citizens of Camden, this great city is in turmoil on the eve of a very important election for a sheriff to head up and guide this city's police force. Yet, this very morning another one of our citizens was taken from us by a serial killer who has been running roughshod over your police department. The leader of the Camden police, Sheriff Richard Winston, has not kept our citizenry informed on the possible capture and conviction of this brazen killer. Now, is that the kind of sheriff you want representing the people of Camden? I say no. It's time for a change. It's time for transparency. It's time for the police department to step up to the plate and let the people know what is happening within this vital service on behalf of the people. I have with me a man still grieving from the death of his beloved wife, Roberta, at the hands of this serial killer we know nothing about. Why? Because the sheriff refuses to inform us. Well, let me tell you right here and now: that will not happen on my watch."

Sporadic cheers could be heard throughout the crowd. Carl continued, "Tomorrow I ask you to cast your vote for the candidate who will give you transparency, timely information, and a reduction in the budget because this service can be run more efficiently. To demonstrate the reality of what I am saying, I give you one of Camden's most prominent citizens, a man whose wife dedicated her life in service to others, a man who has helped build this city with more efficient buildings and safer parks. I'm talking about Mr. Brandt Waverly. Here also is a man who personifies the meaning of being kept in the dark about a crime; a crime in which his wife was slain in this very park. A park that used to be safe. A park that used to welcome its visitors with a place to relax, exercise or picnic without fear of being murdered. But yet, we know nothing about this most heinous crime because there is no transparency in our current administration of the police force. I have been campaigning on a platform of efficiency in the police department, for budget cuts, and new jails to hold criminals so that they may not walk the streets to commit more crimes. But, most importantly, I have been campaigning for transparency and communication between the police force and the citizens for whom they work. Ladies and gentlemen I give you a victim of the abuse this administration has so blatantly tossed aside. I give you Mr. Brandt Waverly."

Brandt approached the podium, his head still low and a defeated look on his face. "Two months ago," he started, "my wife was jogging in this park as she did every morning before she went to work with one of her many charities. I had no fear for her to come here alone. Her life was taken from her and she was taken from me because of a serial killer. A killer the police knew was in the Camden area, but never let the public know about it. Had I known a killer was amongst us I would have never let her come alone to this park and she would still be alive today. But even months after her death, I know nothing about the murder from the police. I am sorry, I can't say any more. The memory of her death and the lack of information on finding the killer have taken a severe toll on me."

The reporters all starting asking questions at the same time. "I will leave my case in the more capable hands of Carl Brisbane."

The reporters again started shouting questions at Brandt, but with a forlorn look he left the podium in tears as he retreated back to his chair. Carl Brisbane once again took the podium. "Fellow citizens, this brave man who has lost his wife and knows absolutely nothing on the progress of the case, could very well be you if this serial killer working among us is not captured. I say inform the citizens and we will gladly help in their efforts but because Sheriff Winston refuses to divulge information we are left helpless and vulnerable. Tomorrow when you go to the polls make the right choice for Camden because closely guarded police secrets will be a thing of the past and these killings will not continue, not on my watch. Thank you."

The reporters started their ritual of shouting out questions. Carl waved to them and left the stage. Carl and Brandt were escorted back to their car by campaign workers and the three security guards Carl had hired to be with him while out in public.

Carl and Brandt then drove to Brandt's home, and Brandt asked Carl to come in for a while.

"I really must be going, Brandt."

"Carl, I need to talk to you. Please come in just to hear me out."

Carl got out of the car and the other four cars, parked two in front and two behind the candidate's car, waited.

Brandt asked if Carl would like a drink but Carl refused. "Big day tomorrow," he said.

"That is what I want to talk to you about."

"So, what's on your mind?"

"I let you use me for this little publicity stunt you just pulled off."

Carl looked at him with questioning eyes.

Brandt continued, "I don't mind helping out a friend, as you well know."

"What's this all about, Brandt?"

"Carl, you and I have been friends for a very long time. I have supported your campaign with a lot of money. Money I have given to you directly so you wouldn't have to report it."

"Is this a shake down?"

"No, no my friend. I was just stating facts. Now I didn't care one bit how you used the money and whether it was reported as campaign contributions or not. That's not what I'm talking about."

"Then what are you getting at?"

"I'm coming to that."

***

# Chapter 10
# The Election
*November 2012*

Carl Brisbane left the home of Brandt Waverly knowing what he had to do for his friend. Carl didn't like to be indebted to anyone but that is the position he found himself. Carl would have to ensure that Waverly Building and Contracting would be awarded the contract for constructing the new jail. Brandt had stopped just short of blackmail when Carl agreed to sway the contract Brandt's way. Carl got into the waiting car and the small processional wound its way back to Carl's campaign headquarters. Tomorrow would be a critical day in his life because it was Election Day. He was very optimistic about his chances for being elected.

Sheriff Richard Winston spent less than $200,000 on his campaign whereas Carl had reportedly spent one point three million dollars. Carl also had an additional $450,000 in his coffers contributed by Brandt Waverly 'under the table', as it were, in addition to the $85,000 Brandt had contributed directly to the campaign.

Early on Tuesday morning, November 6, 2012, the polls opened at 7:00 a.m. All of the news stations were repeating segments of yesterday's press conference held at Garden State Park. Unfortunately for the incumbent, the news of another brutal murder connected to a serial killer in Camden, New Jersey was also being aired. The morning newspapers ran front page reports about the murder of Yosef Rabinovich. For the first time there was mention of letters being sent to the police department after each slaying and a similar note was found on the body of the dead man.

The sensational reports led Carl to call in reporters from all media sources to his campaign headquarters. There was a live feed at noon to the local television stations where Carl was speaking about how he was not satisfied with the current sheriff's way of running the police force.

As he stood in front of the cameras he said, "I am no longer campaigning on this crucial day of decision. However, whether I am elected or not, the sheriff must create more transparency to the public. This is no longer just a difference in policy platforms, this is vitally important for the public safety that transparency takes place immediately. If I am not fortunate enough to be elected, I urge the sheriff to move in that direction. However, if the good people of Camden elect me there will be disclosure and the safety of the public will be foremost on my agenda by achieving transparency. There should be no more hidden secrets from the public. The citizens of Camden should not be left in the dark and that will not happen on my watch. I implore each and every voter to go to the polls and let your voice be heard. Thank you."

The reporters were clamoring for more information. "Mr. Brisbane, have there been any new developments concerning the serial killer?"

"I do not know because I, like you, have been kept in the dark."

"Was yesterday's killing of a Jewish jeweler related to the series of unsolved murders which have taken place since June and linked to a serial killer?"

"Once again, the only information I have is a reported note on the body similar to others delivered to Detective Gil Clifton in the past."

"How did you come about finding that out?"

"I read it in one of the local newspapers and I also heard it on one of the local news networks. But to remain impartial I will not say which station I listened to." Carl laughed at his own joke.

"Is Detective Clifton the investigator assigned to the serial killer cases?"

"I believe so."

There was more bellowing out of questions but Carl ignored them. Soon all of the reporters and cameras left the campaign headquarters.

It was a very short press conference; nevertheless the damaged had been done. Carl succeeded in releasing the information about the letters being tied to the murders. He also got in a jab against Detective Gil Clifton; for that he felt quite satisfied. The story was immediately broadcast over several local stations. A special edition of the evening paper ran a report of letters connecting several murders since last June that were associated with Detective Gil Clifton's name. One editorial aired on a local station demanded that Sheriff Winston immediately withdraw from this election.

The Jewish community was up in arms when they learned that the death of Yosef Rabinovich was directly attributed to a serial killer. Talk show hosts on local radio stations were fielding calls demanding to know more about a killer working in the Camden area. Brandt Waverly was interviewed and he repeated that for almost two months no information about his wife's murder was given to him by the police. Brandt looked like the successful businessman he was and no longer had that look of deep sadness on his face.

Around 4:00 p.m. everyone at the Brisbane Headquarters started heading to the luxurious Royal Manor Hotel and Spa where the

Elizabethan Room had been rented to accommodate more people after the election. Tables were decorated with red, white and blue napkins and balloons in anticipation of a celebration. The podium was draped with the same cloth displayed during the Garden State Park press conference. Large pictures of a smiling Carl Brisbane were attached to walls throughout the room.

Early election reports were filtering into the Brisbane Campaign Headquarters showing their candidate was ahead 53% to 47% per the exit polls being conducted. The six o'clock news reported that Carl Brisbane was leading by a margin of 58% to 42%. It looked as if it were going to be a landslide victory. Carl was elated and started rehearsing his acceptance speech. The polls closed at 7:00 p.m. and the returns were streaming in from all the voting precincts.

At 8:15 p.m. Sheriff Richard Winston appeared before the media from the Camden Inn. The Elizabethan Room got eerily quiet and all eyes focused on several television sets scattered around the room as he went on air and conceded the election to his opponent and wished him well when he became sheriff on December 1. The standing room only crowd was loud and boisterous cheering for Brisbane as he took the podium after watching his opponent concede the race.

Carl started out, "The good people of Camden have spoken loud and clear!" A raucous cheer filled the room. "I would like to personally thank Sheriff Richard Winston for his many years of service to this community and I am positive that we will have a smooth transition of administration during the next few weeks." There was a polite applause from the biased audience in the Elizabethan Room.

"My first priority will be to form a task force to rid this community of fear, apprehension and anxiety, and to capture the sick and demented serial killer who walks among us without fear, without apprehension and without anxiety." Loud cheers and clapping erupted.

"I would like to thank my many supporters and campaign workers who diligently and tirelessly worked on my behalf so that our vision could be fulfilled." Again the cheers. People started chanting over and over, '*Not on my watch. Not on my watch. Not on my watch*' and continued for several minutes until an elated and smiling Carl held up both of his hands and called for quiet.

"Today is an important day for the police department of Camden. Today is an important day for the city of Camden but most notably, today is an important day for the people of Camden." Cheers and applause followed.

"Why is this an important day? Because we have a new sheriff in town!" The tired old cliché was accepted with loud cheers and applause as the audience started their chant once again.

"I have heard the citizens' overwhelming mandate and most humbly hereby accept the office of sheriff for the City of Camden, New Jersey!" The celebration began with horns blowing, supporters cheering and congratulating one another and balloons popping. The hotel staff brought in bottles of champagne and started handing out small portions to the jubilant crowd.

Police Captain Joseph McCadry went to his friend and offered his congratulations. "You will make a great sheriff, Carl. I look forward to working with you."

Carl kept the huge smile on his face as he leaned over and whispered loud enough for only McCadry to hear, "Let me correct you on something. On December first you will be working *for* me." He backed away to watch McCadry's reaction and then left the captain standing alone as he continued shaking hands with those in attendance.

McCadry was stunned by what he heard and didn't know quite how to take Carl's remark. He thanked the waitress as she handed him a glass of champagne and drank it in one fell swoop. He threw the tiny plastic flute on the floor and left the Royal Manor Hotel and Spa.

Gil and Cassandra were watching the election returns on television from Cassandra's house. Gil had arrived about 5:30 p.m., and Cassandra was already there preparing a small evening meal. They had decided earlier to not attend a party given in honor of Richard Winston. They had declined an invitation to the reception to listen to the election results being held at the Camden Inn - where murder victim Harold McDonald's wife, Arlene, worked.

Neither Gil nor Cassandra were overly hungry so she served grilled ham and cheese sandwiches and baked tater tots, accompanied by a glass of pinot grigio. They saw the results and concluded that Winston would not remain in office after the election. That was confirmed when the incumbent sheriff conceded the race to his opponent.

The cameras were now running at the Royal Manor and a reporter was trying to talk over the crowd noise. "We are here at the Royal Manor Hotel and Spa where we have just heard the televised concession speech of Sheriff Richard Winston. This crowd is loud so I hope you can hear me. We are waiting for Carl

Brisbane to take the podium and accept the office of sheriff."

"I bet that son-of-a-bitch hired all those people to be there just for show." Gil announced.

"I don't think so, dear."

The cameras now focused on Carl Brisbane as he stepped behind the podium.

Gil commented, "Here we go, another round of bull from this idiot."

Gil heard Carl say that this was an important day and he added his own words to that of the smiling Brisbane, "Yeah, it's important all right. It's the day the police department started going to hell."

Cassandra grabbed the remote from the coffee table and was about to shut off the television but Gil stopped her. "I want to hear what this idiot has to say."

She put the remote back on the coffee table and put her arms around her lover. "I just don't want you to get all worked up. You knew he was going to be elected."

They finished watching his speech and Gil shut off the television and said, "Let's go to bed."

Gil and Cornell arrived at the precinct at the same time the next day. They talked about the election and what it would mean to them. Cornell was angry that Carl got elected. "What were people thinking?"

"Budget cuts are always fair game in politics. Carl just played it to the hilt. But if he really goes ahead and tries to cut overtime, this city is in for a heck of a ride."

"I imagine every criminal in Camden voted for that jerk."

Gil agreed, "I bet you're right."

They walked into the squad room then to the roll call room where Captain McCadry was waiting to give the morning briefing. When the detectives and squad room personnel were seated McCadry started.

"I suppose you all saw or heard about the election results last night. I haven't spoken to Carl yet but there may be some changes around here." Soft grumbling could be heard from the attendees. "I don't know what those changes may be but I expect one hundred percent cooperation from my department. If you have a complaint or grievance you can, as always, come to me and I will follow up."

A couple of coughs and someone clearing his throat could be heard. McCadry scanned the room with his eyes to see who it was, but could not identify any one in particular. He looked at Gil but did not say anything. He continued, "I will be meeting with the transition team during the next few weeks and I will assure the sheriff-elect that he can count us on his team. Does anybody have anything to add?" The room was silent. "Okay, dismissed."

Everyone was leaving the room when McCadry called out to Gil, "Detective Clifton, could I see you a minute?"

Cornell was going to wait for his partner but Gil shooed him away. "I'll meet you in a bit."

Gil walked up to where Captain McCadry was standing and asked, "What's up, captain?"

"I want a progress report this afternoon on any unsolved murders you and your partner are working on."

"You just got the month end report a couple days ago," Gil complained.

"Do I always have to ask you twice to comply with a direct order?"

"No, sir. You will have it this afternoon."

"Thank you. You are dismissed."

Gil returned to his desk. Cornell asked him what had happened.

"Do you have a copy of last month's month end report?"

"Sure."

"Change the dates on it to today's date and let me have a copy. McCadry wants a full up-to-date report on our cases. That should do, shouldn't it?"

"Of course. He won't know the difference."

"What a perfect ass he is." Gil shook his head in dismay and sat down at his desk.

"I don't know if he's perfect or not but you are right." They both laughed.

Gil pulled out the file on the Rabinovich case and started looking through the notes. Nathan was delivering mail and Gil thought this would be a good time to get a little bit better acquainted with the shy lad. When Nathan reached the detective's desk Gil asked him, "You know Detective Bush don't you?"

"Yes, sir. Detective Cornell Bush, sir." Nathan looked at Cornell and added, "Good morning, sir."

"Good morning to you, too, Nathan," replied Cornell.

"I have forgotten your last name, Nathan," said Gil.

"It's Bowen, sir. Nathan Bowen."

"You can drop the sir thing. Just call me Gil."

"Yes, sir. I mean yes, Gil."

"That's better."

Nathan nodded his head yes.

"Well, Nathan Bowen, are you feeling better today?"

"Much better, sir."

"Gil."

"Sorry. Much better, Gil"

"You see Cornell over there? Well, he and I have a small bet. I bet him I could talk you into getting a beer with me sometime after work but he said you wouldn't. So what do you say that you and I go have a beer after work today? Alright?"

"I don't drink beer, sir."

"Then you can have a soda or coffee or Shirley Temple if you want, it doesn't matter. Just you and me hanging out a little bit. Maybe I can get you jump started on your career in law enforcement. What do you say?"

"I would like that, sir, but I can't tonight. Maybe some other time."

"How about tomorrow then?"

"Maybe. I have to deliver the rest of this mail, sir."

"Okay. Nice talking to you, Nathan."

"You too, sir." Nathan's face was flush as he departed.

When Nathan was out of ear shot Cornell said, "Where's my money? Looks like I won the bet."

"If we had a bet I would win eventually."

"Okay, then let's make it legal, A ten spot says you can't get him to have a drink with you."

"I'm just trying to help the kid. And it wouldn't hurt you either if you were a little friendlier to him."

"Yes, sir, Mister Congeniality!"

The month of November brought no changes to the homicide department. Gil and Cornell were called to a scene involving a domestic dispute which ended in the shooting death of a husband who came home drunk and started abusing his wife. She got a loaded gun and pointed it at her husband but he lunged forward and the gun went off. The bullet went through the victim's chin and exited out the top of his head. Forensic evidence and recreation of the scene as described by the wife exonerated her. It was declared an accidental shooting resulting in death and the case was closed two weeks later.

Brandt Waverly usually called at least twice per week, but Gil had not heard from him since the election. That was two weeks ago, but it was okay with Gil as Brandt would only complain about inactivity and wouldn't listen. However, Gil was feeling low with the approaching holiday season. Thanksgiving was only two days away and there were six unsolved murders for which he couldn't catch a break.

Cassandra had decorated her house traditionally for the holiday season. She had cornucopias filled with dried flowers and leaves, vases with fall colored flowers and Pilgrim figurines placed on side tables. She and Gil had decided to have a traditional Thanksgiving dinner at the NJ Shore Café. Their reservation was for 5:00 p.m.

The NJ Shore Café was full but Gil and Cassandra found one barstool open at the bar. Cassandra sat down and ordered two glasses of pinot noir. After a brief fifteen minute wait, their table was ready. They were seated at a window table looking out at a beautiful landscaped garden with mature trees, flowers and a small path meandering though the entire area.

They filled their plates at the buffet and had casual conversation while eating.

Cassandra first brought up the subject of the murder cases Gil was working on. "Are you having any luck in catching the serial killer?"

Gil looked around the room to see if anyone overheard her and scowled, "Not really, but that's not a subject I wish to discuss right now."

"I'm sorry dear. I was just curious, that's all."

"I know. Everybody is. Unfortunately, there isn't much to talk about. We have so few clues."

"Okay. I'm sorry I asked. I don't want to ruin our dinner. How is yours?"

"Very good."

"Yes, mine is too." She lifted her glass of wine and said, "Happy Thanksgiving, sweetheart."

He touched her glass with his and replied, "Happy Thanksgiving, dear."

\*\*\*

# Chapter 11
# The Inauguration
## *December 2012*

Several officers of the Camden police force, some members of the county commission, city dignitaries and of course the press were all assembled on the sprawling courtyard in front of the Camden Municipal Courthouse. On this Saturday, December 1, 2012, Mayor Alonso Veluchi would be the keynote speaker and Circuit Court Judge William B. Bannerman would administer the oath of office to the incoming sheriff. Brandt Waverly and Gabriella Rabinovich had reserved seats in front of the stage that had been put up for the swearing-in ceremony. Captain McCadry sat with other officers of the police force.

Gil Clifton and Cornell Bush were only invited through a bulletin board post citing the place, date and time of the ceremony. They weren't going to attend even if they had an engraved invitation. Nobody from the homicide division from sergeants on down attended. Most of the uniformed officers also boycotted the ceremony.

Gil was off-duty and had stayed at Cassandra's Friday night. Gil had been hounded by the media ever since Carl Brisbane mentioned his name as the lead investigator during the impromptu press conference on Election Day. Gil was thankful he was at Cassandra's house because he doubted the press would find him there. He turned on the television as Mayor Veluchi was speaking.

". . . . and for many years I have known and worked side-by-side with Carl. We have agreed and we have disagreed on many subjects, but at the end of the day we worked together for the betterment of this city. I know in my heart that Carl will continue to work diligently to preserve the integrity of the law enforcement department, that his leadership will fortify the safety of the community he serves and he will foremost, set the standards high not only for himself but for those under his command."

The audience applauded and Mayor Veluchi continued, "I would now like to call upon the Honorable Judge William B. Bannerman to administer the oath of office."

As Carl was approaching the podium the camera turned and slowly swept the crowd.

Gil spotted two familiar faces seated in the front row. "My God, he invited the spouses of two of the victims!"

"Why would he do that?" Cassandra asked.

"For publicity if nothing else. He's already started using his office as a platform for his own personal vindictiveness."

Carl faced the judge and placed his left hand on the bible held by Judge Bannerman and raised his right hand with his wife, Elaina by his side. He repeated the oath: "I, Carl Frederick Brisbane, do solemnly swear that I will support the Constitution of the United States and the Constitution of the State of New Jersey, and that I will bear true faith and allegiance to the same and to the Governments established in the United States and in this State, under the authority of the people, so help me God."

By 2:15 p.m. the new sheriff was officially installed in his elected office and with that a new era for the law enforcement personnel of the city of Camden, New Jersey began. The entire police force was bracing for sweeping changes; changes in policies, changes in procedures, changes in their lives and changes in their bank accounts. Gil turned off the television before the new sheriff was to give his speech. He had heard enough from Carl over the last several months.

Cassandra slid closer to Gil on the couch and put her arms around him. "No matter what he tries to do I have faith in you to do the right thing."

Gil looked at her and they gently kissed. "Thanks for the support, but this is going to become a nightmare if we don't catch this killer soon."

"You will, dear. I know you will." She rose up from the couch and said, "Let's take a drive to Rancocas State Park. It's not too cold outside and it would be better than moping around the house. Would you like to do that?"

"Yeah. Maybe it will take my mind off everything for a little while."

The temperature was in the low 40's, a typical winter day. Any snow that had fallen was mostly gone. They changed into warmer clothes and headed out for the park. The traffic was rather light for a Saturday afternoon, and the 34 mile drive took just less than 50 minutes. They entered the park and headed for the nature center.

They passed what was left of the afternoon viewing the nature center and walking in the park until the temperature dropped and a chilled wind started blowing. Their return trip to the house was spattered with light conversation. The winter nightfall had arrived as they reached their destination. Cassandra entered the house first and went straight to the kitchen while Gil started the gas fireplace. The couple settled in for a nice quiet supper and restful evening.

The party was boisterous and lively as a jazz band played in one corner of the huge ballroom at Bavarian Luxury Suites Hotel and Convention Center where Sheriff Carl Brisbane was holding court. Champagne was served generously by white gloved waiters in black tuxedos with burgundy bowties and matching cummerbunds. Specialty hors d'oeuvres were sitting delicately on trays transported by waitresses dressed in burgundy suits and black ribbons tied neatly in bows in their hair.

A lavish dinner of Chateaubriand in béarnaise sauce was accompanied by roasted asparagus and garlic Hasselback potatoes had been served. A light dessert of chocolate mousse with vanilla yogurt had been well received. Young men and women all dressed in white hurriedly cleared the tables of dishes, glasses and silverware. At the center of each table was a stunning arrangement of burgundy and white flowers with baby's breath and fern leaves.

Conspicuously missing from the invitation-only gathering was Captain McCadry. When Mayor Veluchi asked Sheriff Brisbane about the homicide division captain, he was told that the captain needed to spend his valuable time doing police work rather than socializing and letting a serial killer run rampant amidst the population of Camden. The mayor was taken by surprise by the sheriff's abrupt and sarcastic answer and made a mental note to be watchful of Carl and how quickly he could turn on a friend or associate.

Carl took to the podium and asked everyone to sit down. He looked over the well-dressed assembly and a broad smile enlivened his face. He began to speak, "Ladies and gentlemen, I am honored and pleased that I may serve you for the next two years as your new sheriff." Applause interrupted. "Thank you." He continued, "I am privileged to have some of the best and most astute law enforcement officers in the country serving right here in Camden, New Jersey." More applause.

"As I humbly stand here before you I can assure you that my commitment to the public for a more open dialogue will be the leading factor during my administration and we will no longer hide behind the thin blue wall of silence. The future of Camden will be cloaked in security. A security that comes with the eagerness and professionalism of a ready and able police presence. A security in the knowledge that the government agencies working for the people of Camden are indeed working *for* the people of Camden and not in the smoke-filled back rooms of seclusion and secrecy. A security that comes from openness, communication, honesty and integrity."

Everyone at the tables stood up and exploded in a standing ovation as Carl waved both hands high over his head in triumph. The audience acted as if they had just nominated their candidate for the President of the United States at the Democratic National Convention. Mayor Veluchi joined in the celebration but with a slight feeling of trepidation due to Carl's previous comment about Captain McCadry.

The festivities concluded around 1:00 a.m. on Sunday morning. Brandt Waverly and Elaina Brisbane were walking together as they approached the table where Carl was slouched in his chair wistfully swirling a scotch and water.

"Tired, honey?" Elaina asked.

Carl looked up plaintively at his wife and then at Brandt. He said nothing then looked away and continued to swirl his drink.

Brandt spoke up, "Well, Carl, I would say you had a very successful inauguration as a prelude to a very successful administration."

"I guess," replied Carl without so much as glancing up but kept his drink swirling in his glass.

---

Carl Brisbane received a call from Captain McCadry Sunday afternoon regarding a suspected murder near the college campus at a sports bar. Carl flew into a rage and called McCadry all kinds of disparaging names. He told the captain to meet him at the precinct around five o'clock. Carl slammed the phone down and dialed Judge Bannerman. When Carl hung up, he said goodbye to his wife as he was preparing to leave the house.

"What time will you be back?"

"I haven't the foggiest idea."

Elaina said, "I will probably go over to my sister's and hang out with her for a while this evening, if that's okay with you."

"That would be fine. Be careful of those Philly drivers because I think the Eagles are playing at home and if they lose, people go crazy."

"I will."

"Give your sister a big hug and kiss from me, too. I'll probably be late." He banged the door shut as he left the house.

Carl could see a few people gathered at the court house steps as he approached..

*No reporters, thank God*, he thought. The people said nothing to him as he passed them and entered the courthouse where Judge

Bannerman had agreed to meet. Carl wanted to get an injunction against the news media for reporting anything further on the actions of an alleged serial killer. The judge told him no over the phone, but Carl insisted they meet.

Carl could not persuade the judge to issue an injunction or any other support to suppress the news media. His hands were tied and Carl grew angry.

"Carl, this is a police matter and as sheriff you need to handle it. This is not a matter for the courts. There is nothing I can do."

The sheriff thanked the judge for seeing him on a Sunday and especially for coming down to the office.

"It's the least I can do for you until you get your feet wet," the judge said.

After the forty-five minute meeting that produced no results for Carl, he headed over to the police precinct and to the confines of his office on the third floor for the first time as acting sheriff. He saw the gathering of people in the courtyard growing and diverted his escape from the courthouse through a back entrance and walked the two blocks to his office building.

Once he arrived at his office he saw Captain McCadry already waiting for him.

Carl started screaming at the top of his lungs, "I've only been in office for twenty-four hours, have not even set foot inside my office officially and now we have another murder that's all over the news and people are gathering down the block."

"There has been no determination that a murder...."

"I don't give a crap about a determination. The news media is already calling it a murder and tying it to the serial killer, and here I sit caught with my pants down before I even get to work! Now what is being done?"

"Detective Gil is assigned to the case and he is at the scene as we speak."

"I want you to take the lead on this. Get down there and catch me this killer! Now!"

---

The El Toro Bistro, an upscale Mexican restaurant in East Philadelphia, was busy as usual for the early Sunday night seating. The infamous bistro was known as one of the very few non-Italian restaurants catering to made-men from the Antonio Palovani crime family. It was the restaurant where the notorious Vito

Veluchi, a capo with the family and brother of Alonso Veluchi, mayor of Camden, NJ, was brutally murdered eleven years ago. The murder was an obvious mob hit; however, no one was ever arrested in connection with the slaying.

The El Toro contained an atmosphere of darkened conspiracy with its dim lights, dark mahogany tables, black tablecloths and rich textured couches and chairs all done in dark subdued colors contrary to the traditional bright colors for the décor of most Mexican restaurants. Small flashlights were given patrons so they could read the menus. The candlelit tables afforded only enough illumination for conversation. The only truly well-lit area was the barroom that peeked around one corner of the main section of the restaurant.

Racially mixed couples were forbidden in the Bistro in the early 60's but East Philly had changed over the years and by the year 2012 there was an acceptable tolerance for such relationships. In a corner booth sat a prominent black Camden businessman with a beautiful white female with an obvious taste for expensive clothing and jewelry.

A waiter dressed in a black Mexican styled tuxedo took their drink order and scurried off to the kitchen.

"That was a very nice party last night," said Brandt.

"Yes it was, but only because you were there," replied Elaina.

Brandt Waverly and Elaina Brisbane had been frequenting the El Toro for over two years, well before Brandt's wife, Roberta, was murdered. The torrid love affair between Brandt and Elaina was well hidden from the public eye and they were careful to keep it that way.

"Did Carl say anything after you got home? He seemed kind of out of sorts there at the end."

"He said he was tired and I guess I believed him. It was quite a tiring day."

"He doesn't suspect anything, does he?"

"No. And let's not talk about him and ruin our evening. I only have a few hours tonight."

The waiter brought their drinks and left the dinner menus for them to look over.

They toasted, "To us."

"To us."

From his position in the booth Brandt saw a small gathering in the bar area becoming rather animated.

"I'm going to the bar. Something is happening. I'll be right back."

Brandt left Elaina at the booth and headed for the commotion. He stood in the back as everyone was focused on the television behind the bar. Brandt listened to the news program.

". . . . during the telecast of the football game between the Eagles and Giants," a female reporter was frantically stating. "It is not known at this time if this is related to the series of murders in the greater Camden area or not. All we have now is that a male, approximately twenty-five years of age and reportedly a student at the nearby Rutgers University lies dead inside the Booster Club Sports Bar and Grille."

"Sarah, do you know how the young man was murdered?" asked the studio news anchor.

"The Camden homicide division is on scene here at the sports bar as well as the coroner, but they have made no public comment. To make sure we are accurate, it is not known if this is a murder or if the victim died of natural causes. That will be determined by an autopsy to be performed later on. However, we have spoken to friends of the victim and they say that while he was drinking his beer he had commented that it tasted funny and died several minutes later. That is unofficial and all we have on the situation at this time. This is Sarah Larsen reporting for WCAM, Camden Action Media, on scene here at the Booster Club Sports Bar and Grille near the campus of Rutgers University."

"Thank you, Sarah," the news anchor said. "Let's take you now to Mike Carriden outside the Camden Municipal Courthouse. Mike, I see a crowd gathering behind you can you give us an update on what is happening there?"

"From the information I have so far, it was shortly after the first reports surfaced of a student being allegedly murdered when a few protesters started forming outside here in the courtyard around 4:00 p.m. It has now grown to what looks like over two hundred angry citizens. I'm going to try to get someone to talk with me if I can." The reporter walked to the edge of the crowd as the camera followed close behind.

"Excuse me sir, I'm Mike Carriden with WCAM. Could you tell me why everyone is gathering here?"

"Yeah. We elected a new sheriff and one day after he gets sworn into office a young kid gets murdered and not a peep out of him."

"Are you speaking about the incident at the Boost Club Sport Bar?"

"I wouldn't call it an incident. I would call it a murder" the man with a baseball hat on backwards said rather nastily.

"We are not certain if the young man you are referring to was murdered or died of natural causes. So why the protest?"

"Mark my words, that kid was murdered. Murdered in broad daylight and in the middle of a crowded bar and the police still can't catch this serial killer. We want to know what is going to be done to protect us!" The man started chanting with the other protesters, "It's on your watch! It's on your watch! It's on your watch!"

"It was only yesterday in this very courtyard where Sheriff Carl Brisbane was sworn into office after being elected on a platform of transparency," reported Mike Carriden. "They haven't given the new sheriff much of a chance, but for now, these people want information and action."

"Has there been any indication that Sheriff Brisbane will make a statement soon?" asked the anchor.

"Sheriff Brisbane was seen entering the courthouse earlier in the day. We have learned that he has since left and is reportedly in route to his office. This is Mike Carriden reporting on scene at the municipal courthouse for WCAM, Camden Action Media."

The news anchor continued with the report, "During his campaign for sheriff, Carl Brisbane used the slogan 'not on my watch' which in a matter of twenty-four hours has viciously turned against him as the public is now chanting 'it's on your watch'. This was the scene at the courthouse yesterday at the inauguration ceremony of Sheriff Brisbane." The television was now showing shots of the ceremony with a clear picture of Elaina beside her husband. The camera also showed pictures of the audience in attendance with a clear view of Brandt Waverly sitting in the front row.

Brandt lowered his head and retreated back to his booth.

"We need to get out of here right now," he whispered to Elaina. "There were pictures of both of us on TV just now from the ceremony yesterday."

He left a fifty dollar bill on the table and he and Elaina were about to leave when Salvatore Moratino and three of his associates approached their table.

"Brandt. Mrs. Brisbane," Salvatore said politely. "You're not leaving are you? I was hoping that I might have a word with you."

The underboss of the Palovani crime family slid into the booth while his three associates sat at a nearby table where they had a full view of the entire restaurant and front door.

***

# Chapter 12
# Hikaru Yoshi
*December 2012*

Detective Gil Clifton was just checking in to the precinct when he got a call on yet another murder. He called Cornell and told him to go directly to Booster Club Sports Bar and Grille only three blocks from the main campus of Rutgers University. When Gil arrived, he found that Cornell had just started talking to the Manager on duty, Martin Porter, 6'6", 263 pound 26 year old former football player from Rutgers. His dark hair and complexion made him a very striking figure and his good looks also swayed the female customers to compete for his attention. He had been the manager for the past three years and was running a very profitable establishment for the corporate owners in Philadelphia.

Detective Gil took Martin over to one corner of the bar area where they were seated in a booth and Gil started questioning him. Cornell continued his part of the investigation with the crime scene photographer and briefly talking with potential witnesses.

"Was there anyone here that looked out of place?" Gil asked Martin.

"No. Not really." Martin seemed shaken by the events that had happened less than an hour ago.

"How about the way they were dressed? Anyone dressed for instance, in military garb or a business suit? Anything you may have noticed that was unusual."

"It looked like a typical Sunday football crowd. The place was packed. We have pregame specials and half time giveaways which are very popular with the students. But when the Eagles play the Giants it just goes nuts in here, if you know what I mean?"

"Yeah. I see you have four security cameras in the bar area, are there any more?"

"We have two in the restaurant and three in the kitchen."

"I'll need to get the data from all of them."

"I believe a police officer has already done that."

"Now tell me what happened."

"I had just come out of the kitchen and I was behind the bar when someone started yelling that Yoshi had passed out."

"You're referring to Hikaru Yoshi, the victim?"

"Yeah. Everyone called him by his last name. He was pretty much a regular. I think he was a pre-law graduate student. Smart kid, always playing practical jokes. So I got awful angry because I thought it was one of his stunts."

"Had he done anything like that before?"

"No. Nothing like faking being passed out. He would play small jokes on his friends, though. He was well liked. He never caused any trouble in here at all."

"What happened then?"

"When I got to him his buddies were saying that Yoshi had commented to them that his beer tasted funny, but he drank it anyway. He started to quiver, and they said it looked like he was having convulsions. Then he just fell to the floor. We all thought he might have had a heart attack so I had my bartender call for an ambulance."

"Did anyone else complain how the beer tasted?"

"No. I immediately stopped the bartenders from serving any more tap beer just in case something got into a keg. You never know about what people might do these days."

"I know. I will need a sample of the beer he was drinking."

"They already took samples of all the taps. It couldn't have been in the taps because others would have gotten sick or at least reported it or. . . ." Martin's head dropped into his hands and tears began to flow.

Gil asked, "Is there something else?"

"I was just thinking about how many people could have been murdered if something had gotten into our beer keg."

"Try not to think about what might have happened. We don't know if this was a murder or something else. Please don't presume anything before we have a chance to understand fully what happened here."

Martin lifted his head and agreed.

"Now, Martin, is there anything thing further that you can think of to tell me."

Martin thought for a second and shook his head no.

"Okay. We'll be in . . . ."

"Wait a minute, I just remembered something. There was one guy who came in and had the hoodie pulled up over his head. I didn't think much of it at the time, but I think he is the first person I have seen in here wearing a sweatshirt with the hoodie pulled up. I don't know if that means anything, but I did think it was strange. Then again I guess I thought the guy must be cold or something and left it at that."

"Do know who he was?"

"I don't think so. He had the hoodie pulled forward so I couldn't get a good look at his face."

"Do you remember the color of the hoodie?"

"Yeah, it was black."

"Can you describe the guy? Was he fat, tall, old? Anything like that?"

"I guess you could call him average height with a medium build. Nothing unusual about him."

"Did you notice if he had contact with the victim at any time?"

"Not that I recall. I just saw him at a glance and then went about my business. Sorry."

Detective Gil thanked Martin for his cooperation and sought out his partner.

"Cornell, do you have the data from the cameras?"

"Yes."

"If you have everything else wrapped up let's take a look at the film."

It was nearly 6:00 p.m. that Sunday night before they got back to the precinct and went into a conference room to start reviewing the data from each of the cameras. They started with the cameras located in the main part of the restaurant. Gil was looking for a guy wearing a hoodie.

---

Salvatore Moratino was a very handsome looking 54 year old Sicilian. His jet black hair was full and shiny. He was well dressed, but not overly stated so as not to bring a lot of attention to himself. He stood only 5'7" and weighed a physically fit 195 pounds. His chiseled facial features befitted his reputation of having an unstable and volatile disposition countered with a quiet but assertive personality. That combination made him a very dangerous man.

He started out, "Perhaps, Mrs. Brisbane, you would like to go and powder your nose or have a drink at the bar while Brandt and I discuss some very boring business." He took out a fifty dollar bill and gave it to her. "Here, your drink is on me." He turned to his associates seated at a nearby table and added, "Mario, why don't you escort Mrs. Brisbane to the bar so she doesn't get so lonely."

The two left the restaurant and headed for the bar. Salvatore then turned his attention to Brandt. "So, how have you been? I mean, since your wife was murdered and all?"

"I don't need the chit chat, Mr. Moratino. What's this all about?"

"That's what I like about you, Brandt; you like to get down to business right away. Okay, so we got a few things to go over. First, I appreciate you for sending me the money every month. You do good. Second, have you closed the deal on the new jail?"

"I'm about ninety-five percent sure I got the contract."

"Well, the way I look at it, ninety-five percent of nothing is still nothing. I need you to be one hundred percent sure you have the contract. Understand?"

"Yes, sir."

"Next, I think our little talk with Brisbane, helping him get elected and you as our point man will be good for the famiglia. But you guys have a problem over there that's not good for business, you know what I mean?"

"What's that?"

"You got some crazed guy going around killing people for no reason. That gets the cops all excited. Then, the DA will get excited and the next thing you know, they might be poking their noses into places we don't want them. But what's worse is that someone got it at one of our own places of business and that's not good at all. Understand?"

"Sure, but what can I do?"

"You're gonna set up a meeting between me and my associates here and Brisbane and Mayor Veluchi. We're gonna offer our help, you see?"

"Mayor Veluchi . . . ."

"Alonzo will be no problem. Just mention my name, kind of casual like. Tell him I said to remember Vito. You see, Vito didn't get straightened out which caused him to get sideways with the famiglia. Just mention my name and that I said to remember Vito. Don't go using any threats or think you are some big shot. Just do as I say. You got that?"

"Yes, sir."

"All we're trying to do is to help. That way the mayor will be happy, the cops will be happy and the good citizens of your fair city will be happy. But most important, we will be happy. See, it's a win-win situation all around."

"Okay," said Brandt. He knew full well what Salvatore was talking about; after all, it was in this very restaurant where Vito Veluchi was gunned down by the Palovani family because he didn't follow the rules and pay his fair share to the bosses. He assumed that they owned the sports bar where a guy presumably got himself killed.

Brandt was not a member of the Palovani family and never would be, but they helped him when he needed it. Consequently, they had made him a very wealthy man so the $85,000.00 monthly stipend, even though it was a great deal of money, was gladly paid by Brandt on time each and every month.

Salvatore continued, "We will meet here Tuesday at nine o'clock." He leaned in closer to Brandt's ear and whispered, "I don't care if you go banging Brisbane's wife, just don't screw this up."

---

It was Sunday night and Gil and Cornell were huddled together intently watching the security tapes from the Booster Club Sports Bar and Grille. Suddenly, and seemingly out of nowhere, stood Captain McCadry.

"Is this about the incident this afternoon?" McCadry asked nonchalantly.

Both Gil and Cornell, startled, looked at the captain.

"What are you doing here?" Gil asked.

"I do occasionally work on Sundays"

"Since when?" Gil stated sarcastically.

"Since I am your boss and I can do what the hell I want and what I want is all of the information on today's case. I am taking the lead on this one."

"The hell you are!" shouted Gil.

"I will not stand for any more of your insubordination, detective. I said I am taking the lead and that is not up for debate. Do you understand, Detective Clifton? Or would you like to be called Patrolman Clifton?"

Gil's eyes were beaming with hatred as he looked his boss up and down and finally concluded this was not a battle he was prepared to wage. "Suit yourself."

"That's better. Now what do you have?"

Gil filled him in with the bare minimum of information. He didn't want his boss, who hadn't investigated a murder for over seven years, to mess anything up.

"What are you looking for in these tapes?"

Gil looked at McCadry with disdain and spoke slowly and deliberately. "We are looking for what you might call evidence, Captain."

Cornell turned the tapes back on and he and Gil resumed their search while McCadry stood behind them and watched.

When the last tape was inserted Cornell said, "Captain, if you are just going to stand there and watch, you're not helping."

"Watch your mouth, detective. I will do what I want, when I want and where I want. Period."

They were about five minutes into the tape when Gil pointed out a guy in a hoodie. "I think that's him."

They watched as the hooded guy brushed up against Yoshi. They stopped the tape and rewound it several times.

"Stop. There. Back a little. There. Watch his right hand. It comes out of his sweatshirt pocket and looks like it's over Yoshi's glass for an instant. Do you see it?"

Cornell stopped the tape and rewound it a few frames and played it back in slow motion.

Both watched attentively. "Stop. Right there."

Cornell kept rewinding and playing that small portion of the tape in slow motion repeatedly several times. "It sure does look like his hand is over the glass. It's not that clear and you can't actually see his hand over the drink, but the angle sure looks like he could have put something in the glass."

Captain McCadry said, "Are you suggesting the guy was poisoned?"

"We are not suggesting anything, Captain. We are merely trying to piece together evidence and if it is supported by an autopsy finding, then we will suggest poison. Until then, it is just suspicious activity."

"Keep me up-to-date on everything. This is my case, detectives." He left the two sitting and went up to his office.

"Thought he'd never leave," said Cornell.

"What a pain in the ass. Let's see the rest."

The two kept a vigil on the rest of the tape.

"My God, did you see that!?" exclaimed Cornell.

"Yeah. Rewind and let's see it again."

They watched the hooded man put an envelope on the bar. A few seconds later Martin picked it up, looked at it and then stashed it alongside of the cash register.

Gil looked at his watch. "It's only eight-thirty. I'm going back over there and ask Martin why he didn't say anything about that."

"I'll go with you."

When they got to the sports bar Martin was still there. The place was empty except for two people sitting at the bar. Martin was taking inventory or something.

"Hi, detective. What can I do for you?"

"You mentioned a guy in a hoodie, right?"

"Yeah." Martin looked confused.

"Did he ever hand you an envelope?"

"No."

"Was there an envelope left on the bar?"

Martin's face became puzzled as he was trying to recall. "Oh, shit, yeah. I forgot all about it. All I can remember is that it had urgent written on it and some guy's name but I didn't recognize the name."

"Can you let me see the envelope?"

"Sure. If I can remember where I put it."

"Try the side of the cash register, but don't touch it. We want to preserve any fingerprints that might be on it," said Cornell. Although he knew they wouldn't find any incriminating prints, he still wanted to be cautious just in case the killer slipped up.

Martin looked astonished but then his face lit up with recognition. "Yeah. Now I remember." He quickly escorted Gil and Cornell to the register and pointed to where he had stashed it. "There it is. I didn't recognize the name, so I put it alongside the register and was going to deal with it later. We were too busy at the time."

Gil took the note and saw his name typed in the middle with <u>URGENT</u> typed on the bottom left. He opened it and slipped out the note very carefully. It read:

*'Cowards die many times before their death*
*the valiant never taste of death but once*
*of all the wonders that I yet have heard*
*it seems to me most strange*
*that men should fear*
*seeing that death*
*a necessary end*
*will come when it will come'*

Gil slipped the note back into the envelope and said, "I am Gil Clifton. Thanks."

"I'm sorry detective. I forgot all about it," said a contrite Martin.

Brandt Waverly was waiting for Carl Brisbane to come into the office on his first official Monday morning.

"Good morning, Brandt. What brings you here?"

"We need to talk right away."

They walked into Sheriff Brisbane's new office and before the sheriff was even seated, Brandt asked him if he knew Salvatore Moratino.

"Yeah. I know him. Why?"

"He wants to meet tomorrow at the El Toro Bistro in East Philly. No choice, Carl."

"What do you mean no choice? Are you threatening me?"

"He wants to meet with you and Mayor Veluchi. Nine o'clock. He's not messing around."

"The mayor? Is he crazy?"

"He might be but he's not kidding."

"Okay, okay."

"Another thing, Carl. You know how we talked about the new jail contract, right? You are going to make sure I get that contract. One hundred percent!"

"Who do you think you are coming...."

"I'm not kidding either. Just make sure you are there tomorrow at nine." Brandt turned and left the sheriff's office and headed to seek out the mayor.

Brandt knew his way around the municipal building and went straight to the mayor's office.

"Tell him I have a message from Salvatore."

"Yes, sir, Mr. Waverly." The secretary went into the mayor's office and a minute later returned and asked Brandt to come right in. Brandt passed her as she held the door open and then shut it on her way back to her desk.

"Mayor, thank you for seeing me."

"You're dropping a pretty big name around, Brandt."

"He wants to see you tomorrow night at El Toro's."

"Impossible."

"He asked me to remind you of Vito."

The mayor looked forlorn and said he would be there.

"Nine o'clock. The sheriff and I will be there, too."

Monday afternoon former sheriff Richard Winston knocked on Sheriff Brisbane's office door. "May I see you a minute?"

"Sure, come right on in. What's on your mind?"

"I just wanted to personally congratulate you on the election. I hope you and your friends from Philadelphia have a successful tenure."

"What the hell are you talking about, Winston?"

"You know full well why I didn't campaign. That's okay. I might enjoy retirement. But, let me warn you, if you get in too deep you might not see retirement."

"Get out of my office. Now!"

"Sure, Sheriff. Politics make strange bedfellows they say, so best of luck."

"Get out!"

\*\*\*

# Chapter 13
# The Agreement
*Tuesday, December 4, 2012*

Tuesday, December 4, 2012 Detectives Gil and Cornell were viewing the tapes from the Dorothy Coel, Adin Williamson and Hikaru Yoshi cases. They were trying to match physical characteristics from the three images showing a possible suspect in a hooded sweatshirt. They concluded that the images in all three were similar in build, height and appearance in so much as the suspect kept his face hidden at all times. They also had the notes, and when Cornell looked up the message from the Yoshi case, all were connected to plays written by William Shakespeare.

The two detectives felt they had connections but couldn't understand what they all meant.

"Okay, we have a guy in a hoodie at three locations where they had security cameras. We also have a witness who saw a man in a hoodie walking away from the Rabinovich Jewelry Store. We have notes sent to me immediately after each incident - except for Josef Rabinovich, where the note was left on the body and the Yoshi case, where the note was left at the bar. All have quotes from Shakespeare. Do you see a connection between the quotes and the victims? I don't," said Gil.

Cornell replied, "Not really. But here's what we do have. We have Allen Venter killed in an alley on June first at close range, and you get a quote from Shakespeare's Hamlet. Harold McDonald is shot by a sniper in front of a convenience store on July fifth, and you receive a quote from Othello. On August first, we have Dorothy Coel, suffocated in her own apartment and a quote from King Lear. September fourth, Roberta Waverly is found strangled in a public park and the quote is from Henry VIII. October third, we find Adin Williamson stabbed in a crowded gay club and you get a quote from The Tempest. November fifth, Josef Rabinovich is bludgeoned in his own jewelry shop and the killer leaves a note from Shakespeare's As You Like It. Finally, on December second, Hikaru Yoshi is apparently poisoned in a sports bar and a note is left with the bartender addressed to you from Julius Caesar. By the way did the coroner verify yet if Yoshi was poisoned?"

"No, but I think we need to talk to him today, though."

"You're right. Now let's continue. Each murder takes place at the beginning of a month. Meaning?" Cornell was searching for help.

"Meaning that the suspect may not be available during the latter part of the month because he is in some kind of work release program or something?"

"Each quote is from a different play. What does that mean?" Cornell was trying to ignite the probative juices of his partner.

"I've been going over and over that and I don't know if it's the plays themselves that are important or the quotes. I can't make the connection. I do know from high school that Julius Caesar was stabbed by Brutus, not poisoned. So things just don't make sense unless we rearrange the quotes to fit the crimes; but I've tried that and they still don't make sense."

Cornell said, "There must be something there as to why he is only killing at the beginning of each month. That too, is strange. Only one a month. Usually serial killers crop their killings together or spread them out over a long period of time. Why does this guy only kill consistently at the beginning of a month? That's the pattern we have to figure out - hopefully before January."

"Agreed. Let's go see the coroner."

Gil and Cornell went over to the coroner's office. Dr. Ingersoll was there and reluctantly took time to speak to the two detectives.

"I haven't made any final conclusions as of yet. I am waiting on some test results. I should have them in a few days."

Cornell asked, "Can you tell us what kinds of tests were conducted? It would help to know if you are looking at a possible poisoning."

"You are getting to be just like your partner over there. It's always hurry, hurry, hurry."

Gil and Cornell both produced a small smile.

Cornell continued, "If I promise I won't ask you to hurry with the results, would you at least tell me if you suspect poisoning for any reason?"

"This is not scientific. I found no bodily injuries; due to that discovery and information on the police reports, I am looking at several possibilities including heart attack."

"Is poisoning a possibility, also?"

"You detectives can't even wait a few days. Yes, I am looking into that possibility but I have no proof of anything until the test results come back. Now please go and let me continue with my work."

"Thank you, doctor," said Cornell. "Just let us know the results as soon as you get them."

"Yes, yes. Now please go and issue some parking tickets or something."

Gil and Cornell huddled in the hallway outside earshot of Dr. Ingersoll.

"I say that, for the time being, we assume we have a poisoning. What do you think?"

Gil answered, "It doesn't matter what I think at this point. But I'll go along with that assumption until the results come back."

They returned to the precinct to review each file in detail once again. They would select witnesses, such as they were, and mark to re-interview those selected for a second or third time. Each detective would read a complete file and then they would trade and discuss the two cases and move on to two more.

Nathan was delivering the last mail run of the day as he approached Gil's desk.

"Good afternoon, Nathan."

"Good afternoon, sir."

"Gil, remember. Please call me Gil."

"Good afternoon, Gil," said Nathan weakly.

"How about having that drink after work tonight and maybe I can help you prepare to get into the academy if you want?"

"I don't think so, sir. My mother doesn't think that I should get into police work."

"Why is that?"

"She thinks most all law enforcement people are dishonest and they just protect themselves and not the people."

"Really? You don't think that way, do you Nathan?"

"I don't think so, sir. But she knows much more than I do so I am not sure what to think."

"I would be glad to talk to her if you want me to."

"I'll ask her. But I don't think she likes the police too much."

"Does she know you are working here?"

"Yes. But I just sort and deliver the mail and stuff so she doesn't mind as long as I don't get involved with policemen."

"Okay. Just keep an open mind and if you decide you would like to apply for the academy, I will be here to help you. Okay?"

"Thank you, sir."

"Gil."

"Thank you, Gil." Nathan's head hung low as he shuffled away from Gil and continued on his round.

"I wonder why he is working here. He sounds like such a mama's boy," asked Cornell.

"Yeah. I could be wrong about him. He might be a little too weird. Maybe he wouldn't be much of a detective, although you got in," kidded Gil.

"Ha ha."

They returned to their work.

---

Mayor Alonso Veluchi, Sheriff Carl Brisbane, and Brandt Waverly were waiting at nine o'clock at the El Toro Bistro in East Philadelphia under a reservation name of Angelo Bondini. At nine-fifteen, Salvatore Moratino and three rather hefty associates entered the bistro. Salvatore had the Maître d' ready a table for four in a secluded corner reserved only for special guests. Salvatore Moratino was a special guest. The three associates were not introduced but guided the mayor, sheriff and Brandt over to the table.

Once they were all seated Salvatore lit a cigar and started, "We have a problem, gentlemen. A mutual problem. Quite frankly, I don't like problems." He looked at his three invited guests, one at a time. There was no reply.

"The problem is that you have a serial killer running loose in your city. Most of the time I stay out of police matters, but recently it became personal for the famiglia. We have an interest in a certain sports bar in Camden and now there has been some problem there that involves the police. I don't like the police to be involved in my problems." He let that settle in before he continued. "So in order to solve our mutual problem, I want to know everything about the investigations and I will use my resources to catch this killer which, of course, would be mutually beneficial to both parties. Agreed?"

Sheriff Brisbane spoke up. "It would be very difficult to get all of the information on the investigations without raising internal suspicions. I could, however, supply you with an overall generic view with as much detail as possible. But most importantly, I will stop any investigation into who the owners are of the sports bar in question, if it arises.

Brandt added, "If I may say, I think if you were to use your resources on the street we could then feed that information to the detectives as an unnamed source and that would not raise any internal questions."

Salvatore sat back in his seat puffing on his cigar, contemplating what the sheriff and Brandt had said. He looked at Mayor Veluchi and asked, "What do you think, Alonso? Do you have an opinion on this matter?"

"Yes, sir. I agree with Carl and Brandt. On my end, I will start putting more heat on the homicide division to get this solved so any information coming in as unnamed will not be questioned. I'll give them enough heat to burn themselves if I have to." He now knew that his longtime friendship with Captain McCadry would come to an end. An end he didn't like to see but an end that meant personal survival.

"That's not what I had in mind, but . . . ." Salvatore looked intently at each person seated at his table. "I'll try it your way for now. But rest assured, if there is any mention or inference about my famiglia, each of you will be held accountable. Do you understand?"

Each nodded their head in affirmation.

"Good. Now I have one more piece of business. Alonso, you sit on the City Council and the building committee. You will be hearing the recommendations for the new city jail as presented by our new sheriff. As I understand it, the sheriff is going to highly recommend Waverly Building and Contracting. I support that choice one hundred percent and I hope you do too. Now if there is no other business I suggest we adjourn this meeting so that I can get on with my evening meal. Thank you for coming. I will be in touch."

Alonso, Carl and Brandt left the El Toro Bistro and drove back to Camden with their 'marching orders' as presented by the underboss of the Palovani famiglia. None of the trio had the means or propensity to oppose such a formidable influence that had crept into their lives very slowly. Their obligations to Salvatore Moratino, however, were now irreversible.

## ----*Wednesday, December 5, 2012*----

Early on Wednesday morning, Gil and Cornell were summoned to the sheriff's office for a meeting and asked to bring their files on the cases they were working. When they arrived, they were surprised to see Mayor Veluchi and Captain McCadry already with the sheriff.

"Are we too early?" asked Gil.

"No, come in. We would like to talk to you," said Sheriff Brisbane very cordially.

Gil and Cornell took seats alongside the mayor and captain, all facing the sheriff, who was seated behind his desk.

The sheriff spoke. "How is the investigation going into this serial killer? Do you have any suspects?"

"All we have, basically, is a possible person in a hoodie and the notes I received after each incident."

"I would like to go over each case. The mayor is very interested in getting this serial killer put away and relieving some of the tension with the citizens of Camden. I am sure you understand. So please, let's get started. After all, we are all on the same team."

Gil opened each file and gave known facts about the case. He didn't, however, give any information that wasn't already known. He kept his and his partner's observations private. Gil spoke without interruption for about forty-five minutes when he finally concluded his impromptu dissertation.

Mayor Veluchi said, "Sheriff, do you think we should form a task force with other law enforcement agencies such as the Camden Crime Unit and the gang unit to give these detectives more support?"

Gil replied, "I don't think that a task force would . . . ."

"I'll state it another way. I insist that a task force be formed. You haven't produced any results for six months and this has been going on far too long." The mayor's voice sounded forceful and angry.

"I was thinking along those same lines, Mayor." The sheriff turned to Gil and asked, "Would you head up this task force? I will give the necessary orders for it to be created and I'll provide you at least three or four other resources. We need to get this solved right away."

Captain McCadry interjected, "Don't you think I should be in charge of the task force? After all, I am a captain and in charge of the homicide division."

Mayor Veluchi answered, "And that is precisely why you are not going to head it up. You've also been in charge while all of these murders have been taking place with no results. I believe Detective Gil would be an excellent choice to supervise the task force."

Captain McCadry looked unbelievably at his friend of many years and felt a sting of betrayal throughout his body.

Gil also felt the betrayal of the mayor and almost felt sorry for his boss. Gil asked, "Sheriff, how much of the information we learn will be made public? I mean, because of your campaign about transparency."

"I will only announce that we have created a task force but the details we will keep to ourselves for the time being. I want to assure the citizens we are working diligently but there is no use creating undo panic with details they may not understand. Do you agree?"

Gil looked at the new sheriff, realized how much of a hypocrite Sheriff Brisbane could be and made a mental note to be careful of him. "Yes, I agree."

Days later Gil and Cornell were meeting with two members of the CCU (Camden Crime Unit), one member of the CAGE (Camden Area Gang Enforcement) and one member of CLEAR (Camden Law Enforcement Arterial Resources). Gil gave each of the task force members a copy of the files. They all sat in a conference room and went over the points for which each person would be responsible. Gil was happy about the additional help, but had reservations about the timing and reasons behind its formation.

Later that afternoon, Dr. Ingersoll called Detective Gil and informed him that Hikaru Yoshi had been poisoned with a lethal dose of potassium cyanide. He had found at least 500 milligrams in the blood work of the victim. A lethal dose would be in the range of 150 to 200 milligrams.

"How does one go about getting that much potassium cyanide?"

"I'm not a criminal. I am a doctor," Ingersoll retorted gruffly.

For the next two weeks the task force had interviewed every witness for a least a second time if not a third. No one on the force thought of looking into the ownership of the sports bar because the manager was cooperating completely and he did not send up any red flags. There was no new evidence that came out of the interviews and even with new sets of eyes closely examining the files, they still came up empty as to a possible suspect.

The homicide department's Christmas party was held on the snowy afternoon of Christmas Eve and members of the task force were invited. Sheriff Brisbane, Captain McCadry and Jacob Feinstein (the Camden Police Chief) were all in attendance on the second floor where Gil solemnly joined in, but mostly stayed at his desk.

Cornell came up to him and said, "Are you being antisocial today?"

"Maybe. I want to run something by you that I've been thinking about."

Some of the party guests started singing Christmas carols. As they broke into an out-of-tune rendition of Jingle Bells, Cornell got closer to Gil so he could hear. "What are you thinking?"

Gil had a distressed look on his face as stared at his partner. "I've been wondering if we should go see The Professor." Gil lowered his head and gazed at the floor without any further comment.

"You've always been against that. Why now?"

"I'm just thinking that my pride has prevented us from using any and all resources. We need to give these victims our very best and if that means talking to The Professor, well, then I guess that is what we will have to do."

"The Professor could be a good resource and then again, maybe not."

"I owe it to the victims to at least try."

"I'll support you in any decision you make, partner. But let's put it aside for right now and enjoy the Christmas party. Okay?"

"Okay. But I'm not singing."

"That's the spirit. Besides, I've heard you sing and you are doing us all a favor."

Gil joined the festivities but avoided getting close to the sheriff or Captain McCadry. He didn't want them to spoil any holiday joy he could muster up. Some of the detectives had their wives join them. Sheriff Brisbane had his wife, Elaina, join him and they both were busy doing what Carl did best - politic. Alcohol was not served at the gathering, but it was evident that some of the employees had access to it and were getting a little loud and animated.

The party broke up around 5:30 p.m. Cornell and Gil were the last to leave and Cornell said, "Are you going home now?"

"I will in a bit. I just want to think in private. I hope you understand."

"Sure. Let me know what you decide about The Professor. Like I said, I'll support any decision you make. Don't stay too long, the snow is building up out there. Merry Christmas, partner."

"Have a Merry Christmas, Cornell."

Cornell shut off all of the lights except one set over Gil's desk and left.

\*\*\*

# Chapter 14
# The Professor
*Wednesday, December 26, 2012*

The week between Christmas and New Year's was slow for the Camden homicide division as was per usual for that time of year. The good news for Camden was that there was little traffic to hinder the snow plows from clearing the streets from the Christmas Eve snow storm. The bad news was the Camden Killer Task Force did not have a suspect nor were they even close to having one. The dread of the approaching January was foremost on the minds of Gil and Cornell. Would the killer strike again? Where would the killer strike next? Who would be the next victim? They needed a break and none was forthcoming.

On Christmas Eve Gil had confided in Cassandra that he might have to solicit the help of The Professor. She neither approved nor disapproved what he did in his job, but she told him she would support him in whatever decision he made. On Wednesday morning, December 26, Gil had made arrangements for Cornell and himself to make the 80 mile trip from Camden, NJ to Rahway, NJ where James 'The Professor' Macklevy was housed. The Professor, as he was always referred, was serving a life sentence without the possibility of parole for five out of seven counts of murder he committed back in 1985. Gil Clifton was the key law enforcement officer responsible for The Professor's current permanent address. Gil was not even sure if The Professor would speak with him, but he had to try. He had to try for his victims.

The hour and a half it took to drive to the prison was filled with conversation between Gil and Cornell as to how they were going to approach the infamous James Macklevy. One troubling area for Gil was how to address the killer. Should they call him James, Mr. Macklevy or Professor? They decided that Mr. Macklevy would be appropriate. They didn't want to have the familiarity of calling him James nor give an edge to the prisoner by calling him Professor and therefore, by silent insinuation, imply that he had a superior intellect.

The Professor, however, was a very intelligent individual. At the time of his arrest, he was a professor of English literature at the University of New Jersey – Camden. His students said he was very challenging during his lectures and always tried to spur them into thinking of English literature from different perspectives rather than the old tried and true versions usually taught at that level.

The detectives checked in and signed the register. They left their guns and ammunition with security and were subjected to a routine 'pat-down.' Once they passed inspection, they were escorted to a room where a long line of Plexiglas was dividing connected cubicle desks from a like set on the other side. There was a telephone attached on each side hanging on a wall. As they were waiting, other visitors were talking to prisoners. Some were in the middle of conversations while others were either beginning or ending their visits.

Thirty-five minutes later, they had their first glimpse of James Edward Macklevy - known to all as The Professor. He was much heavier than Gil remembered. He attributed the excess weight to the three square meals per day and not much in the way of exercise as it was up to the prisoner to keep in shape. The Professor didn't strike Gil as the type of person who would indulge in any sort of rigorous activity. His skin was prison pallid and his head was almost completely bald save for a small ring of gray hair surrounding the side and back of his head. He now sported a grayish goatee which made him look like the devil incarnate.

Gil picked up the phone's receiver and held it against his ear waiting for The Professor to do the same. The Professor sat back in his chair and stared continuously at his visitor from the homicide division. He then leaned forward, resting his left hand on the desk, and slowly reached for the phone.

Gil started, "I am Detective Gil Clifton from the Camden, New Jersey Police Department,

Homicide Division. This is my partner, Detective Cornell Bush. We wish to thank you, Mr. Macklevy, for talking with us."

The Professor started out slow and deliberate. "First of all, I request that you call me by my societal given name, Professor." There was slight pause, "Secondly and most notably, my good man, I have very few subjects about which I have aspirations to converse with you as I recollect the name Gil Clifton most distinctly."

That is not exactly what Gil and Cornell were hoping to hear. Nevertheless, Gil pressed on. "We have been investigating a series of killings in our area and with each killing I have received a quote from one of William Shakespeare's plays. We were wondering if, because of your illustrious and learned background as a professor of English literature, you might give us some insight into the meaning of the quotes and how they are tied to the murders."

"Are you suggesting to me, my good man, that I should attempt the formidable undertaking of interpreting for you a collection of scholarly compositions by the venerable and learned William Shakespeare in an abbreviated and capsulated form thus rendering his works of no more dignity than a dime store novel?"

"I'm sorry, Professor. I have wasted your time." Gil hung up the phone and was about to leave when, on the other side of the Plexiglas, a lonely man waved him back to the phone. Gil picked up the receiver.

"Mr. Gil Clifton from the Camden, New Jersey Police Department, Homicide Division, I may be of some assistance to you. After all, the scholarly William Shakespeare shan't be taken lightly by amateurish individuals trying to intellectually interpret his complex writings and relinquish it as some insidious drabble."

"If you're saying you will help, then, thank you, Professor." Gil was trying to be respectful.

"Do not try to placate me. What I am revealing to you is that I would be desirous to have an illustration of your dilemma."

Cornell whispered in Gil's ear, "I think the pompous ass wants to see one of the quotes."

"Mr. Cornell Bush of the same police department and division, I kindly entreat you to make all commentary aloud for all to appreciate. Secrecy can be assessed as such a devious behavior."

"Sorry, Professor," said Cornell as he leaned over and spoke into the receiver, "I was just telling my colleague to tell you how much we appreciate your cooperation."

"I have, with the utmost of certainty the belief that the words conveyed to your associate were less than complimentary and falsehoods shall hastily dissolve our association; of that, I assure you."

"Okay. I've gotten off to a bad start. I am sorry and it won't happen again." Cornell said and slumped back into his chair.

Gil asked permission of the guard to show the prisoner a piece of paper with a quote. The guard looked over the paper and handed it back to the detective. "Do you mind if I take another look at your credentials. I don't want any secret messages being passed to the prisoner. I hope you understand."

"Sure, I understand. We have a special request of this prisoner to interpret some Shakespeare quotes we are having difficulty understanding."

"Why don't you just go to the college and ask them?"

"The notes are connected to a criminal investigation."

"I see. You need the point of view from a criminal's mind," said the guard.

"That's about it." Gil and Cornell presented their credentials to the guard and were granted permission to show the note through the Plexiglas to the prisoner.

Gil said, "This is the first one we got. It coincided with the murder of a man named Allen Venter, a white male, 42 years old who was killed at close range by a .45 caliber pistol in an alley between the hours of 4 and 7 p.m. on June 2, 2012."

"Oh yes," The Professor said and then continued with a loud and slow but purposeful voice, as if he were acting on stage, "Doubt thou the stars are fire, doubt that the sun doth move, doubt truth to be a liar, but never doubt I love." He held his hand over his heart and his eyes closed as if he were in a trance.

"So what do you think?" asked Gil.

"This rather short couplet was uttered by Lord Polonius to Gertrude, Hamlet's mother, but written by Hamlet to Lord Polonius's daughter, Ophelia. Gertrude and Lord Polonius were discussing the sanity of Hamlet as he was explaining to her his position that Hamlet was crazy. Lord Polonius was reading this love letter which was given to him dutifully by his daughter for which Hamlet was merely saying to Ophelia that you may doubt many things, but never doubt that I love you."

"Do you see any connection between the note's content and the murder I told you about?"

The Professor looked at Gil with a peculiar expression. "To interpret Shakespeare's Hamlet is excruciatingly exigent due to the incessant vicissitudes of the sands beneath the foundation from scene to scene and from act to act."

"Meaning?"

"It is difficult to give a finite definition to a singular quote as it does not reflect the entirety of the composition. This follows that ambiguous succession because in the very next scene Hamlet says he does not love her."

Gil cautiously asked, "Then what is the connection?"

"My good man, as eager as you are to make a connection from one of Shakespeare's more daunting plays, one might ask, why was the most famous quote from Hamlet not alluded to in this mysterious annotation?"

"What is that? The 'to be or not to be' thing?" said Gil.

The Professor replied indignantly, "Would you please afford me the simple pleasure when referencing quotations from one of the most profound playwrights of human existence not to call his illustrious writings .... things?"

"I apologize, Professor."

"I assume you have approached me because you are in want of the perspective from a criminal mind. Is that not so?"

"I believe, Professor, you may have a unique perspective, yes."

"My good man, I would like to espouse my complete and utter innocence for crimes which were indubitably perpetrated by others however unduly promulgated upon my person. Nonetheless, I have been subjected; unfairly mind you, to those who have a criminal propensity for vicious behaviorisms in this most unholy of all places. Ergo, because of the situation for which I find myself, I have the unique dispensation to more fully examine the raison d'être for their acts."

"I'm sorry, Professor, but are you saying that you will help us make a connection?" Cornell asked.

"You have solicited my assistance and I shall acquiesce as such benevolent challenges are far and few between in this forlorn domicile of which I find myself needlessly incarcerated. So, to answer your question more succinctly, yes."

"We will be back tomorrow when we have more time."

"The timeless in you is aware of life's timelessness. And knows that yesterday is but today's memory and tomorrow is today's dream." The Professor looked at the puzzled faces on the other side of the glass. "A quote from Khalil Gibran's philosophical essay entitled 'The

Prophet' which is an inspirational illustration of literary fiction composed in elegiac English prose. Gentlemen, I bid you good day."

The Professor hung up his phone and scooted his chair back. As he rose he tilted his head slightly forward and gave his visitors an almost imperceptible salute and a sly smile. A guard came to his side and escorted him once again to his prison cell.

Cornell looked at Gil, "I still say he's a pompous ass."

Gil smiled, "A pompous ass who might be able to help us get inside this killer's head."

Gil and Cornell asked permission to see the warden. They were led to his office and the warden graciously agreed to see them. Gil explained the purpose of their visit and inquired about having a room where they could have closer access to The Professor. There are rooms with tables that have hooks where the prisoner's hands can be handcuffed.

"The Professor has been a model prisoner and I see no reason why I can't grant your request. He will have to be handcuffed to the table but will have some room to operate. However, be ever so mindful as he is still a killer and in all probability, always will be."

They thanked the warden but were surprised by his answer. It sounded to them like the warden did not believe in rehabilitation. They returned to the precinct and started to prepare for the next day's meeting with The Professor. They wanted to ferret out any information they thought The Professor shouldn't have knowledge of, such as witness names, addresses and the like.

The phone rang and Gil answered. The mayor was on the line and wanted to know the progress in the case.

"We are working hard at getting a resolution. I am sure we are going to catch this guy soon, mayor."

"Make sure you update Captain McCadry every day. I understand he is not the lead on the task force but from what I hear you are not keeping him in the loop. He is a very valuable resource so please take advantage."

The mayor hung up the phone.

"The mayor?" asked Cornell.

"Yeah. He wanted to make sure we keep Captain McCadry in the loop because, as he put it, he is a very valuable resource."

"Resource? My ass!"

"Things are getting weirder every day," observed Gil.

## ----*Thursday, December 27, 2012*----

Gil and Cornell met with the task force early Thursday morning. They updated everyone, including Captain McCadry, on the contact they had with The Professor. Cornell stated how enthusiastic they are about what The Professor might be able to contribute to the investigation.

McCadry asked, "So you're telling us that a guy you arrested twenty-seven years ago is willing to help you find some kind of meaning and connection with these notes you have been receiving? Just how in the Sam Hill do you think that is going to look to the public? Do we have to rely on prisoners to help us catch one killer because we can't catch him ourselves, is that it?"

"I think to utilize every resource available is the prudent thing to do. We have asked the local FBI to help us with a profile so we are effectively using the whole spectrum of ideas to be put on the table."

"Well, I don't like using a criminal for police work."

The rest of the task force participants agreed with Gil and the captain abruptly left the meeting.

Gil continued, "Where are we on the re-interviews? Have we contacted everyone at least one more time?"

"I have contacted Bonita Rodriquez from the Quick-E-Stop about the Harold McDonald case," reported one member. "She said about the same thing as she did before; that he victim bought a few items, didn't say much and left. When she happened to look out the window from behind the cash register, she said the next thing she knew was that the victim fell. She thought he had a heart attack."

The member from the gang unit spoke up. "I talked to Arlene McDonald. She spoke more about their marital problems than what was in the report from before, but it sounded like it was just the way they lived. You know, some people just love to argue. But with all of their arguing, I believe her when she says she loved her husband despite everything. On the good side, the Camden Inn where she works has been giving her more hours so she's getting by a little bit better. I also got in touch with Lil' Mac, their son. What a piece of work he is. He hangs out down by the river front with the homeless. He wasn't too cooperative but I ran a check on him and he was in jail for three days including the day his father was shot. I talked with a few of the people at the river and no one really knows too much about Lil' Mac other than to say he kept to himself and he didn't say much to anyone. I don't think he would be capable of shooting a gun, much less a high powered rifle from a distance. He's pretty much a hardened alcoholic more interested in his beer and whiskey than Shakespeare."

"I have done some follow-up on the Allen Venter case, but all we know is that the victim was shot at close range with a .45 caliber pistol. Because his car was found several miles from the crime scene, I guess we can conclude it was some kind of abduction which led to murder. No word on the street from my informants about this one at all. Kind of unusual that it's so quiet out there. Usually somebody knows something." He shook his head. "Nothing."

Another member of the task force updated everyone on the August murder of Dorothy Coel. "I didn't get much more out of Dorothy's roommate, Amanda Samuels. She said that Dorothy's boyfriend, Richard Sawyer, was a very nice person and that he and some of his friends went on a fishing excursion. I spoke with Richard and that checked out. He also stated there were no problems between Dorothy and him. As a matter of fact, he was going to propose to her. He showed me a ring he had just purchased. Not a likely candidate to want her dead. I also went to the Red Bird Lounge and tried to locate the guy by the name of Darryl. His name is Darryl Jorgenson. He admitted having sex with Amanda the night of the murder. He said it was kind of a quickie. He's been going to the Red Bird for about two years. He remembers seeing Amanda's roommate there but she was always with another guy. I showed him a photo of Richard and he said that was the guy always with Dorothy. The bartender remembers Dorothy and her boyfriend but not much of anything in particular. Everything was a dead-end."

He continued his update, "I have also been looking at the Adin Williamson case and there seems to be nothing but dead-ends on that one too. I did have one of Adin's friends tell me that he was talking to Adin when he was stabbed. All he remembered was some guy in a hooded sweatshirt bumped into them, and right after that, Adin went down. The guy looked around after he realized that Adin had been stabbed but couldn't find the guy in the hoodie. A few other witnesses remember a guy in a hoodie, but nobody said they knew who he was, mainly because they couldn't see his face."

Cornell spoke next. "I've been on the Roberta Waverly case. There's not much in the way of forensic evidence. She was strangled, but the perp used gloves and probably wore a hat or hooded sweatshirt because the coroner didn't come up with any hair fibers or prints of any kind. However, when I started looking at her husband, Brandt, there are some rumors that he was having an affair. I found one person who lives in the same neighborhood and she confided that she thought she saw Brandt Waverly with - now get this - Sheriff Brisbane's wife at a restaurant over in East Philly. She said she and her husband went to the El Toro Bistro because they heard it was a mob hangout and they wanted to go and be part of it for one night." Everyone at the conference table chuckled and shook their heads in disbelief about how some people got their kicks.

"Be that as it may, she said she recognized Brandt and wanted to say something to him but her husband told her to let it be. I've done some more checking and it looks like Brandt and Elaina Brisbane are some type of hot item."

Gil asked, "You say this El Toro Bistro is a mob hangout?"

"Yeah. It seems that it is the only non-Italian restaurant they use."

"I've heard that too," said Bryan Martinson a member from the Camden Crime Unit. "It's used by the Palovani crime family. They control East Philly and western New Jersey."

Gil perked up, "Do they have any influence here in Camden?"

"I was going to fill everyone in when we got to the Yoshi case, but, they are the silent partners who own the Booster Club Sports Bar and Grille where Yoshi was murdered."

Cornell said, "That probably didn't set well with them. Have you heard of any repercussions yet?"

"Not yet," said the investigator.

"Keep on top of that one. With Brandt being seen there and them owning the bar, it just raises a red flag to me. Probably nothing, but stay on it."

"Will do."

The task force was looking for new ideas but the cases were not producing any new evidence. The meeting broke up at 11:15. Gil asked Bryan Martinson to stay for a minute.

"Bryan, what is your feeling about this El Toro Bistro connection?"

"I think it's worth taking a harder look at."

"Stay on this one and if anything new develops or you need some help, let me know. My gut is telling me something but I'm not sure what."

When Bryan left, Gil approached Cornell. "So we have a connection with the Booster Club and the mob. We should take a little closer look at our friend the manager. What's his name. . . . Martin?"

"Martin Porter."

***

# Chapter 15
# The Meeting
*Friday, December 28, 2012*

Sheriff Brisbane was talking to Mayor Veluchi in the mayor's office on Friday, December 28. The mayor said, "I just heard from our friend in Philly and he told me one of his contacts on the street had heard somebody from Rahway was asking about potassium cyanide a couple months ago. He was wondering if it tied into anything we had. I told him I would get back to him. What should I say?"

"I understand the kid who was killed at the sports bar was poisoned with potassium cyanide. Tell him that it might tie in and to give you the name of the prisoner and the contact. We will take it from there."

"Should I tell him anything else?"

"No. Just play it cool. If word ever gets out we're working with him and his associates, you might as well stick a fork in us because we're done. How are you supposed to get in touch with him?"

The mayor said, "I am supposed to make a reservation at the El Toro Bistro under the name Angelo Bondini again."

"Kind of a corny name, if you ask me. Sounds like an Italian James Bond. But anyway, you make the arrangements and as soon as you get back, let me know about everything that took place."

"You aren't coming with me?"

"No. I think it is better if we're not seen together as much for right now."

"Listen, Carl, you are up to your neck in this the same as I am. And if you think for one second that you are going to hang me out to dry on this, you are sadly mistaken."

"Alonso, don't get so defensive. I'm just saying that I don't want us to be looked upon as having some kind of an ulterior motive. We need to hang this on Gil Clifton and Captain McCadry."

"I'm just saying, don't try double-crossing me."

The sheriff left the mayor's office and returned to the precinct. He called Captain McCadry and told him to come to his office immediately. The sheriff had an important assignment for him.

Mayor Veluchi called the El Toro Bistro and made a reservation for 9:00 p.m. on January 2. Four hours later, his secretary gave him a message that the dinner reservation was changed to 9:00 p.m. on Sunday, December 30.

"He said you would know what he was talking about," his secretary informed the mayor. "I don't have anything on your calendar, Mayor."

"I know you don't. This is an old friend from college I haven't seen in years and I didn't want this to be construed as a business meeting."

"Should I put it on your calendar so you don't forget?"

"No. That's okay. I'll remember."

---

Gil and Cornell reached the East Jersey Prison, formerly known as Rahway State Prison, at 1:15 p.m. They were escorted to a small conference room where a table sat that had a large circular piece of metal secured to its middle. There were two chairs on one side and one chair on the other. Large Plexiglas windows were set into the door and a large smoked glass mirror was on one side. They knew this was a two-way mirror and that they would be monitored by prison staff during the meeting.

The Professor entered the room accompanied by two guards. He took a seat and the guards unlocked the cuffs from behind his back and shackled him to a hook protruding from the table. His feet were secured to the legs of his chair by chains. The guards took their leave and locked the door behind them.

"Good afternoon, Gil Clifton and Cornell Bush," the Professor acknowledged, then turned his head and smiled at the mirror, "and to you, too, officers of this unholy institute, whoever you may be."

Gil started, "I have a series of notes here with quotes from various plays written by Shakespeare. I have also put the pertinent information about each crime. What we need your help with is to find some sort of connection between the crimes and these quotations, if you can."

The Professor took the notes and read each one in silence. After several minutes he said, "The antithesis of good is evil, of want is need, of charity is selfishness. I am not an evil, nor needy, nor even a selfish person. However, I perceive no advantage for my participation in your quest for edification of these profound writings. With that being avowed, I gave you my word as a gentleman when you solicited my services and I shall abide by my understanding of your requirements. It would be most benevolent on your part to afford me some form of mundane compensation. I am, of course, not speaking of monetary recompense or remuneration, but perhaps a humanitarian gesture would be in order. The ball, as they say, is in your court."

Gil was confused, "Are you saying you won't help us unless we do something for you?"

"Your comprehension of the English language is suspect at best. I declare and aver once again that I will help but it would be nice if you were to help me in some way. Is that plain enough?"

"What would you suggest?"

"The access to books with any substantial relevance is a scarcity in this abominable institution. I would be most desirous of obtaining tomes of a scholarly temperament to nurture my curiosity of the intellectual side of humanity. I am most positive that with something more than a parochial visionary attitude, this could be accomplished with relative effortlessness."

"You want us to bring you some books?"

"Precisely, my good man. I shall compose a list of those which I am most anxious to indulge my aspirations and profession. I believe I could enlighten these helpless humanoids incarcerated in this unhealthy and intellectually bereft institute to perhaps gain some semblance of insight, by some sort of remedial form, into the philosophical existence of mankind."

"I think we can help as long as we get the warden's approval," said Gil.

"Thank you. Now, I would like to peruse these prolific illustrations and the accompanied data in a more in-depth manner, if you please."

"You need time to study them?" asked Cornell.

"Once again your astute perception is much like the Swiss founder of analytical psychology, C.G. Jung, when he wrote, 'everything that irritates us about others can lead us to an understanding of ourselves.' I do aspire reach a formidable and intellectual conclusion."

Cornell got angry. "I don't know whether I should thank you or bash your head in."

"Your pugilistic tendencies would most assuredly gain the attention of those who so steadfastly keep sentinel upon us." He gestured towards the mirror.

Gil spoke up, "Detective Bush means nothing by it. Sometimes you say things we don't quite understand as we have not had the privilege of a broader education, as you have."

"Do not pacify me with encomiums."

"See," said Gil, "that's exactly what I mean."

"I shall restate my contention." The Professor leaned forward, and with eyes that were squinted in a fierce and threatening manner which could almost penetrate the very soul, he whispered very slowly, "Don't bullshit with me."

The guards took notice and became tense, ready to spring into action should the situation escalate any further.

"That we understand," commented Gil.

The guards relaxed as The Professor repositioned himself back in his chair and continued, "I shall examine the notes, which I now have in my possession, with diligence and accord. I shall render you my understanding whether it is right or 'the assertion that you are in falsehood and I am in truth is the most cruel thing one man can say to another' as Leo Tolstoy said in his writing of A Confession."

Gil countered, "Didn't he also say in that same book, 'wrong does not cease to be wrong because the majority share in it'?"

"I am astounded, my good man!" The Professor said in amazement.

"We will be back next week. Will that give you enough time?"

"Yes. Would you please write down these books and, if you would be so kind, bring them with you the next time we meet."

Gil opened his notepad and was ready to write.

"My short list consists of the following works: The Divine Comedy by Dante Alighieri. Don Quixote by Miguel de Cervantes. Hunger by Knut Hamsun. Leaves of Grass by Walt Whitman. But without fail and above all else, please obtain a copy of The Brothers Karamazov by Fyodor Dostoevsky. I feel this prolific writing would be most apropos because of its philosophical passion regarding the ethical debates of free will, morality and God and the spiritual drama it creates with the struggles of faith, doubt and reason."

"We'll do our best but first I have to check it out with the warden."

The guards entered the room and looked at the notes before handing them back to The Professor. The meeting was over and Gil and Cornell headed for the warden's office when Cornell asked, "Where did that highfalutin quote come from?"

"Why should you be surprised? I read."

"You read Tolstoy?"

"Naw. It was a favorite saying of one of the nuns in high school. She would say that almost every day if the class got something wrong."

"Nice touch, partner."

"I thought so."

The warden granted their request to let The Professor have the books provided they pass the x-ray test.

## ----*Sunday, December 30, 2012*----

Bryan Martinson, an investigator on the Camden Killer Task Force on loan from the Camden Crime Unit, was spending his third consecutive night at the El Toro Bistro. On Friday he ate with his wife, Luanne, as he kept an undercover vigil in the notorious restaurant. Luanne knew she would not be in harm's way as her husband would not have any confrontations with any person from the underground.

He kept his silent surveillance, but there was nothing that captured his attention. He had small photos of known associates of the Palovani family and committed them to memory as best he could. Nothing noteworthy happened and he and his wife left the bistro after several hours of ultra-slow dining.

On Saturday night he sat in the bar nursing his drink and trying to keep an eye on the restaurant, but because of its location it was harder to do than he expected. Surveillance was such a tedious, time consuming and boring way to make a living, but he knew that eventually all covert surveillance activities mostly paid off. However, this Saturday was a bust.

Tonight, he made another reservation at the El Toro and was accompanied by his sister. Luanne didn't like that Bryan would use his sister, but he explained to her that a 'girlfriend' was never suspect in that place. As a matter of fact, it may even enhance his status. Nevertheless, he would not do anything conspicuous to draw attention to himself.

His sister, Jennifer, was 23, very cute and unmarried. She would make the perfect decoy 'girlfriend'. They arrived at 7:50 p.m. for their eight o'clock reservation. They had a before dinner cocktail, read the menu slowly and ordered some appetizers. They were looking at the menu for the main course entrees when Bryan spotted Mayor Veluchi enter the restaurant.

"Okay, this might be something. Play it real nice and quiet."

Jennifer understood.

He overheard the mayor say that he had reservations for nine under the name of Angelo Bondini. The maître d' had him follow to a secluded table, out of earshot of Bryan. At 9:15 p.m. Salvatore Moratino and four associates walked in and went directly to the table where the mayor was evidently waiting for them. Bryan hurriedly scribbled names and times on his pad and returned it nonchalantly to his breast pocket.

Bryan and Jennifer slowly finished their dinner and had an after dinner cocktail. When they were done the waiter came to their table and asked if they needed anything else. At the same time Mayor Veluchi was leaving the restaurant so Bryan asked for the check. As he was paying for their evening meal, he noticed out of the corner of his eye that their waiter speaking in confidence to Salvatore Moratino.

"Let's get out of here fast," he whispered lowly to Jennifer.

They quickly got into their car and as they were leaving, Bryan looked into his rear view mirror and watched as the four associates of the Palovani family run out of the restaurant and suddenly stop as they watched his car speed off into the night.

## ----New Year's Eve 2012----

On the morning prior to the big New Year's Eve celebration for all off-duty law enforcement personnel that was to take place at the Camden Inn, Gil Clifton received an urgent message to call Bryan Martinson as soon as possible. Gil and Cassandra were having breakfast in her kitchen and he had heard his voice mail beep from his cell phone. He looked at the number but didn't readily recognize it. He listened to the voice message and immediately dialed Bryan.

"What's the emergency?"

"I've been scouting out the El Toro Bistro. I was there Friday, Saturday and Sunday. It paid off because on Sunday Mayor Veluchi had a meeting with Salvatore Moratino, the underboss of the Palovani family. The mayor got there at nine and when Moratino and four of his big goons arrived, they went right over to the mayor's table and sat down. I'm sure the mayor was expecting them. They met for about forty-five minutes. I left right behind the mayor, but as I was leaving I saw our waiter whisper something to Moratino so we hightailed it out of there pronto like. The four guys came running out and watched me pull away. I just made it out of there with my life in the nick of time."

"Well, needless to say, the surveillance over there is done. Did you hear any of the conversation?"

"No, they were too far away. But I did get this little tidbit of info. When the mayor first came in he called himself Angelo . . . . Let me look at my notes for a second. Yeah, he called himself Angelo Bondini."

"The only connection we have with the serial killer is that the Palovani family has an interest in the Booster Club Sports Bar and Grille, right?" Gil asked.

"Yeah, but you can throw the mayor, Brandt Waverly and Elaina Brisbane into the mix, somehow. All have been seen at the El Toro Bistro."

"They could have easily gotten the potassium cyanide, but it doesn't make sense they would off a nobody kid, especially in their own house. That is, unless Yoshi has more behind him than we think," Gil wondered out loud.

"We'll take another look at him, but he came up clean. Wrong person, wrong time, wrong place."

"Yeah. Good job, Bryan. Sometimes things happen and we don't know why, so we've got to keep this to ourselves. Let's not let the sheriff get hold of this. Not even the rest of the task force. I'll update Cornell, but that's all for now unless you can think of a reason to not keep it quiet."

"I agree. We've got a hot potato on our hands, that's for sure."

They ended their conversation and Gil hung up the phone.

"Who was that, dear?" questioned Cassandra.

"Bryan from CCU. He's on the task force. Looks like there might be a tie-in with the mob over in Philly and this serial killer."

Cassandra looked concerned. "A serial killer and the mob?"

"We're not sure yet. A lot of names are coming up. I think we're closing in on the killer if we just keep pecking away."

"You never told me how your meeting went with The Professor."

"He's looking at the quotes."

Cassandra put her arms around Gil's neck and said, "Do you think he will be of any use?"

"You never know."

Gil and Cassandra attended the New Year's Eve dance at the Camden Inn and returned home around 2:00 a.m. on New Year's Day. They slept in until almost ten o'clock. Gil prepared breakfast as Cassandra made a couple of telephone calls and watched the Rose Parade on television.

Gil was thinking about the connection between the mob and Mayor Veluchi. He also wanted to interview the manager of the Booster Club Sports Bar, Martin Porter, again. This time he thought he would put a little more pressure on him. He was also thinking how The Professor was coming along and whether or not he had found a connection.

After the breakfast dishes were securely in the dishwasher, Gil was antsy. He told Cassandra that he wanted to go the office for a couple hours.

"Of course, dear. I have a few things to do also and today is as good as any to get them done. What time do you think you'll be home?"

"Probably around six."

"See you then."

---

Gil arrived at the mostly deserted office at a little after noon. There was only a front desk officer on duty and one homicide detective reading some files.

"What brings you in today, Gil?"

"Nervous energy, I guess."

"I know what you mean."

Gil sat at his desk and started writing up notes from the conversation he'd had with Bryan Martinson. When he finished he called his partner, Cornell.

"What time are you coming in tomorrow, Cornell?"

"I thought I'd be in around ten or so. Why? You got something?"

"Can't tell you over the phone but this thing is getting big."

"I'll be there at eight."

"Good. I want to meet again with the manager of the sports bar and then drive over to the prison and see what The Professor has for us."

"Did you get his books yet?"

"Oh, crap. I forgot. I'll do that now."

"It's New Year's Day, partner. They're probably not open."

"You're right. Okay. We'll stop on our way over to the sports bar."

"Did you check to see if the manager is on duty that early in the morning?"

"No. I guess I didn't."

Cornell said, "Listen, Gil, You need to settle down. You're not thinking clearly. Take the rest of the day and do something with Cassandra to take your mind completely off the cases for the rest of the day."

"I guess you are right. I'll see you around eight then?"

"See you then. And take it easy."

Gil drove back to Cassandra's but she was not there. He flopped on the couch and drearily dozed off thinking of catching a serial killer.

\*\*\*

Randy L. Hilmer

# Chapter 16
# The Investigation
*Wednesday, January 2, 2013*

Gil was already seated at his desk when Cornell arrived, and the two exchanged pleasantries. Once Cornell took his seat, Gil updated him on the conversation he'd had with Bryan about the mayor. Cornell was shocked and wanted more details, but Gil said they would talk in the privacy of their car on the way to the prison. They started to go over the files Gil had opened individually on the shared abutted desks.

There was one new file which contained the compilation of the Camden Killer Task Force findings. Each case was documented with brief sentences and showed time tables. It also had the relationships of the witnesses to the victims, witness statements and if any forensic evidence was found. They had also cited the notes pertaining to each case, but there was no comment in the connection section of the notes to the crime. They were relying on The Professor. Gil was beginning to have second thoughts about that reliance.

"Gil, I was thinking," Cornell said out of the blue, "what was the latest day of the month that a killing took place?"

"The fifth. What's on your mind?"

"I was wondering if there is a mathematical connection. Look, we have June first, 6-1 then July fifth, 7-5, then August first, 8-1, September fourth, 9-4, October third, 10-3, November fifth, 11-5 and finally December second, 12-2."

"Meaning?"

"Well, I've been playing with these numbers. I first added them up to come up with 7, 12, 9, 13, 16 and 14. Nothing logical there."

"How did you get those numbers?"

"I added the month and the day together to see if there was some kind of pattern. Then I took the day of the week, and I got Friday, Thursday, Wednesday and Tuesday. That was for June, July, August, and September. October's murder happened on a Wednesday, but if that was the pattern then the next date should have been Monday. No sequence there. Also there was no sequence between the numbers."

Gil concluded the same.

"But here is an interesting connection. Take the dates for June and July, which is the first and fifth. The difference is four. Then, take August first and September fourth; the difference is three. The difference between October third and November fifth is two. Now we have a pattern of 4-3-2. So if this holds out, then a January murder should have been committed on January first because December happened on the second, and the difference would be 1 so we would have 4-3-2-1."

"Interesting, except today is January second," countered Gil.

"Maybe a murder on January first hasn't been discovered yet?"

"Oh my God. Look who's coming with the mail."

"Do you think there might be a letter marked urgent? I would rather be wrong on this one," said Cornell.

As Nathan approached the two detectives, Gil's heartbeat started to increase as the tension rose between his heart and his mind.

"Good morning, Nathan."

"Good morning, detective."

"Still can't call me Gil, huh?"

"Sorry. Good morning, Gil," replied Nathan softly.

"Anything for me this morning?"

"Just the usual, sir."

"Good."

Nathan handed the mail to Gil and started to leave but turned around and faced Gil again.

"Sorry, sir. I misrouted this one. It also has your name on it." Nathan handed a type written envelope with Detective Gil Clifton across the top and <u>URGENT</u> in the lower left corner.

"Thanks Nathan."

"Have a good day, sir." Nathan then continued on his rounds.

"Is that what I think it is?"

"Unfortunately, yes." He showed the envelope to his partner.

Gil opened it and read:

> ***'Good friend, for Jesus' sake forebear***
> ***To dig the dust enclosed here;***
> ***Blest be the man that spares these stones,***
> ***And curst be he that moves my bones'***

"Look this up."

Cornell went to his computer and typed in the saying as Gil read it to him.

"It's coming up as the markings on Shakespeare's grave."

"Do you think it is saying that this case is dead?" Gil questioned.

"Maybe the killer is thinking of ending his killing spree, or we haven't heard about a murder that may have happened, according to my mathematical theory, yesterday. Did you get any results from the FBI profiler yet?"

"Not yet. Let's get up to the prison and find out what The Professor has to say."

"How about the sports bar manager?" Cornell asked.

"We can let that go until later."

They made a quick stop at a nearby bookstore and purchased copies of The Brothers Karamazov and Don Quixote, but had to order the other three books requested by The Professor. On the way to the prison Gil elaborated on the connection between the mob and Mayor Veluchi.

"I believe the mayor's brother was murdered in the El Toro," said Cornell.

"I'll let Bryan follow up on that, but as I said before, this case is getting weirder by the minute."

"Did you bring the latest note?" inquired Cornell.

"Yes, I brought it with me but I want to wait on presenting it to him."

They made a beeline for East Jersey Prison and were once again in the conference room where The Professor was being shackled to the table and chair.

Gil placed the two books on the table, to the delight of The Professor.

"My good man, you have made a generous bestowment to the enlightenment of the under achievers for with whom I am saddled."

"Before you take possession of these, do you have anything for me?"

"If you are quite ready to take notes, then yes. I do not repeat myself when expounding on the topic of English literature whether it be in a lecture theater for unappreciative students or law enforcement officers seeking vengeance upon an individual who may be seen as an opportunistic creature of disillusionment or perhaps one indulging in self-abnegation. Either way I shall begin with my humblest of pronouncements."

"We're ready."

The Professor postured himself upright in his chair as best he could and began his oratory. "The first note, as we stated previously, was taken from Hamlet, act two, scene two and we have discovered its origin and meaning hence I shall not expound further on the details of that particular couplet."

The Professor set those notes to one side and picked up a second set of notes. "In July a decrepit little man by the name of Harold McDonald died, presumably at the hands of a sniper, with the following quote from Shakespeare's Othello, act five, scene two, 'Then must you speak of one that loved not wisely, but too well', which was Othello's swan song or his endeavor, before killing himself, to justify having suffocated his blameless wife Desdemona. It reveals one side of Othello's personality of being calm, cool and collected. Here, Othello seems to have recovered from the passionate jealously that drove him to commit murder. Some view this as a compassionate way for him to say that he loved deeply, but did not love the right person. However, I am of the opinion that Othello was rash, brutal and overconfident in his self-delusion and that he was susceptible to jealousy. He never gave Desdemona the opportunity to defend herself and I shall render the conclusion that his foolish credulousness is not compatible with loving his wife too well at all."

"How does that connect to the murder?"

"These are all a concatenation; consequently, I shall come to that supposition upon my conclusion, dear sir."

"They're a what?"

"Your questions are exasperating. I said they are connected."

"Okay, thank you. Continue, please," urged Gil.

"Your indulgence is most gratifying. Now, with the untimely death of the beautiful Dorothy Coel we see a note from King Lear, act one, scene one wherein King Lear is conversing with the Duke of Burgundy, who wants the hand of marriage to the king's daughter, Cordelia. However, his daughter would not fully declare her love for her father other than as a daughter should love her father - no more or no less. She also says she will owe her devotion to her husband as well. King Lear decides not to give her any part of his kingdom, which he is dividing amongst his daughters. Therefore, he tells Burgundy to do what he will with his daughter as she has all but been disinherited. The Duke cannot marry Cordelia without her dowry. However, her other suitor, the King of France finds Cordelia's position intriguing and promises to marry her. Therefore King Lear tells him to 'take her or leave her', meaning that she is of no consequence to him."

"Does that mean that the killer knew Dorothy Coel and couldn't care less about her?"

"It has been stated many times over, my good man, that to assume makes an ass out of you and me. Detective Gil, I am not an ass now nor shall I ever be; therefore your postulation only foretells of the problematical road which lies before us. It is incomprehensible to me how you fathom to leap to such extraordinary inferences. I shall further like to reiterate my previous statement that I intend to render my conjectures at the end of my dissertation."

"I am sorry, Professor."

The Professor once again laid the note he had been using to one side and picked up another one. He studied it carefully and put it face up on the table in front of him.

He looked at Detectives Gil and Cornell and started, "The ebony beauty of Roberta Waverly is in juxtaposition with that of a queen in a fairytale and not of a Shakespearean play. Although it is in alliance with this quote from Henry VIII, act four, scene one, 'she had all the makings of a queen', meaning that a queen should be of royal characterization befitting the temperament of the times. Henry VIII broke his ties with Rome which did not condone annulments, and then had his marriage to Catherine of Aragon annulled because she produced no male heir to the throne. He proceeded to marry his mistress, Anne Boleyn, but Henry later accused her of adultery, incest and witchcraft and she was beheaded four days later."

"Brutal," said Cornell.

The detectives were enthralled with the presentation of the plays, but were not yet satisfied that The Professor had provided any answers - although he so much as said he would at the end.

"So the killer thinks that Roberta is so beautiful that she could be a queen or perhaps was a beauty queen?" questioned Gil.

"You are an unvarying drain on my patience with your inexorable and unremitting pursuit of simplistic answers to composite and multifarious questions. I shan't be able to continue due to your infantine drivel."

"We are sorry if we have caused you any consternation, Professor. We will go now and return on Friday once you have rested."

The Professor glared at Gil and while he held his stare he yelled out, "Guards!"

The guards quickly came into the room and, with The Professor's constant and unrelenting stare fixated on Gil, unshackled him. The Professor rose unwavering in his fanatical preoccupation of Gil, but then turned and accompanied the guards back to his cell.

As they were headed back to their car, Cornell asked, "Sorry if we have caused you any consternation! Where did you come up with that line?"

"I told you, I can read, too."

"Sure. Another nun's story?

"Actually, yes. She kept saying that to our class all the time. I finally had to look it up to see what she meant because I thought it meant she couldn't go to the bathroom."

———

Gil and Cornell reached the Booster Club Sports Bar sooner than they had anticipated due to the sudden ending of the meeting with The Professor. The detectives walked up to the bar and asked if the manager was available. They got lucky because Martin Porter was on duty. The bartender left from behind the bar and walked the few steps through a double swinging door. Shortly afterward, he and Martin came to the bar.

"Detective?"

"Yes. You remember my partner, Detective Bush? We would like to ask you a few more questions concerning the afternoon Yoshi was murdered. Let's go over here and sit in this booth, okay?"

"You're sure he was murdered? No one told me he was, although I assumed so," said Martin as he slid into one side of the booth across from Gil and Cornell.

"Do you know who owns this bar? I believe you said a corporation out of Philadelphia, is that correct?" asked Gil.

Both investigators could sense a change in Martin's demeanor at the mention of a corporation from Philly. Martin started rubbing his fingers together and there was a slight twitch in his neck as he searched for an answer.

"All I know is that this place is owned by a company called Good Eats, Incorporated. At least that's what's printed on my check every week."

"Have you ever met any of the corporate officers from Good Eats?"

"No."

"Who hired you?"

"Some guy by the name of John Smith. He said he was the acting manager until they got someone to take over."

"Can you describe this Mr. John Smith?"

"I think so. He was in his fifties and had black hair that looked kind of greasy but he was dressed in a nice suit."

"Was he fat or tall?"

"He wasn't fat at all. I thought he was an athlete. He was around 5'7" to 5'10". I'm not too sure about that."

"What were his facial features?"

"He looked like he could be mean but he was real nice. He was very polite and hired me right away."

"Did he train you, too?"

"No. There was another guy, short, bald and kind of grumpy. He managed a sports bar over in New York. He spent a week with me and then I was on my own."

"Do you remember his name?"

"Sure. Tony Douglas."

"You seem to be sweating a little bit. Is there anything wrong?"

"No. I was just working in the kitchen and it was a little hot in there, that's all." He took a napkin and wiped his brow. "Is there anything else? I need to get ready for the evening crowd."

"Just one more thing." Gil brought out a picture of Salvatore Moratino he had gotten from the CLEAR unit and placed it facing Martin. "You described this man to a tee. Is this the man, John Smith, who hired you?"

Martin took the picture and examined it. The detectives could tell he was very tense looking at the picture of the underboss. "No. That's not him."

"Are you sure?" Cornell asked.

"Yes, I'm sure. Now if you don't have anything else, can I get back to work?"

"Sure, Mr. Porter. Thanks for your time, you have been a big help."

Martin scooted quickly out of the booth and disappeared behind the swinging doors to the kitchen.

Cornell said, "Looks like you hit a nerve."

"He wasn't too imaginative in his description. He nailed Moratino's features."

"Yeah, that's what I would call a perfect match. He didn't even catch on that we didn't ask any questions about the murder. And, he couldn't come up with anything more original than John Smith?"

The detectives left the Booster Club, headed back to the precinct and decided to call it a day. They were preparing for their next meeting with The Professor.

"Are you going to give him the latest quote?" asked Cornell.

"Yeah. I think once he gets done, if he gets done tomorrow. I am wondering if it is just a prank note or is it really from the killer."

"Why would you think it is a prank?"

"It doesn't fit even the sparse evidence we have. Something's not right about it."

Cornell was going to argue logically, "Okay, let's see what we have. One, if it is real then either a murder has been committed and not reported or, two, the killer is telling us that the killing spree is over or three, it is a cruel prank. The fourth possibility is that it's not the fifth of the month yet and maybe we got this one early."

"We can't rely on the fifth as being some sort of deadline."

"I know, Gil. Let's just give it to The Professor and see what he thinks."

---

Martin Porter had a number and dialed it.

"Hello."

"This is Martin Porter, the manager over at the Booster Club Sports Bar in Camden. May I speak to John Smith please?"

"He's busy right now. I'll have him call you back."

Fifteen minutes later Martin's cell phone rang. "Hello."

"This is John Smith," said Salvatore Moratino.

"Thank you for calling me, sir. I had a couple of investors interested in buying this bar and wanted to know about the ownership. They showed me a picture of the owner. I told them I could not authorize any meeting until I heard from you."

"You did right, Martin. I'll make a reservation at the restaurant for tomorrow night. Do you think you can be there?"

"Yes sir."

---

"I have Sheriff Brisbane waiting for you, mayor. I don't have an appointment for him. Do you wish to see him?"

"Sure. Send him in."

Once the office door was closed Sheriff Brisbane started, "Alonso, how did your meeting go on Sunday?"

"You waited three days to ask me?"

"Hey, I told you we need to play it cool and besides, you were supposed to let me know what went on. So now I'm asking."

"I told him the kid at Booster's was killed with potassium cyanide and that it might tie in. I also asked him the name of his guy on the street. That didn't go too well."

"Why?"

"He threatened to kill me like they did my brother if I don't mind my own business."

"So all we have is that someone on the street knows about someone up in East Jersey Prison who was asking about this poison. Is that about right?"

"That's all I got. How close are you to catching this killer?" asked the mayor.

"We formed a task force, but nothing concrete yet."

"Sheriff, do you think I should put more pressure on the task force?"

"We need to get at Captain McCadry."

"How do you propose to do that?" the mayor inquired.

## ----Thursday, January 3, 2013----

Gil was getting out of bed as Cassandra was making breakfast. He turned on the television.

". . . . that seems to have the Camden Police Department fragmented. Sheriff Brisbane clearly set the blame of the lack of an arrest squarely on the shoulders of Captain Joseph McCadry. The captain is a twenty-three year veteran and reportedly is close friends with Mayor Veluchi. However, this morning in a brief news conference held outside the mayor's office, Mayor Veluchi sided with Sheriff Brisbane, blaming inept leadership in the homicide division as the reason for not producing a suspect in the serial killing cases that have been plaguing this city since last June. This is Sarah Larsen reporting for WCAM, Camden Action Media."

Gil quickly got showered and dressed. He went to the kitchen to join Cassandra. "Did you hear that news cast a little while ago?"

"You mean about the sheriff and mayor blaming your captain?"

"Something's falling apart upstairs at work. I don't know what it is, but it is not going to be pretty."

Cornell was waiting for Gil when he entered the precinct. "Gil, I've been upstairs since I got here about a half hour ago. The captain wants to see you. He seems a little different."

"What do you mean?"

"I don't know. He wasn't sarcastic, or yelling or being a bully. Something is up. Be careful."

Gil went straight to the captain's office. "You wanted to see me, captain?"

"Yes. Please shut the door and have a seat."

Gil obliged and sat in front of the captain's desk.

"How is the investigation coming along with the task force?" The captain sounded very contrite.

"I think we are progressing."

"Is there anything I can do to help?"

"What's this all about, captain?"

"Gil, I know we have been at odds for some time now and I am sorry about that. I realize now that things weren't like they always seemed. I was doing as the mayor and sheriff asked me.

That was wrong and for that I hope you accept my apology. Have you heard the news reports today?"

"I have."

"Then I think you know what I am talking about. They are trying to hang me on this one. I need your help."

"We've been working hard and developing different leads and suppositions."

"Is there anything that can help me with the press?"

"This thing is pretty big and encompassing, but if you can wait a few days we may have something."

\*\*\*

# Chapter 17
# Finding A Connection
*Friday, January 4, 2013*

Gil and Cornell were waiting for the guards to come in and shackle The Professor to the table so they could continue their investigation. After waiting twenty minutes, The Professor was ushered into the conference room. He had a huge grin on his face. Once he was secured, Gil asked, "Looks like you are in a good mood."

"My good man, one is never in a good mood in this contemptuous environment. Unless, of course, you have forayed your way here to foretell of my impending emancipation back to the freedom of conformist sovereignty."

"It just looked like you had a smile on your face, Professor. Will you continue with the notes?"

"I shall continue your edificational development. Where did we leave off?"

"The last time you talked about Roberta Waverly and Henry VIII."

"Yes, indeed." He picked up the folders lying before him and thumbed through them. He laid them all down except for one and began, "With the demise of young Adin Williamson and the ardent views of homosexuality that prevailed during the time of Shakespeare's writing of this play entitled The Tempest, written circa 1611, the prevalence of men loving was not counter-culture. In act three, scene two it is written 'he that dies pays all debts'. Thus, we find Stephano, a drunken butler, being spooked by Ariel's music but at the same time coveting the music for when he could control the island and have music for free. Ariel is a non-gender entity servant to Prospero, the former Duke of Milan. Stephano muses that he shall kill this man Prospero and rule the island. Prospero's daughter, Miranda, shall be his queen and his co-conspirators, Trinculo and Caliban, shall be viceroys. However, Ariel is invisible to Stephano and he is looking at his own mortality by saying 'he that dies pays all debts' meaning that the bright side of potential death is that the dead are debt-free; used as a metaphor only."

"Is that all?" asked Gil.

"Is that all, you query? My good man, that is but a snippet of the story which has to do with the quote you gave me. I would like nothing better than to explicate upon the entire interpretation of this most judicious and intricate play. My time is of no consequence, however, and you are mired in the daily routine of human existence and, like students biding their time until graduation, have little or no interest in the true art of prose and therefore covet knowledge as a whimsical trek for passing time. You see, I am of the opinion that few need to learn, fewer want to learn and even fewer ever learn. Alexis de Tocqueville said 'history is a gallery of pictures in which there are few originals and many copies' and I am afraid the students of today shall be mere copies of their predecessors."

"Well said, Professor. Do you have anything about Yosef Rabinovich, the 61 year old Jewish jeweler who was bludgeoned to death on November fifth?"

The Professor took another folder in his hands and opened it. "The note that reads, 'the fool doth think he is wise, but the wise man knows himself to be a fool' is from Shakespeare's play written between 1598 and 1600 called As You Like It. A young clown or fool, as they were referred to, was in the court of Duke Frederick. His name was Touchstone and it was his job to criticize the behavior and folly of others. But, he is, in point of fact, hopelessly vulgar and narrow-minded. In act five, scene one we find Touchstone speaking with William, a country boy in love with Audrey, a simpleminded goat tender. However, Touchstone is also in love with Audrey. Here we find Touchstone mocking William, his rival; with innuendo by asking first if William was rich and then if William was witty, to which William replies that he is fairly witty.

Then Touchstone answers with the quote thus attached. Although Audrey understands little of what Touchstone tells her, she later agrees to marry him."

"Thank you, Professor. The last victim we know about was Hikaru Yoshi a 25 year old student at Rutgers who was poisoned on December 2nd in a sports bar."

"Do not spoil what you have by desiring what you have not; remember that what you now have was once among the things you only hoped for." The Professor looked at the two detectives as they remained silent. "A quote from the Greek philosopher Epicurus, which is as apropos today as it was in 250 BCE."

"BCE?"

"Yes. Before the Common Era. By using this notation, the abbreviations avoid reference to Christianity and, in particular, avoid naming Christ as Lord. Thusly, do not presuppose faith in Christ and hence are used for interfaith dialog rather than the conventional BC and AD."

Gil looked at Cornell who shrugged his shoulders. "I didn't know that."

"Any fool can know. The point is to understand," The Professor replied. "From the wisdom of Albert Einstein, gentlemen."

Neither Gil nor Cornell replied. The Professor picked up the one remaining folder and opened it. "Cowards die many times before their deaths; the valiant never taste of death but once. Of all the wonders that I yet have heard. It seems to me most strange that men should fear; seeing that death, a necessary end, will come when it will come." He laid the folder back down on the table. "That, dear gentlemen, is from one of William Shakespeare's most famous plays entitled Julius Caesar, act two, scene two finished in 1600. Here we find Caesar wandering throughout his house dressed only in a dressing gown as he is being kept awake by his wife, Calpurnia, with her nightmares. She has screamed three times in her sleep about the impending murder of her husband. She warns him not to leave the house because of what had happened earlier that night. Although she did not believe in omens previously, she says, she saw dead men walking, ghosts throughout the city and terrific lightning. She also tells of a nightmare where she sees a bleeding statue and Romans washing their hands in the blood which, according to her, portends danger."

Cornell interrupted, "What do you mean by portends?"

"My good man, is there no such a thing as a dictionary any longer? Is there no such thing as common courtesy? Is there no such thing as patience? I may be pedantic in my teachings but here I am giving only the briefest of explanations to satisfy your requisite for swiftness of answer. Now you have the audacity and impudence to interrupt me by catechizing me for a simple delineation of a word I use for complete and precise accuracy of one of the world's most renowned authors!"

Cornell's face turned red with embarrassment as he was being chastised by The Professor. "My mistake, sir. I should have written it down and looked it up later so to not have interrupted you. Please accept my sincere apology."

"Portends means to foretell or foreshadow such as an omen does. Now may I continue?"

Cornell shook his head yes and Gil looked at his partner's discomfort and smirked ever so slightly as if to say *ha-ha, you've been set in your place.*

"Your alacrity is most welcomed. Now, where was I? Yes, in this scene Calpurnia is telling Caesar that he cannot afford to ignore the obvious omens. He says that nothing can change what the gods have in mind and that omens are for others. He believes that they certainly do not apply to him, wherein he replies that only cowards imagine their own death and because they do, they die many times over. However, a brave man, like himself, does not dwell on death and consequently only dies once. He further postulates that he cannot understand why men fear death because it will come to all eventually and therefore he does not think of death."

The Professor picked up the folder, placed it with the other discarded and completed folders and sat back with an air of superiority, pride and fulfillment. Gil and Cornell waited for The Professor to make a conclusion, but he sat there in complete silence casting an eerie gaze from one detective to the other.

Gil reached into his jacket pocket and pulled out a piece of paper and handed it to The Professor. "We received this the other day. We know it is the grave markings of Shakespeare but right now we do not have a murder, thank God, to go along with us receiving this. It breaks the pattern. So we're wondering if you, as you do your summary, would explain its meaning."

The Professor took the note and read it. "Good friend, for Jesus' sake forebear, to dig the dust enclosed here; blest be the man that spares these stones, and curst be he that moves my bones." He put the note on the table and stared at Gil. "This simplistic verse is not understandable to you, is that correct?"

"We think it means his grave should be left alone and not dig up his bones or there will be a curse on the one who does. Is that correct?"

"Generally speaking, yes. During the life of William Shakespeare it was conventional tradition to bury a human for a period of five years to allow the natural decomposition of the body to occur. The bones would then be exhumed from the burial plot and transferred to an ossuary or charnel house, thus allowing the burial plot to be reused. The playwright did not want this to materialize, ergo; he more than likely paid a prodigious amount of money to have the talisman engraved with a curse."

"What we are asking you is how do you think it ties in with the other quotes?"

Gil and Cornell waited as The Professor once again looked disconcertingly from one to the other still not saying a word. Gil and Cornell took quick glances at one another but neither felt like they should say anything at this point. They waited.

The Professor finally broke the awkward silence and said, "If you have no further quotes for me to decipher than I feel our business shall be concluded for the day."

"Professor, you said that you would summarize their meaning at the end. That is why we came to you." Gil said rather gruffly.

"Gentlemen, gentlemen. I am by profession an educator and by nature an inquisitive creature. You have given me a platform by which

I could engage in my aspiration to teach. This I have done and I would be remiss in my responsibilities to you, my students, if I were presented this quandary and simply regurgitated the retort for you. I have painstakingly and with disquieted alarm, because of the brevity for which you demanded, given you a succinct synopsis of the notes you have presented. I have given you, in epigrammatic form, the play, acts, scenes, circumstances and meaning. If I were to lay the answer upon your feet what would you have learned? My purpose would have been ephemeral and that is not the rationale for which I chose this profession. It chose me. So I ask you to take your copious notes and return with your answer. I have funneled your attention directly to the answer and it is now upon you to present it to me. Gentlemen, I hope I have made myself laconically clear. Guards!"

The guards came in and unshackled The Professor. When he stood up he spoke directly to the two detectives, "I will say that you have partially understood the grave markings. However, you must give everything else more supplementary thought."

Martin Porter arrived at the El Toro Bistro at eight o'clock. He knew he would not be able to meet with the underboss until nine, but he wanted to have one cocktail to calm his nerves. He had met Salvatore Moratino only on two other occasions. The first was when his uncle, Alonso Veluchi, the mayor of Camden, introduced him. Salvatore had a football scholarship for Rutgers so that Martin could attend Rutgers even though his grades were not acceptable to the college. The second time was when Salvatore hired him to front for the Booster Club. Martin didn't graduate and his football eligibility ran out so he needed a job. Salvatore came to his rescue with certain 'understandings'.

As Martin sat waiting for the underboss, he thought this would be a good way to fulfill part of those commitments to the mob. He may not be very smart, but he knew that if he had their protection he would have no worries in life. Martin wanted to keep it that way.

Anna Veluchi, the sister of Vito and Alonzo, married Joshua Porter and they had a son, Martin. Martin was seventeen and had extremely poor grades at the time Vito was killed. He barely graduated from high school but his uncle, Alonso, took the young boy under his wing. That led to the football scholarship at Rutgers and the beginning of Martin's obligations.

Salvatore Moratino strode into the bistro and took his regular table before the maître d' had an opportunity to greet him. Martin joined him as soon as Salvatore and his two associates sat down.

"Young Martin, how are you, my boy," said Salvatore enthusiastically.

"Fine sir."

"So let's get down to business. Tell me what happened yesterday."

"These two detectives, Gil and Cornell came in and were asking me about the ownership of the Booster Club, who hired me, who trained me and things like that. Then they put your picture on the table and asked me if that was the guy who hired me. Naturally, I said no." Martin started fiddling with his fingers.

"Do you know their last names?"

"Yeah." Martin reached into his pocket and pulled out a business card Gil had given him and handed it to Salvatore.

Salvatore looked at it and handed it to one of his associates. "Okay, then what happened."

"I told them I had to get ready for the evening crowd and they left. I called you as soon as they left the parking lot."

"Good. Here's what I want you to do. I want you to call this.... what's his name?"

His associate read the card, "Detective Gil Clifton."

"Okay, give him back the card." Salvatore returned his conversation to Martin, "Call this Gil Clifton and tell him that you found out that this kid was poisoned by people in a chemistry lab over at the college because he owed them money on some football bets. You got that?"

"Yes, sir."

He turned to his associates and said, "That should keep them busy for a while. In the meantime, I want you two to get the name of the guy over at Rahway who asked about the potassium cyanide. Do whatever you have to do, just get me the guy's name."

Martin asked Salvatore, "Is there anything else I can do?"

"No. Go ahead and go back to Camden. Call me if anything turns up that I should know about. Same routine, okay? Good job. Thank you."

"I will. Thank you, sir."

———

On Saturday morning, January 5, 2013 Gill and Cornell were at the precinct writing up their notes.

Cornell said, "What do you think we should do about Martin Porter? I really didn't like the way he acted at our second interview."

"I agree," said Gil. "Why don't you see if you can get a little background on him? I'll get together with Bryan Martinson before our next task force meeting to see what we have with Mayor Veluchi and his little meeting with the Palovani family."

"So, Gil, are we going to go over the quotes so we can answer The Professor's questions?"

"Why don't you take a copy and I will take a copy. Monday we'll see if we can put together an answer. I thought he would be more cooperative and not on this 'I'm an educator' kick."

Gil made a call to Bryan Martinson and they scheduled a meeting for 1:30 that afternoon. Cornell started searching the internet for information on Martin Porter. Ten minutes later he started reading something very interesting.

"Gil, Martin Porter is the son of Anna and Joshua Porter."

"Great piece of information, Cornell. Thanks for letting me know," Gil replied with a little sarcasm.

"You will thank me. Do you happen to know Anna Porter's maiden name?"

"No."

"Try Veluchi."

Gil looked up in sudden surprise. "Excuse me?"

"Anna Veluchi, sister of Vito and Alonso."

"You've got to be kidding."

"No. Says he attended Rutgers University for four years."

Gil rhetorically asked, "I wonder what a Rutgers grad is doing as manager of a sports bar?"

"I think I'll go over to the practice field and have a little talk with Coach Fielding," suggested Cornell.

"Good idea. I'm meeting with Bryan at 1:30. Do you want to circle back here this afternoon?"

"Okay. I'll call you if I dig up anything interesting from the coach."

Cornell met with Coach Fielding right after practice. The Rutgers football team had one more game against their rival, Princeton University, only 16 miles away, in the Jersey Bowl on the following Wednesday night. As Cornell sat across from the longtime coach of the Scarlet Knights, he noticed the coach's rugged facial features from being in the sun for hours upon end. His silver hair accentuated his round face. He stood at 5'11", but the young athletes under his tutelage towered over him. He was known and respected around the league for being demanding but fair.

"Coach, I thank you for taking a few minutes for me," Cornell said as he sat down in front the of coach's desk.

"Anything to help the Camden police. What is it you need from me?"

"I would like to ask if you remember a player by the name of Martin Porter."

The coach got up from behind his desk, walked over and closed his office door. He returned to his seat and sat down. "Most vividly."

"Why is that?"

"One of the dumbest kids I have ever coached."

"He attended her four years, isn't that correct?"

"Yes, for four goddamn years I had to carry that son-of-a-bitch's scholarship on my books. I could have used that scholarship money on a better benchwarmer than that idiot."

"Did someone force you to give him a scholarship?"

"Absolutely. Two big thugs came in here one night and threatened me. They said they had my wife and would kill her if I didn't cooperate. They gave me the phone and when I called my wife Helen, she was hysterical. She was crying and pleading with me to do what they wanted. I had no choice."

"Could you identify these men today?"

"Even if I could, I wouldn't. You can't possibly imagine the terror they put my wife through. I believed them when they said they would kill her."

"Did Martin have the grades to keep the scholarship?"

"He couldn't wash his own hands without asking for help. He was dumber than a pile of rusty nails but I kept him on scholarship." Coach

Fielding was becoming flush with embarrassment as he lowered his head. "I finally explained to the school dean what the situation was and he helped me. We kept it pretty much to ourselves. There were questions from a few teachers, but they pretty much stayed out of my business so the dean and I got through the four years. There was nothing illegal about keeping a fourth rate benchwarmer on scholarship, mind you. It just irked me, though."

"I can imagine."

"Do you know if he graduated?"

"I doubt that he even graduated kindergarten."

---

When Bryan and Gil met at the precinct, Bryan expanded on his observations of the evening.

"I heard Sheriff Brisbane on the radio again on the way over here. Sounds as if he is after you and the captain."

"Yeah, I know. He's a big blow-hard and I'll have to deal with him later. Right now we have another connection with the mayor. Seems his sister's kid is Martin Porter, the manager over at the sports bar where Yoshi was murdered."

"Do you think that has any bearing on who the serial killer is? Could be just coincidence," Said Bryan.

"Yeah, a coincidence. A deadly coincidence."

\*\*\*

# Chapter 18
# Closing In
*Monday, January 7, 2013*

Martin Porter called Detective Gil on Monday morning. He said he had heard some information concerning Yoshi that he thought Gil would be interested in knowing. Martin wanted the detective to meet at the sports bar, but Gil insisted he come to the precinct. Martin hesitated, but then agreed to meet there. Gil wanted Martin on his turf so he could question him without being disturbed and, at the same time; put Martin into a position of vulnerability and intimidation.

Martin showed up thirty-five minutes late and was escorted by the desk sergeant to an interrogation room where he was left sitting alone at a solitary desk. Two chairs were sitting across from him and a smoked-glass mirror was affixed to one wall. Gil watched from the other side of the mirror as Martin sat there nervously looking around.

"Good," said Gil. "We want him a little worried."

Cornell and Gil watched for a few more minutes and then saw Martin start to fiddle with his fingers.

"Now," said Gil.

The two detectives entered the interrogation room and each took a seat opposite Martin. Cornell had updated his partner on his conversation with Coach Fielding. They were counting on breaking Martin and hoping to find a connection between the mob and the murderer.

Gil started, "Thank you for coming in, Mr. Porter. I understand you have some information for us."

"Yeah. I overheard a couple guys talking about Yoshi and how he owed money on some football bets to some guys over at the chemistry lab and Yoshi refused to pay them. From what I heard, the chem lab guys were real mad and made up some poison and put it into Yoshi's drink when he wasn't looking."

"What were the names of the couple guys who you overheard talking?"

"I don't know. I didn't recognize them."

"And you say they were talking and you happened to overhear them, is that correct?"

"Yeah."

"Were there other customers in the bar?"

"Only a few."

"So the place was pretty quiet, is that correct?"

"Yes. Not too loud at all, that's why I could hear them real good."

"How far away were you?"

"Probably ten to fifteen feet away. I pretended to be washing glasses but I was really listening to them."

"Did you actually wash glasses or just pretend?"

"No, I actually washed them. I didn't want them to think that I was listening."

"How are the glasses washed?"

Martin looked at Gil rather oddly, "I put them in a cleaning solution and turn on the brushes. The brushes clean the inside and then I rinse them in two different solutions of sanitizer."

"How many glasses were there to wash?"

"I don't know." Martin was getting mad at this line of questioning. "Probably about thirty or so. Enough so I could stand there and listen to them."

"Did they mention the name of anybody from the chemistry lab?"

"No. They just said a couple of chem lab guys."

"Can you describe the two guys at the bar?"

"One was a white guy, pretty average looking, about 150 pounds and the other was a black guy about 280 pounds. They both had on Rutgers football jerseys."

"How much money did Yoshi owe them?"

"About two hundred dollars."

"Wait here. We'll be back in just a little while."

Gil and Cornell left the interrogation room. Gil said, "He is lying through his teeth."

Cornell replied, "Yeah, and he is not very good at it. Somebody wants to send us on a wild goose chase."

"Let's put some real heat on him."

Gil and Cornell waited for another fifteen minutes before they walked back into the interrogation room. Gil sat down while Cornell stood in a corner facing a jittery Martin Porter.

Gil opened his new notebook and his badge was facing Martin just as Cassandra said. "I just want to get this straight. You say two guys, you presume were from Rutgers because they both had on a Rutgers jersey, who were never in your bar before, came in a relatively quiet bar and started talking loud enough with you running the noisy glass washer fifteen feet away and with thirty glasses to wash from only a few customers so you could hear them talking about two other guys who the victim owed two hundred dollars for some football bets and were mad enough to kill Yoshi with poison they supposedly mixed together in a chemistry lab?" Gil said in one long breath as his voiced rose with the unbelievabilty of what he was saying.

Martin looked strangely at the detective. "Yeah. That's what happened. I heard the two guys talking about Yoshi owing some chemistry students money and they got mad and poisoned him."

"Do you think that the chem lab guys would kill a guy who owed them only two hundred dollars? How would they get their money back if that were true?"

"I don't know." Martin started twisting his fingertips together.

Cornell walked over to the desk and slammed both of his fists on the desk, leaned in close to Martin and said rather loudly, "Do you know what obstruction of justice is?"

"Yeah, I guess so," Martin answered meekly as his body instinctively backed away from the imposing figure glaring at him.

"Do you think lying to the police is obstruction of justice?"

"I don't know."

Cornell stood up and addressed Gil calmly, "He doesn't know. Maybe you should enlighten him."

"Martin," Gil said in a fatherly manner, "obstruction or giving false statements to the police during a felony investigation can get you two to three years in jail. Is that something you think you could handle?"

"I'm not lying," Martin insisted.

"Martin, we know better. I think it's time you told us the truth."

Martin's head lowered and he stared at his hands as he fretfully intertwined his fingertips.

Cornell barked out loud, "How did you get the football scholarship?"

Martin looked up with an alarmed look on his face. "What?"

"Didn't your uncle Alonzo Veluchi have Salvatore Moratino get you a football scholarship at Rutgers?" Cornell put his face closer and closer to Martin's with every question. "Didn't you earn that scholarship by sitting on your ass on the bench for four years? Didn't Moratino get you a cushy job at the sports bar? Who told you to come up with this cock and bull story about two guys at the chem lab? What are you hiding? Who are you protecting, Mr. Porter?"

Martin sat there dumbfounded and scared.

"My partner's not happy with you, Martin," said Gil. "It seems he has a little more information than you figured on. You see, we seldom ask a question that we don't already know the answer to. It's time to come clean for your own sake."

The good cop bad cop routine actually worked. Martin broke down and told the detectives everything he knew.

---

Gil and Cornell didn't get any information from Martin that shed light on the serial killer. They found a strong connection between the Booster Club Sports Bar, Mayor Alonso Veluchi, Brandt Waverly and the Palovani crime family of Philadelphia. They knew now that the mob was interested in the poisoning of Yoshi and deduced that the mob wanted the police out of the way on some misguided scavenger hunt. It was all very intriguing but they were no closer to finding a suspect than before. They were relying on The Professor to help lead them in the right direction.

They gathered all of the files and headed for the bookstore to pick up the three remaining books The Professor had requested. They each had their own theories about the quotes and discussed them on the drive to the prison.

"I say it has to do with that mathematical connection I told you about."

"I was thinking about that," said Gil, "and I don't see the connection. It is true that you found some kind of formula for 4-3-2 but that's where it ended. But why use Shakespeare quotes? I don't think it is mathematical unless there is something neither of us has thought of."

Cornell asked, "What do you think?"

"I think it has something to do with the explanation of what the quotes mean."

"Do you think they have any ties with the mob? Seems we have a connection there with Yoshi's murder."

"But not with any of the others. I think where Yoshi was murdered was just a twist of fate. I say it's the meaning behind the quotes that is important."

Cornell said, "I took all of the quotes and looked at the first letter of each word to see if they spelled anything. I ran them forwards and backwards but nothing. I tried to see if there was a connection between the characters in the quotes and the victims. I didn't come up with anything."

"I know. I did almost the same thing. Nothing for me either."

"So what are we going to present to The Professor as our answer?"

Gil took one hand off the steering wheel and reached for the top file that was sitting next to him on the console and handed it to his partner. "I wrote some ideas down. I don't know if they will pass as answers or not but we have to give him something. Read them over and see what you think."

Cornell studied the file carefully. They were at the prison parking lot and Cornell said, "Go with it. I can't think of anything better."

When they were checking in with security, one of the officers asked them to wait. Gil and Cornell took two seats outside of the security office. Five minutes later they were asked to go to the warden's office.

"What's up?" Gil asked the security officer.

"I don't know. I was just told to escort you two to his office."

The warden was seated behind his desk and asked the two detectives to have a seat. Once they were settled the warden asked, "How many times have you seen The Professor?"

Gil answered, "I believe this is our fifth visit."

"Precisely. You are logged in on Wednesday, December twenty-sixth and Friday the twenty-eighth and also on Wednesday, January second and Friday the fourth."

"Is there something the matter, Warden?"

"Have there been any conversations about other prisoners in your dealings with him?"

"Nothing more than he wanted some books so he could teach some of the other prisoners about English literature. But you know that."

"I know about the books."

Gil looked at his partner with a puzzled expression and then asked the warden, "What's this all about? Did we do something wrong?"

"I'm not sure, yet. All I know is The Professor is in the prison hospital. He got beaten up pretty severely last Saturday."

"How is he?"

"He'll survive but won't be let out of the infirmary until later today. We have the guy who beat him up, but he isn't talking."

"Do you have any idea why he would be beaten up?"

"It happens in here all the time. It could be as little as he looked at another prisoner wrong or wouldn't give another prisoner a piece of bread. It could have been something that happened in the yard or maybe someone didn't like the way he talked. It could be just about anything."

"It wouldn't be because we were interviewing him, could it?"

"It could. We just don't know. The possibilities are almost endless."

"Has The Professor said anything to you?"

The warden answered, "He can barely speak, but I doubt he would say anything. Prisoners are pretty closed mouthed when it comes to talking to officials. That's why I was wondering about your conversations with him."

"We've only talked about the quotes. He has been explaining their content and meaning."

"But the other prisoners don't know that."

Gil questioned the warden, "Are you saying we can't talk to him anymore?"

"Of course not. That would be up to him. I have to try and protect the inmates and it's not always easy to protect them from themselves, let alone others. But I caution you to end your visits as soon as possible. If something else happens I will be forced to end them. Do we have an understanding?"

"Yes. We need to see him at least one more time. When do you think we can do that?" Gil asked

"He should be available tomorrow, but remember, the decision to talk with you is entirely his."

"Understood."

Cornell set the three books on the warden's desk. "The Divine Comedy, Hunger and Leaves of Grass. Quite an eclectic selection," the warden commented.

"We already gave him Don Quixote and The Brothers Karamazov."

"I'll run them through the x-ray and see to it that he gets them."

"Thank you."

---

It was late afternoon by the time the detectives were back at the precinct. Sheriff

Brisbane was just walking out when he ran into Gil and Cornell. "I was looking for you two."

"If you don't mind, Sheriff, we're kind of beat and...."

"Follow me over to the mayor's office. He is expecting us."

Gil and Cornell reluctantly followed the sheriff. The trio went directly into the mayor's office without a word to the stunned secretary sitting at her desk.

"Mayor Veluchi," Sheriff Brisbane started, "I have the two detectives here who, as you know, are heading up the Camden Killer Task Force."

"Yes, I want to talk to you two," said the mayor. "Sit down. What is this nonsense I hear about some mob affiliates being involved with this serial killer?"

"Where did you hear that?" asked Gil.

"The where or how doesn't matter. I want to know if it is true."

"We have some information that may or may not be connected. We are investigating it as part of a theory."

"And exactly what is that theory?"

"Mayor Veluchi, it would be unprofessional of me to speculate without proof. We cannot possibly give you hearsay evidence; at least not until it becomes fact and everything can be confirmed," answered Gil.

"As mayor of this city, you ultimately report to me and I am asking you about this theory of yours."

Gil looked at his partner and started out, "We think there may be a possibility that events that took place at a restaurant in East Philadelphia called the El Toro Bistro and the murder of Hikaru Yoshi may be connected."

Gil and Cornell saw the troubled expression on the mayor's face. "What are those events?"

"Well, sir, with all due respect, that is why it's called a theory. We do not have any names yet but we have heard there was some kind of meeting over there on . . . ." he turned to his partner and asked, "What day was that meeting."

Cornell answered, "Sunday, December thirtieth."

"Yeah, that's right."

The mayor stole a quick glance at the sheriff and loudly said to Gil, "This theory is preposterous. Sheriff, what are you going to do about these two running around with stupid theories that are getting us nowhere when we need to concentrate on finding a serial killer?"

The sheriff turned to Gil, "Detective Clifton, I think your efforts should be concentrated on rounding up a suspect rather than wasting taxpayer's money on some foolish theory."

"You're right, sheriff. It probably would have been nothing anyhow. We'll drop that theory and get back with the task force to see if we have any more clues."

"Thank you. Let me know what the task force has to say tomorrow. You are meeting with them, correct?"

"Yep. Tomorrow morning, first thing. Is there anything else?"

"No, detective. You can leave now. And keep your focus on the serial killer. We have other agencies that deal with mob connections and are better equipped to handle various situations of that nature." The mayor's voice returned to a calm reserved tone. "I agree it probably would have been nothing. Keep up the good work and bring in the killer."

"We will."

***

Randy L. Hilmer

# Chapter 19
# The Quotes
*Monday, January 7, 2013*

Unpredictability is not unique when it comes to investigating homicides, but these murder cases were giving that word an entirely new meaning. Gil and Cornell made their way back to the precinct in silence. Each was trying to digest what had just happened in the mayor's office. They didn't want to say anything out loud where someone might overhear them. They knew each other very well and worked like a team knowing what the other might be thinking.

Once they arrived at the precinct they huddled at their desks.

Cornell said, "Partner, I'm glad you're not a dentist because you operated on the mayor without Novocain and hit a nerve."

"Did you see him look at the sheriff? I think the sheriff is in with Mayor Veluchi and Brandt Waverly on something. I hate to say it, but I think they are all connected to the mob somehow."

Cornell exclaimed, "That's it! The murder of Roberta Waverly may be linked to the serial killer and the mob. That's two. Could the others be connected but we just haven't found the association yet?"

"That's a long jump but worth considering. We'll run it by Bryan Martinson in the morning. He saw the mayor with Moratino."

The FBI profiler, Dr. Ingrid Rolfheiser, stopped by just as they were leaving.

She handed Gil a report, "Here are my findings. If you need anything else please let me know."

"Thanks." Gil took the report and settled back in his chair. He skipped the long foundation of the report and went to the last page where the actual profile was stated. After he read that portion, he handed the report to Cornell. "You can read the whole thing. Make copies and bring them to the meeting tomorrow. I'm leaving."

Gil and Cornell departed for the day and Gil headed to Cassandra's for the night. He found her in the kitchen preparing supper. He came up behind her and gave her a big hug. She turned around and they kissed.

"How was your day, honey?" she asked as she went back to the stove and stirred the noodles that were beginning to boil.

"Exhausting." Gil sat at the kitchen table. "We went to see The Professor but somebody from the mob got to him and beat him up pretty bad."

Cassandra whirled around, "Is he all right?"

"I don't know. We didn't get to see him. Why the big concern?"

"No big concern. I just thought that whoever did that to him might also come after you."

"I wouldn't worry about it. We think there is a possible connection with the assault on The Professor and the poisoning of a victim at a mob owned bar.

Cassandra went back to tending to the noodles. "Are you going back to see him soon?"

"The warden said we could probably see him tomorrow. Cornell and I will head up there after the task force briefing in the morning."

"How is the case coming along?"

"I am hoping that after we meet with The Professor we'll be nearer to catching this killer. We just need to get into the killer's head. So far the FBI profiler has come up with just a generic description."

"What's that?"

"The profiler said the killer would be in his twenties or thirties, quite agile, probably has a very high IQ and is well versed in police procedures. Because the murders all had different M.O.s, she said the killer had an obsession with how each murder took place. The lack of physical evidence leads the profiler to believe the killer is almost like a student of murder. A pretty weird guy if you ask me."

"The profiler is a woman?" asked Cassandra.

"Yes."

"Is she pretty?"

"She is gorgeous. She has a long hooked-nose with a wart at the tip and wears a long pointy black hat and a black cape. She flies on some kind of broom."

Cassandra turned, glanced at Gil and let out a small giggle. "You're such a liar. Do you have any suspects yet?" she asked as she returned her attention to the noodles.

"Not yet but I don't feel like talking about it tonight. Can we just have a nice supper, a glass of wine and maybe some quiet time?"

"Sure, baby. Whatever you want."

*----Tuesday, January 8, 2013----*

The Camden Killer Task Force met at 8:00 a.m. on Tuesday. Cornell gave each member a copy of the profiler's report and presented, in synopsis form, the profile of the killer as described by the FBI. "We need to hit the streets and give this information to your informants to see if they come up with anyone."

Gil added, "Cornell and I are heading back to see The Professor. Once we get his take on how the killer is thinking we can compare it to the FBI's profile, find this guy and put him away. Bryan are you still working on your angle?"

"Yes."

"So that everyone knows, Bryan is working on kind of a farfetched idea but we don't have enough information to bring to this task force yet and waste everyone's valuable time. Are there any questions?"

Detective Arthur Farnsworth, a member of the task force on loan from CLEAR, Camden Law Enforcement Arterial Resources, added, "I had a conversation with Phyllis Fullerton, the Waverly's neighbor and she said she has seen another woman frequenting the Waverly home. She said she was going to take her picture, but I strongly advised her not to do that. However, last night, Mrs. Fullerton called me and said she had some pictures of the woman. I'm going to see her today." He looked at Cornell and continued, "Cornell, you said at one time that Elaina and

Brandt Waverly were spotted over in East Philly, so if this turns out to be a picture of Elaina, should I interview her too?"

Cornell looked at Gil for comment. Gil thought for a minute and then said, "If it is a positive ID by you, then get with Bryan Martinson and both of you can decide whether or not to interview her. Just keep in mind, once we start asking the sheriff's wife questions, we're going to get real heat from the sheriff himself."

All of the investigators nodded their head in agreement.

"Any other questions?"

Everyone was leaving the room when Gil pulled Bryan aside. "Be careful when and how you interview Elaina Brisbane because we have a suspicion the sheriff and mayor may both be linked to the mob. There could be a possibility that all of the murders are associated with the mob. Only speculation now, so just keep that in mind."

"I will. Thanks."

Gil and Cornell started their drive to the East Jersey Prison.

The Professor was brought into the interrogation room in a wheel chair. His right cheek was bandaged from ear to chin. His left eye was swollen shut and surrounded with a deep purplish blue and brown coloring. Several stitches could be seen in his eyebrow. The left side of his face showed cuts that were just beginning to scab over. His lips were a darkened red with abrasions protruding along the top and bottom; they were so inflamed that they bordered on appearing grotesque because of his surrounding goatee. It was hard for him to speak clearly.

He was wheeled in front of the desk but his handcuffed hands were not shackled to the table. He simply sat there in a sullen and defeated silence.

Gil asked, "Do you know who did this to you?"

The Professor shook his head yes.

"Do you know why?"

He looked up and with his right eye only partially shut Gil could sense the hatred The Professor was harboring. However, there was only silence.

"Are you able to talk?"

Once again he nodded his head yes while he uttered a muffled, "A little."

"It's very important that we continue our discussions about the quotes, but if you are not up to it we can come back another day."

"We shall continue." He grinned as best as his injuries would let him and said, "Do you have a solution?" He barely moved his lips, much like a very good ventriloquist.

Gil opened his folder. "We have an answer we think is plausible. When we looked at the quotes and your explanations of their meanings, we found vague connections to some of the murders. But, for others we couldn't find any concrete similarities. For example, 'Doubt thou the stars are fire, doubt that the sun doth move, doubt truth to be a liar, but never doubt I love' was the first quote and the murder of Allen Venter. He was married and we found out he took his divorce rather hard at first. That's about all we could come up with. In July the quote 'Then must you speak of one that loved not wisely, but too well' could mean that even though the victim and his wife argued a lot, they still loved one another." Gil paused for a response from The Professor but he only sat listening in silence.

"Shall I continue?"

The Professor nodded his head affirmatively.

"The death of Dorothy Coel had the quote; 'Take her or leave her' which we think meant that her fiancé should either marry her or let her live her life without him. The September murder of Roberta Waverly had 'She had all the royal makings of a queen.' Roberta was a beautiful woman and was extremely helpful spending most of her time working for a variety of charities."

Still no reaction from The Professor. Gil looked at his partner for guidance. Cornell shrugged his shoulders as if to say he didn't know what to do.

Gil continued, "The October note said 'He that dies pays all debts.' We didn't find that the victim owed money or was deeply in debt so this one still baffles us. Although all people have debts, it may just be saying that Adin Williamson was now free from all debts he may have had. Even though you told us it was a metaphor, we still couldn't come up with a good solution for this one."

Gil was getting frustrated with The Professor's complete silence. "Professor," he said, "if we are not on the right track could you please let us know."

The Professor nodded his head slightly and uttered softly, "Continue."

"The note, 'The fool doth think he is wise, but the wise man knows himself to be a fool' was attached to the victim's clothing and we think it means the victim and his son were intelligent people, but the killer thinks that owning a jewelry store is a foolish way to make a living and the victim and son loved their jobs and so the killer thought they were fools."

Gil took a deep breath and plodded forward with the answers. "Finally, 'Cowards die many times before their deaths; the valiant never taste of death but once. Of all the wonders that I yet have heard, it seems to me most strange that men should fear; seeing that death, a necessary end, will come when it will come' simply states the victim, in the killers eyes, was a coward and the killer views himself as a hero."

An uncertain stillness filled the room. The Professor's right eye shifted between Gil and Cornell. "The last?"

"Shakespeare's grave markings, we feel, indicate an end to the killings. That's all we have, but we do not understand the association to the killer, only to the victims." Gil closed his folder and laid it on the table.

The Professor motioned very slowly with his handcuffed hands for the detectives to move in closer. Both pulled their chairs tight to the desk and leaned forward to better hear The Professor, his voice being almost inaudible as he spoke slowly and deliberately, "You have entirely and miserably missed the point of the quotes and therefore shall collect an F for your efforts. However, you have certainly been an immense source of amusement for me. Your floundering vividly conjures up images of freshly caught fish flapping pointlessly in the bottom of a boat. You have given me such a wonderful diversion from this temporal enslavement."

"We're glad we were funny to you, but this is not a funny situation to us. Are you going to make a connection and tell us how this killer is thinking? I believe that was your promise," Gil said sharply.

"In William Shakespeare's play, Much Ado About Nothing he writes, 'Sigh no more, ladies, sigh no more, men were deceivers ever, one foot in sea and one on shore, to one thing constant never'. This means that men have always been deceivers with one thought being one place, another thought someplace else and never devoted to anything in particular. Gentlemen, you have been deceived by your own imprudence. It is not the quotes that were of importance, but rather the act and scene. Yes, the antagonist and executioner are related but are not of the same mind. One is of a foretelling, the other of a fulfilling."

Gil felt anger swelling up inside but tried to show an exterior calmness. "Are you telling me the quotes were of no importance?"

"You have wandered far too deep amongst the trees thus obstructing the view of the forest. Or to paraphrase what Shakespeare wrote, you were 'hoisted on your own petard'. The unambiguous answer is before you." The Professor reached for the folder and handed it back to Gil. "Guards!"

---

Detective Farnsworth pulled up in front of the stately home of Phyllis Fullerton. The plush green lawn was evenly manicured with immaculately trimmed bushes lining both sides of the walkway leading to the front stoop. Two large pillars stood guard alongside a double entrance door of deep-grained mahogany. An oversized knocker with a ring between the teeth of a vicious looking lion was polished to a golden shine and placed prominently in the middle of the right-hand door. On the left door there was a large shield reminiscent of a coat-of-arms often associated with the great castles from the middle ages and the knights of old.

As he walked towards the front door he noticed a gardener on his hands and knees busily tending to a flower garden that surrounded a large oak tree shading the front yard. Before he had a chance to knock, the front door opened. A very petite elderly lady was standing in the entry. She had silvery silken hair pulled back into a bun and a pearl necklace draped around her neck. Diamond earrings danced brilliantly when the sun hit them just right. "I was expecting you. Please come in."

She had on a light blue flowered dress that brought out her delicate features. "I am so glad you came, Detective."

"I am Detective Arthur Farnsworth, do you remember me?"

"Yes, indeed. You are such a handsome young man."

"Mrs. Fullerton, I understand...."

"Oh, please call me Phyllis."

"Sure. Phyllis, I understand you took some photographs of a woman that you want me to see, is that correct?"

"Oh, yes indeed. The comings and goings at that Waverly house is shameful since the death of Mrs. Waverly. I have been noticing the same woman going into the house at all hours of the day and night. Sometimes she doesn't come out until the next morning." Then she added forcefully, "Dressed in the same clothes she went in with the night before!"

"Phyllis, have you been spying on them?"

She puckered her lips indignantly, scowled and said tersely, "Of course not. I merely happen to be watching, that is all."

"Of course, Phyllis. I understand."

A delighted expression returned to her face. "I did take some good pictures of her. Would you like to see them?"

"What you did is very dangerous and I asked you not to do it, don't you remember?" he reprimanded.

But she eagerly replied, "Yes, but she never saw me take them. I'll go get them for you."

Phyllis Fullerton was a widow and had a charming personality that immediately made one think of her as their own grandmother. He chuckled when he thought of how she thought she was playing detective, but worried that what she was doing could get her into serious trouble. She re-entered the room with small, abbreviated footsteps and excitedly handed the photos to Detective Farnsworth. "Here, Arthur. You can see her face. Unfortunately, some I took a second too late and only got her back." She bent over and lowered her voice as if to tell a well-guarded secret, "She is white."

"Yes, I can see."

She lowered her voice to a soft whisper. "He's black." She stood upright, held her head proudly, folded her arms and was very pleased with her discovery.

"Phyllis, I thank you for these, but please do not involve yourself any further. You could get into serious trouble."

"Oh, heavens, I would never let them see me take their pictures."

"Phyllis, promise me you will let us handle this from now on?"

She looked away like an ostrich that puts its head in the sand so nobody can see it.

"Phyllis? Promise me."

"Okay, Arthur, I promise."

"You don't have your fingers crossed behind your back, do you?"

Being caught with her hands behind her back she said shyly, "Why Arthur, what you must think of me."

"Let me see your fingers and then tell me you promise."

She held her tiny hands out in front of her and said, "Okay, I promise."

---

Detective Farnsworth called his fellow task force member, Bryan Martinson, and told him he had the pictures and they clearly show Elaina Brisbane at the home of Brandt Waverly. Although the pictures themselves meant nothing because they could be easily explained away, the ramifications and fallout could be huge simply because of the implication of impropriety.

Bryan said, "I don't think we should approach Mrs. Brisbane and expose our hand yet. What do you think?"

"I agree. I'll give these pictures to Detective Gil and see what he wants to do with them."

---

Gil was as angry as his partner had ever seen him as they drove back to Camden after the meeting with The Professor.

"The unmitigated gall of that insipid old man. I can't believe he squandered our time like that."

"You're starting to talk like him, partner."

"All that time wasted. Why? So he could get a laugh? I knew better than to involve a guy like that. Five trips to see him. Five! And for what? Absolutely nothing."

"You had to try," consoled Cornell.

"Time could have been better spend!" Gil shot back.

"I know how you must feel. But let's just leave it be for now and see if there is something in our notes that he may have said about the dates and scenes. He did say they were important."

Gil went on a disgusted rant for the next ten minutes and was winding down. "He's so full of crap I wouldn't believe it if he said the sky was blue and grass was green. As far as I am concerned I don't ever want to hear his name again. I hope he rots in that prison or gets beaten up every day for the rest of his life. I'm through with him! Hoisted on my own leotard or whatever the hell he said. He's full of crap. Crap I tell you! Crap!"

For the next hour and ten minutes the only thing that could be heard in Detective Gil's car was the engine running and the occasional swooshing of a car passing. Cornell knew enough to let his partner stew alone.

***

# Chapter 20
# In Check
*Thursday, January 10, 2013*

Gil spent Tuesday night and all day Wednesday at his own apartment. His frustrations with The Professor had churned inside of him and he didn't want to innocently take anything out on Cassandra. He explained to her that he needed to be alone for a couple of days. She said she understood. On Wednesday when Cornell called Cassandra's asking about Gil, she informed him that he was at his own place.

"Is there something wrong between you two?" Cornell asked.

"Not that I know of. He just said he was discouraged about the case and needed some time alone."

Cornell called Gil's cell phone but there was no answer. He decided that Gil needed his privacy so he didn't pursue it.

The Camden Killer Task Force met on Thursday, January 10, 2013 and Cornell was elated when he saw Gil stroll into the precinct.

"How are you, partner?"

"I'm alright. Sorry about not calling you yesterday. I just needed time to think."

"We all need to be by ourselves once in a while."

All members of the task force were waiting in the conference room. Gil and Cornell entered and Gil took his place at the head of the table.

"I am sorry to inform you that our meetings with The Professor resulted in a big waste of time. The inmate did not fulfill his promise, so we are no further down that road than when we began."

All in attendance could hear the exasperation in his voice and could sympathize with his feelings. They have all have trodden down a path that lead to nothing but a dead-end.

Bryan Martinson spoke up, "Gil, we've all been there."

"Thanks but right now you need to go over what you have and don't have. You need to get a new focus." Gil got up and abruptly left the room leaving the team members looking at one another.

Cornell broke the confusion. "My partner is having a hard time coping with the results, or should I say the non-results of utilizing The Professor. He has been getting almost daily phone calls from the sheriff demanding results and, to top it all off, the sheriff's calling for an arrest during constant news briefings with the press. So, he's under a lot of pressure. In the meantime, like Gil said, we do need to refocus. So, let's take this time to go over where we are right now."

The team members expounded on their portion of the investigation. Bryan Martinson and Arthur Farnsworth collaborated on the connection between the mob, Mayor Veluchi, Sheriff Brisbane and Brandt Waverly. They also laid out the theory about Brandt Waverly and Elaina Brisbane. The group came up with a supposition that if the Palovani family had an interest in the Booster Sport Club where a poisoning of a patron took place, they might like to find the killer because of police involvement in the investigation. They would want it solved quickly and without much notice or fanfare.

Bryan speculated, "Okay, we all know that potassium cyanide is hard to come by. What if Moratino used his people to find out who supplied the poison that would lead them directly to the killer? Due to his involvement with the mayor and sheriff, he will turn that information over to them, the sheriff will sidestep us, pick up the killer and come out looking like a hero while we sit here with egg on our faces."

Cornell asked, "Why did Moratino have his meeting with the mayor and not the sheriff?"

"The mayor's brother was a made member of the Palovani family and killed, supposedly, by hit men from the mob. They may have threatened the mayor or maybe the mayor is already involved with them, but that's a different subject. For now, let's just presume the mayor was threatened and got the sheriff to go in on it with him.

"That kind of makes sense," said Cornell, "as a theory goes, anyway. We know, from what Martin Porter told us, the mob wanted us to be investigating some story about a guy from a chem lab. So while we're out spinning our wheels on that cockamamie runaround, they have time to find out who supplied who with the poison. I think you have something there, Bryan. What do the rest of you think? Any ideas?"

Arthur Farnsworth spoke up, "We have circumstantial evidence that Brandt Waverly and Elaina Brisbane are having some kind of affair but I'm not sure that it ties in with the serial killer."

"Yeah, I think you're right on that one," agreed Cornell. "But here's the thing, I think we can use that information to keep the sheriff occupied while we get information on the poison supplier. I'll pursue an idea I have on that. In the meantime, with you stirring up trouble between Brandt and the sheriff I'll be left alone for a couple days. If the sheriff doesn't back off tell him the photos will be sent to the media. And while you're at it, have the sheriff put his buddy, Mayor Veluchi, in check at the same time."

"I'm on it."

Cornell continued, "Bryan, while Arthur is keeping them out of our hair, you go and have a conversation with Brandt Waverly to put him in check too. Take copies of the pictures with you but tell him they were taken by our surveillance team. We don't want to put the old lady in any danger."

Nathan knocked on the conference door and entered, "Excuse me, Detective Bush, but the captain sent me to tell you to report to his office right away."

"Okay, Nathan. Thanks." When Nathan left Cornell finished up, "Is there anything else?"

The meeting was adjourned and Cornell proceeded to Captain McCadry's office. When he got there he saw Gil sitting in front of the captain's desk looking rather dejected.

"You wanted to see me, Captain?"

"Yes. Seems your partner here is trying to submit his resignation."

"What?!" Cornell exclaimed. Cornell looked at his partner and said, "What the hell are you thinking?"

Gil did not look up from his gaze on the floor in front of him. "I think it's time for me to give it up."

"Nonsense." Cornell saw a badge and gun on top of the captain's desk. "Captain, you didn't accept this bullshit from him did you?"

"Of course not. That's why I called for you."

"Okay, partner, pick up your badge and gun and let's talk about this."

Captain McCadry stood up, picked up the badge and gun and handed it to Gil. "Here, take these because I'm not accepting them."

Gil looked at the captain and then his partner.

"Take them and let's go!" insisted Cornell.

Gil reluctantly retrieved both items and left with his partner. They went to their desks where Gil put the badge and gun on top of his own desk.

Cornell said plaintively, "Gil, what are you trying to do?"

"I've lost my touch. I've wasted almost five days and for what? Because I wasn't smart enough to catch a killer? I think it's time for me to hang it up."

"You're smarter than that, partner. You know it and I know it. Now, why don't you take the files, go to Cassandra's and just study them at your leisure for a few days. I'll handle things here. We've got a good group of guys working with us on the task force but we need your leadership to see it through to the end. Once we catch this son-of-a-bitch, then you can retire or resign or whatever you think is best and I won't stop you. You've been working on this thing for seven months and you need to take a fresh look at it, that's all."

"If I do that I will be letting down everybody on the task force."

"Nonsense. No one else knows about this stupid prank you tried to pull just now and besides, we all have assignments to keep us busy for the next day or two so you can regroup. We need you, partner. I need you. Okay?"

"Do you really think it will help?"

"I know it will. You will be relaxed. Just go over the files. When you're rested, I'm sure something will pop out at you and then wham-o, end of the serial killer case."

Gil relented and said, "Okay. I'll try it your way but you will call me if you need me, right?"

"Absolutely. You're our leader, not McCadry, although I am surprised he didn't accept your resignation but we all know who is running the show. Now take these and go relax." He handed the gun, badge and files to his partner and watched Gil leave the precinct.

---

A lovely young girl in her late twenties knocked on the sheriff's office door. "There's a detective Arthur Farnsworth from the Camden Killer Task Force wanting to see you, sir."

"Send him in."

She turned around and held the door open and said, "The sheriff will see you now."

The sheriff stood up and shook the hand of his visitor. "Do you have an update for me, detective?"

"Yes." The detective went back, shut the door and sat in front of the new sheriff for the first time. He had information he knew Sheriff Carl Brisbane would not like.

Detective Farnsworth started laying out the information slowly, effortlessly and precisely. The next twenty-five minutes showed the sheriff in disbelief, then anger, which turned to disdain. Carl Brisbane then flew into a rage cursing out the detective who was accusing him of mob connections.

"You come into my office and accuse my wife of having an affair with somebody who has ties with the mob? You have no proof of anything you are accusing me of! I will have your badge for this and your future will be in prison - not in law enforcement!" He was shouting at the top of his voice and could be heard throughout the third floor.

Arthur sat calmly and listened to the tirade. "Perhaps, Sheriff Brisbane, you would like to settle down before I show you these pictures. You might find yourself looking more foolish than you already are."

"What the hell are you talking about?!"

"We are in receipt of several photographs taken by our surveillance team depicting your wife in the company of Brandt Waverly. I understand he was a big supporter of yours during the recent campaign."

"What's this all about?" His voice was still loud but had a tone of concern.

"We want your cooperation to leave the task force alone so we can do our job. If you don't, you will have personal problems with the media if these pictures happen to fall into their hands."

"Is this some form of blackmail?"

Farnsworth shoved one picture towards the sheriff. "No blackmail. Just an insurance policy that you stay out of our way."

"Where did you get this?"

"Sheriff, you're missing the point. We don't give a hoot about troubles between you and your wife. All we want is your assurance that you will let the task force handle the serial killer without any further interference from you. No more daily media updates. None of us care about your private life. We just hope it doesn't go public."

"Okay, but I want to know where you got this." He waved the photo in the air.

"In due time, sheriff. In due time. But, for now, we also want you to get with your buddy, Mayor Veluchi and tell him to stay out of Philadelphia - especially the El Toro Bistro. Will you do that?" He expected no reply and rose up and left the sheriff's office. Before he shut the door on the way out Farnsworth turned around and said, "Thank you, sheriff," then promptly departed.

---

Bryan Martinson was meeting with Brandt Waverly at the headquarters of Waverly Building and Contracting. The two sat in comfort in Brandt's overly large private office.

"Would you care for a drink, Detective Martinson?"

"No, I'm here on business, Mr. Waverly."

"Business? My, my. So, what can I do for you?" Brandt poured a generous glass of scotch and sat behind his desk. "Have you solved my wife's murder?"

"Not yet, but there is something I can do for you, Mr. Waverly."

"Is that so? So tell me, what is it that the police can do for me?"

"You have been seen in the company of Elaina Brisbane. I believe she is the sheriff's wife."

"Naturally. We have been friends for a long time and she and my wife used to work together on a lot of charitable projects."

"Mr. Waverly, you can sit there and bullshit me all you want, but at the end of the day your being with Elaina at the El Toro Bistro, having her over to your house and, on some occasions staying the night, sounds to us more than you two being friends and working on charitable projects."

"What the hell is this?"

"The police do not care one iota how you run your personal life. However, with the El Toro Bistro being a favorite spot for the Palovani family, you and Elaina dining there, meetings between you and Mayor Veluchi, and him being seen talking to Salvatore Moratino at that same restaurant all seem to have you in a very difficult situation. We are asking you to stay out of Philadelphia and your nose out of police investigations. I hope I make myself clear." Bryan Martinson stood up and said, "I will find my own way out. Good day, Mr. Waverly."

***

# Chapter 21
# A Revelation
*Thursday, January 10, 2013*

Cornell was sad that his partner was taking the outcome with The Professor so hard, but on the other hand, was glad Gil was taking a few days off to be by himself to rethink the case. Cornell had all the confidence in the world about Gil's abilities to logically reason through a case. He also knew Gil would overcome the pressures being applied by the mayor and sheriff.

Cornell called on Dr. Ingrid Rolfheiser, the FBI clinical psychiatrist who did the profile on their cases.

"Doctor, I have read your report and I understand most of it. The profile's conclusion is that the killer would be in his twenties or thirties, quite agile, probably has a very high IQ and well versed in police procedures. Because the murders all had different M.O.s, you concluded that the killer has an obsession with how each murder takes place. The lack of physical evidence led you to believe the killer is almost like a student of murder. Is that correct?"

"Yes, I believe those were my conclusions." The psychiatrist was a rather bland looking woman with short russet colored hair and close set eyes. She had a nose slightly too large for her face, but had a charming smile that she used to hide her unattractiveness. A pleasant personality and extreme intelligence engaged people to her. She was single and devoted her life to her work.

Cornell asked, "Is there anything you can tell me that you couldn't put into the report? I know you have to substantiate everything you write, but what I am asking is for your gut feelings that may provide additional information for me to work with. Of course, it would be held in strict confidence and not brought out in court or any other written report."

She looked at the detective and, in her mind, tried to determine if she should impart her instinctive feelings. She smiled, tilted her head slightly to the left and asked, "If I were to give you my personal feelings about the case, I would need your positive reassurance that I will not have to testify on anything I tell you. Is that understood?"

"Yes, Dr. Rolfheiser. I do have one more thing I would like to show you. We got this after you submitted your report." Cornell handed her a piece of paper. "These are the words of the epitaph written on Shakespeare's grave. However, there has been no murder that we know of associated with it like the others."

Dr. Rolfheiser studied the words carefully. She looked up at Cornell and said, "Let me get my notes. I may have something." She went over to a bank of file cabinets, opened one of the drawers, picked out a file and returned to her desk. The doctor rummaged through the file rather quickly and, upon finding what she was looking for, sat back as if pondering some great philosophical question.

"What is it, doctor?"

"When I was jotting down notes from the crime scene photographs, police reports and the notes you received from the killer, I was trying to make some correlation between the meaning of the note to the crime scene or victim."

"Yes. We tried using a criminal serial killer who happened to be a professor of English literature, but that failed."

"Why do you say that it failed?"

Cornell opened his ever present notebook and as he was thumbing through the pages, he told a short version of how they interacted with The Professor. "He told us that it wasn't the quotes that were important but rather the act and scene. He said something to the effect that the antagonist and executioner are related but not of the same mind. He also said one is of a foretelling, the other of a fulfilling. We took it to mean he wasn't going to tell us if we had the answer correct or not."

The doctor looked at her notes and said, "I think I have something very interesting. This is strictly off the record because there is no logical clinical proof and only my feelings, but look at this." She turned a page of her report so that Cornell could read it.

"Look at the dates of the crime and the acts and scenes."

Cornell scrutinized the document and finally said, "I don't get it."

The doctor began to explain, "When we do a profile we have five basic procedural steps to generate it. First, we examine thoroughly the type and nature of the criminal act and compare it to the types of people who have committed similar crimes in the past. Secondly, we do an in-depth analysis of the actual crime scene. Thirdly, we look at the victim's background and activities to try to connect motives. Fourthly, we investigate possible factors for motivation of the crime. Lastly, we develop a description of the perpetrator founded on the detected characteristics based on previous cases. Do you follow so far?"

"I think so."

The doctor continued, "When I look at all the information given, like I said, police reports, crime scene photos and notes, I came up with a very general description of the suspect characteristics - mainly that he was young, agile, intelligent and a student of murder. I wish I could have given you something like the suspect is 26 years old, 5'10", weighs 189 pounds, has blond hair and blue eyes and lives in an apartment near the college. Unfortunately, that is impossible. What is possible, however, is an understanding of the mind of a serial killer. With what you have just given me, that may prove very beneficial."

"How so?"

"Let me explain. This is not scientific and only is being given to you as a far reaching supposition. The first murder took place on the evening of June first. Correct?"

Cornell nodded his head and cautiously said, "Yes."

"Okay, the quote is from Hamlet act one scene two."

"I still don't see what you're driving at."

"There are six letters in the title, Hamlet, for the sixth month of the year. The murder occurred on the first, act one and between noon and midnight, scene two. Now look at the patterns for the rest of the cases. The second murder took place on July fifth in the afternoon. The quote was from Othello, seven letters for the seventh month, act five for the date and scene two for after twelve noon."

"Does this hold true for the rest of the crimes?"

"Yes. August is from King Lear act one scene one; first day of the eighth month between midnight and noon. September follows the same pattern, Henry VIII act four scene one or the fourth day of the ninth month between midnight and noon. You see, the name of the play corresponds to the month of the year because of how many letters are in the name. The act is for the day of the month. I noticed that only quotes were from scenes one or two. There were no quotes from a scene three or scene four or any other scene which led me to believe the scene seemed to indicate between midnight and noon or noon and midnight."

"Is that what The Professor meant by the act and scene were important and not the quote itself?"

"I believe so. As you can see, the rest follow the same pattern. October, The Tempest act three scene two and the murder occurred on the third day of the tenth month between noon and midnight. November, the play As You Like It, act five scene one. The murder took place on the fifth day of the eleventh month between midnight and noon. Finally, from the play Julius Caesar, for the twelve letters depicting December second in the afternoon for act two scene two."

"So the meanings of the quotes were only some kind of sick game the killer was playing?"

"The killer tried to match them to the victim as best he could but you're right. However, like I said, this is only an abstract theory. It might also be just coincidence."

"My partner doesn't believe in coincidences. But what does it all mean?"

"With what you have told me, and now seeing this epitaph, please give me until tomorrow so I may think about it. I will try to give you an answer by then."

---

Gil called Cassandra and told her he was taking a few days off and asked if she would mind if he stayed at her place so they could be together at night. She welcomed the idea. Gil brought over a small suitcase as if he were going on a 'staycation'. He made himself comfortable and by the middle of the afternoon fell asleep on the couch with all of the files scattered on the coffee table and one lying open on his chest.

---

Cornell called the warden at East Jersey Prison and asked if he could see the security film from people who had visited The Professor within the last year. The warden said he would have it by early Friday afternoon. He also said he would get the log books for the names of the visitors.

Both Bryan Martinson and Arthur Farnsworth checked in with Cornell after their respective meetings and updated him. Cornell jotted down their verbal reports in his notebook and started studying and looking through the files for the hundredth time. However, this time he would use the information that Dr. Rolfheiser had given him and look at the files from an entirely different perspective.

He was reading his notes late into the afternoon when Captain McCadry stopped by his desk.

"What happened with Gil?" the captain asked with genuine concern emanating from his voice.

"I told him to take a couple of days off and just relax and look at the files at his leisure. There was too much pressure on him around here for him to think straight."

The captain said contritely, "I apologize if I have added to the stress around here. Things are going to change. Just keep me in the loop, okay? I'll help if you need me."

Cornell sensed remorse in the captain's tone, accepted his apology and truly believed he was going to change. "Okay, Captain, I will."

Captain McCadry started to leave and Cornell called out, "Thanks, Captain."

McCadry turned around and smiled, nodded his head and went back to his office.

Cornell returned to his files and closed them. He jotted down a note to himself: *Did Martin Porter visit The Professor prior to the poisoning? Was the person who beat up The Professor an associate of the mob?*

## ----Friday, January 11, 2013----

Cassandra made a small breakfast and darted off to work early in the morning. After they ate, Gil cleaned up the kitchen and spent the rest of the morning studying the files. He found something very interesting, but also very shocking. He quickly jotted down notes, double-checked the files, then checked them again and then rechecked them one more time just to make sure he hadn't misinterpreted anything.

By early afternoon his theory was crystal clear. He also remembered what The Professor had said - you can't see the forest for the trees. Could this be it? Could this unbelievable yet almost undeniable revelation be the answer? The pieces fit! He pondered deeply a decision he was about to make. He read over his notes one final time to be absolutely convinced he was right. The circumstances were unmistakable. He would have to place a call to Captain McCadry immediately.

---

Cornell was in a small conference room where the warden had set up equipment so that the detective could view the films of people who had visited The Professor. The warden also gave Cornell the visitors' log books covering the last year. Cornell first scoured the log books looking for the name of Martin Porter, but couldn't find it. When he found the name Kathleen Macklevy, he asked the warden to search the database so they could view the corresponding security film.

"Who are they?" Cornell inquired.

The warden looked at the picture on the screen and saw the time and date on the bottom right-hand side. He then took the log book from Cornell and pointed to the names of the two people were on the screen. "That is The Professor's daughter and her son."

He looked at the other name written below Kathleen's. "You're positive?"

"Yes. They come here often to visit. I have spoken with them a few times."

From out of the blue Cornell asked, "The guy who beat up The Professor, do you know if he has any ties with the Palovani family?"

The warden scrutinized the detective and replied, "Why do you ask?"

"I'm taking a very wild guess, that's all."

"The answer to your question is yes he does. He's been in here for three years and is a known associate of the family. However, The Professor didn't implicate him and he didn't confess, so all we have are our suspicions that he beat The Professor. I need to know, what made you ask?"

"One of the cases we're working has a connection with the mob, but we didn't know how it connected to the serial killer. As you know, we were asking The Professor to make a connection between the Shakespeare quotes and the killer."

The warden sat back in his chair. "I was thinking that maybe The Professor got it because he was talking to you guys. Now I'm not so sure."

Cornell said, "We haven't even mentioned the mob to The Professor." He looked at the screen one more time and asked, "You're absolutely positive that is The Professor's daughter and grandson?"

"Absolutely."

Cornell sprang out of his seat, thanked the warden and ran to his car. Once there, he called Dr. Rolfheiser from his cell phone as he tore out of the parking lot in a mad rush to get back to Camden.

\*\*\*

# Chapter 22
# Exeunt Omnes
*Friday, January 11, 2013*

Gil looked at his watch and saw that it was only 2:48 p.m. He knew Captain McCadry would probably be in his office. He picked up the phone but hesitated before dialing. He questioned himself whether or not he should escalate his findings. He put the phone back into its cradle and stood staring at it as though it was some kind of foreign object. A full two minutes passed before he reached for the phone and dialed the captain's number.

"How are you feeling, Gil?"

"To tell you the truth, Captain, terrible. I've got something that I need to tell you in private. Will you stay around until I get there?"

"Sure. But if it's about your resignation, then just forget about it."

"I'll be right there."

Gil hustled to the precinct and proceeded directly to the captain's office with his folders. The two men were meeting behind closed doors. Gil sat nervously in his seat.

"What's on your mind, Gil?"

"Captain, I want you to take a look at something. I hope like hell that I am wrong, but I need a second opinion."

Gil laid a folder in front of the captain and with slow drawn out words said, "I think the serial killer . . . ." He stopped and looked at the captain.

"Go on, I'm listening."

Gil's expressionless face turned pale white. "Captain, I think the killer is my partner, Cornell Bush."

"What?!" Captain McCadry cried out.

"It's all circumstantial. When we are looking for a suspect we need someone who had the opportunity, means and motive. Now, I don't know what the driving force behind the motive for these murders could be, but I do have these findings." Gil pointed to the dates he had written in the folder. "In June when Allen Venter was killed, Cornell was already on the scene by the time I got there. His whereabouts before the crime are unknown. Because it was an apparent abduction from a different location, who better to persuade an unsuspecting victim to get into a car? Or, he could have made some kind of arrest, handcuffed him, taken him to the crime scene and killed him. He had the opportunity and means. In July when Harold McDonald was killed by a sniper, Cornell missed roll call because he claimed he was chasing down some piece of evidence in the Venter case. Cornell is a marksman and familiar with all kinds of weaponry. When I asked him later what had happened with the lead he was investigating, he said it didn't amount to anything. So, again, his whereabouts are unknown during the commission of a crime. Therefore, he had opportunity and means."

Gil paused, waiting for some kind of response from Captain McCadry before continuing. The captain was listening intently but did not interrupt.

Gil continued laying the foundation for his accusation. "Dorothy Coel was murdered early in the morning of August first. Cornell asked me if he could take an hour or so off to go pick up a girlfriend from work because she didn't have a car. I know that's against regulations, but I told him I would cover for him. Shortly after he returned, we got the call. Once again he had the opportunity. And another thing, he never mentioned that girl to me again. In September when Roberta Waverly was murdered, Cornell didn't get into the office until nine-thirty in the morning, leaving him an opportunity once again. Adin Williamson was murdered in October when we were off duty. Cornell had the opportunity and was on the scene before I got there. It seems odd that he would get the call before me, get dressed and beat me to the scene."

Once again Gil paused. There was still no reaction from Captain McCadry.

Gil kept on. "The November slaying of Yosef Rabinovich found Cornell coming in late. Almost as soon as he got to work we got the call. His whereabouts before coming to the office are unknown and the opportunity is there once again. Finally, in December I was at the precinct alone when I got the call about the incident at the Booster Club when Hikaru Yoshi was poisoned. I called Cornell. Again, he was at the scene before I got there. Whereabouts before? Unknown."

Gil slumped back in his chair, exhausted.

The bewildered captain was silent as he was trying to register the scenario just presented. He took a long deep breath, leaned back in his chair, put his elbows on the armrest and clasped his fingertips in front. "Do you really think he is capable of murdering all of those people?"

"My heart says no but you would think that out of all of these cases, he would not have had the opportunity in at least one. There is opportunity in every case. I first suspected it was an inside person, but I dismissed that notion a long time ago. Now I'm not so sure I should have. I think we need to get a warrant and search his house."

Captain McCadry rose slowly and deliberately from behind his desk and gave a hand to Gil to help him up from his seat. "I will look into Detective Bush's background, but I want you to go home now and give this some more thought. If I find anything suspicious at all I will get in touch with you. You present a very compelling case, but it is very circumstantial and we need to be cautious. I will, however, also think of a way to write up a search warrant."

Gil got up and was about to leave when he turned and said, "I hope I'm wrong and that you find nothing in his background. I am staying at my girlfriend's place."

"I have your phone number but what's her address in case I need to talk to you in person?"

"2311 Willow Lane Drive."

---

Cornell was driving back to Camden at breakneck speed with his siren blaring. It was 5:15 p.m. and nearing dark when Cornell pushed the hang-up button on his cell phone after speaking with Dr. Rolfheiser and then frantically dialed Captain McCadry's number.

"Captain, get somebody over to Gil's place and have them watch his apartment."

"I just spoke with Gil and he is staying at his girlfriend's place. What's up?"

"Oh yeah, I forgot. I'm driving in from Rahway and will be in town in about twenty-five minutes. Do you know Cassandra's address?"

"Yes, Gil gave it to me before he left."

"Before he left?"

"Yeah, he came in to see me about something he wanted me to check on. Are you coming back to the precinct?"

"Not yet. Please dispatch someone to that address immediately. I'll meet you there."

The captain asked guardedly, "Is there something going on between you and Detective Gil?"

"Of course not, we're partners and best friends."

"Then what's going on?"

"It's too complicated to explain over the phone. Traffic is getting heavy so I'll meet you there and explain then."

Captain McCadry called dispatch to have an unmarked patrol car sent to 2311 Willow Lane Drive for surveillance purposes only.

Detective Bush turned off his siren about a mile before turning onto Willow Lane Drive. He rolled up behind the parked patrol officer's car. He also saw Captain McCadry walking swiftly towards him. Cornell exited his vehicle and met the patrol officer and the captain.

"Any activity?" Cornell asked.

The patrol officer said, "There was a woman who arrived and went into the house when I first got here. Then about five minutes ago, another guy knocked on the door and the woman let him in."

Cornell asked, "Did you get a good look at him?"

"Detective Bush, what's this all about?" demanded the captain.

"I'll tell you in a second." Cornell then spoke again to the officer, "Did you get a good look at him?"

"Not really. He had his hood pulled up over his head."

---

Cassandra came into the house around 5:30 p.m. and found Gil sitting on the couch. She asked him how his day went and he was about to explain to her his suspicions of his partner but was interrupted by a knock on the front door.

"I'll get it," said Cassandra.

She walked over to the front door and opened it. A young man in a black sweatshirt with a hood pulled tight around his face pushed her aside and shut the door behind him.

Gil was startled as he looked around. He couldn't recognize the face hidden by the hood, but he did recognize the body style and immediately connected it with the images he had seen on the surveillance videos. He stood silently staring at the menacing figure that had a gun pointed at him.

Cassandra said, "Nathan?"

"Yes, mom. It's time. Here take this rope and tie him to a chair." Nathan Bowen tossed his mother a large piece of fiber rope he had taken from his pocket.

"It will be my pleasure!" she said nastily.

Gil had a look of disbelief etched on his face. "What's going on?"

"I have waited for over three years for this day. Now sit down and it will all be over in a minute." Cassandra spitefully said. "You put my father in prison and labeled him a serial killer.

Then you crawl to him on your belly like the snake-in-the-grass that you are and ask him to help you. The Professor loved me and took care of me after he divorced that the bitch he was married to. He took care of me, taught me how to live and gave me a wonderful childhood. But you needed to inflate your ego, so back in 1985 you arrested an innocent man - my father. I was only fifteen years old and you took him away from me. I was forbidden to see him. My foster parents were mean and cruel and they didn't love me at all. But I had to live with that for three years before I could escape and live on my own. It was a living hell, but the day I got my freedom I vowed to myself to have vengeance on the man responsible for taking my father away from me!" Her voice was becoming almost maniacal and her face was contorted and angry. "Every time you touched me I would almost vomit but I waited. I waited for this glorious day to bring judgment upon you like you did my father!" Her vicious words were spewing forth like venom from a poisonous viper.

"Tie him up, mother!" yelled Nathan as he flung a desk chair towards Gil.

Gil stood beside the chair but would not sit down. "You're going to have to pull the trigger face-to-face, Nathan."

"Mom, come here and watch this guy. I'll get the son-of-a-bitch to sit down!"

Cassandra took the gun, pointed it at Gil and said, "You'd better do what my son says because he hates you almost as much as I do and he is very good at his craft. The Professor has taught him well. You see, my father was never a serial killer, but you put him in a position where the only thing he could think about every minute of his life is how you, Detective Gil Clifton, stole everything from him. His dignity was scornfully thrown to the humiliations of prison life. You stole his life and my life and now you must pay."

Gil turned his attention to Nathan, who stood about five feet away. He could almost see Nathan trying to figure how he was going to maneuver his captive into the seat.

"Why did you kill those people, Nathan?" Gil asked calmly.

Nathan pushed back the hood of his sweatshirt and scowled at Gil. With a mean sneer he said, "Shakespeare wrote in Julius Caesar, 'He that cuts off twenty years of life cuts off so many years of fearing death' act three scene one. I simply relieved them of their fears as I now shall relieve you of your fears. That will be the note you receive at your office tomorrow. You see, this will all be blamed on the serial killer. But you never found out who the serial killer was, and this will be the last murder. If we had killed you first, they may have found a connection to my mother and The Professor. This way, I get away without any suspicions, The Professor receives his revenge and my mother can feel comfort in the fact that you have paid for taking her father away from her. Now sit down!"

Gil controlled his voice, "Nathan, you killed all those people just to get at . . . ."

"Shut up and sit down!" screamed Cassandra as Nathan moved cautiously closer to Gil.

The front door was smashed open in a violent collision with the wall. Cassandra immediately turned towards the door and fired her gun wildly. A shot from Cornell's gun cut through the confusion and hit her in the chest. She fell to the floor in a grotesque heap. Nathan momentarily turned towards the chaos, so Gil jumped and tackled him to the ground. A police officer took control of Nathan and put him in handcuffs within seconds.

Gil crawled the few steps on his hands and knees and picked up Cassandra's head and held her in his arms. The red liquid oozing from her mouth stained his shirt while a small pool of thick blood formed on the floor. The smell of gunpowder was drifting heavily in the air.

With a faint gargled whisper she said, "Let me see my son. The last person I want to see before I die is you." She inhaled with a frantic gasp then slowly exhaled as her head went limp and fell slightly towards Gil's chest with her eyes in a fixated stare.

Gil could no longer hear her shallow, labored breathing. He laid her head on the floor and with two fingers gently pulled her eyelids closed.

***

# Epilog

## Bryan Martinson
## Arthur Farnsworth

Bryan Martinson, from the Camden Crime Unit (CCU), and Arthur Farnsworth, part of the Camden Law Enforcement Arterial Resources (CLEAR) unit, both testified at the murder trial of James Nathan Bowen. During the internal investigation of Mayor Alonso Veluchi the testimony of Bryan Martinson, his wife Luanne and his sister, Jennifer was heard about the events that took place at the El Toro Bistro. Luanne only testified to why she was asked to participate but it was Jennifer's and Bryan's testimony that was most effective. The two detectives still remain in their respective units.

## Martin Porter

Martin Porter was charged with giving false information to the police but because he relented and cooperated with authorities he was given a suspended sentence. He fell in disfavor with Salvatore Moratino and although there was no further mention of mob ties in the media Salvatore wanted to punish Martin for his role in cooperating with the police. Upon advice from his uncle, Alonso Veluchi, Martin left Camden to relocate in southern California. The Palovani family did not pursue the young man. However, Martin had a difficult time adjusting to a completely different life style and was arrested when he tried to rob a gas station in August of 2013. He was given a one year sentence.

## Mayor Alonso Veluchi

Mayor Alonso Veluchi was forced to resign his post in the summer of 2013. It was made public that he had participated in and was the principle architect of a kick-back scheme from Waverly Building and Contracting and several other companies who were awarded contracts with the City of Camden, New Jersey. His association with the Salvatore Moratino was not a crime but played an influential role with the County Commissioner's and during the Special Prosecutor's case against him. Alonso was arrested and on November 20, 2013 was sentenced to five years in prison.

## Brandt Waverly

Brandt Waverly was convicted of bribing a state official. At a special trial in January of 2014, he was ordered to pay the City of Camden a total of $3,500,000.00 for excessive construction costs billed to the city and sentenced to three years in prison. All assets of Waverly Building and Contracting and his home were seized to pay the levied fine. He made a plea deal back in early 2013 with the Special Prosecutor which helped in the conviction of the mayor and the fall of Sheriff Brisbane. He presented evidence of the kick-back scheme and his role in the unrecorded campaign contributions given to Carl Brisbane. He spent nine months in prison and was released in October of 2014. He moved to East Philadelphia and works as a manager of a night club owned by Good Eats, Inc., a front for the Palovani family's many business interests in Pennsylvania and New Jersey. The selling off of all of his assets were not enough to pay the fine because of debt encumbrances. The Camden City Council enacted new laws governing how city contracts shall be awarded.

## Sheriff Carl Brisbane

Sheriff Brisbane was also forced to resign his elected post due to community pressure applied when it was reported that he received undocumented campaign contributions. His marriage to Elaina ended in divorce in July of 2013. On October 12, 2013 he was found dead in his apartment of an apparent self-inflicted gunshot wound to the head. Elaina moved to Portland, Oregon and lived a quiet life in relative obscurity from the public eye.

## Captain Joseph McCadry

When the news broke of the capture of the Camden Killer, Captain McCadry went before the media and gave all of the credit to the task force mentioning each member by name and gave special recognition to the achievements in solving the case to Detectives Gil Clifton and Cornell Bush. Captain McCadry was selected as Sheriff Pro Tem when Carl Brisbane turned in his resignation effective on February 1, 2013 until a special election could be held in November. During his temporary assignment as sheriff he won the praise of his fellow officers. His popularity turnaround was due to his new understanding and his positive personal dealings with those who served under him. The media and an overwhelming majority of the police force were in support of the captain. He won the election and was sworn into office on December 1, 2013. He never mentioned to Cornell the accusation made by Gil and Gil was grateful for his silence on the matter.

## James 'The Professor' Macklevy

During the mob inquiries surrounding a murder that took place at the Booster Club Sports Bar they owned it was discovered that The Professor had solicited information from fellow inmates about obtaining potassium cyanide. His beating took place at the hands of a prisoner who was a member of the Palovani family and was assigned to obtain the name of the person who The Professor contacted. Inmate James 'The Professor' Macklevy confessed to the man that it was his grandson who wanted the poison. Salvatore Moratino was given that information but by the time he received the news Nathan had been arrested on an attempted murder charge involving an incident that occurred at his mother's home concerning Detective Gil Clifton. Later Nathan was also charged with seven counts of murder.

James Macklevy was married in 1969 and a daughter was born one year later. She was christened Kathleen Cassandra Macklevy. After five years of marriage The Professor filed for divorce and received custody of his daughter. She was sent to a foster home when he was arrested and convicted of several murders. The Professor first started getting visitations from his daughter in 1988 when she turned 18.

The Professor started indoctrinating Kathleen little by little with the injustice that was being levied upon him and how Detective Gil Clifton was to blame for his imprisonment because the detective was a self-serving egotist with no regard for human life. Kathleen's first child, named James Nathan Bowen, made the visits to his grandfather every month with his mother.

The Professor started laying the foundation for the murder of Gil Clifton using both his daughter and his grandchild. He groomed Nathan slowly and steadily in all of the subtleties of committing a murder at a very early age. Nathan would read books about forensic science, evidence gathering techniques, police procedures and famous murderers and how they were apprehended. The Professor also taught his grandson to appreciate the renderings of William Shakespeare. In 2006 the visitations became more frequent as The Professor schooled his enthusiastic 12-year old grandson in the minute details in the art of murder. He also practiced psychological brainwashing on his daughter who became utterly subservient to the dictates of her imprisoned father.

After his daughter was killed and his grandson was convicted of the murders of seven people, The Professor steadfastly held to his belief that law enforcement had a vendetta against his family. He never admitted any culpability.

# Kathleen Cassandra Macklevy Marshall

Kathleen Macklevy lived exclusively with her father after his divorce until she was 15 years old. She was very close to her father and idolized him. When he was sent to prison she was forbidden to see him and rebelled against her tyrannical foster parents who treated her badly. It was a traumatic experience and she was at a vulnerable age in her upbringing due to her affection for her father.

When she turned 18 she was pregnant by her boyfriend, Frederick Bowen. Kathleen tried to raise her son, who she named James Nathan Bowen, the best way she could and she always brought him to visit his grandfather, The Professor. In 1997, at the age of 27, Kathleen married Edgar Marshall but the marriage only lasted one year. It was evident to Edgar that his wife had some mental problems. After each monthly visit with her father she would return home with her son and begin a tirade of rambunctious and sinister mutterings. Then out of nowhere she would begin to laugh hysterically like a crazed hyena. Edgar could no longer tolerate her unstable behavior and filed for divorce.

By the time she turned 34, in 2004, and James Nathan was 10, The Professor had his daughter thoroughly convinced that she could avenge his incarceration. Kathleen started using her middle name exclusively and made her son use his middle name so that nobody would connect their names to her father. Kathleen or Cassandra as she liked to call herself now would teach Nathan to hate.

Cassandra was taught by The Professor how to change her personality to fit her surroundings. She demonstrated that she could control her emotions and once she was proficient to fool everyone she actively sought out Gil Clifton and used her newly acquired talent to garner his unfailing love for her.

## James Nathan Bowen

Nathan Bowen dropped out of high school and left his mother's care in 2008 when he was only 14. He still made the monthly visits with his mother to see The Professor. He survived on the streets by committing robberies, burglaries and shakedowns. This was the same year Cassandra met Gil Clifton and mother and son began the plot to kill the man responsible for their existence and The Professor's imprisonment. Nathan was hired by the police department in May of 2012 as part of a program to help teenagers who dropped out of high school develop their sense of worth.

Capital punishment was in effect in the state of New Jersey but the state had not executed anyone since 1963. In 1972 there was a nationwide ban on executions. However, in 1976 the U.S Supreme Court allowed states to start executing prisoners once again. Following in 1982, New Jersey reinstated the death penalty. Under the 1982 statute 228 capital trials were conducted in the state. Of those, the juries returned verdicts of death in 60 cases but 57 of those were overturned.

A series of bills were introduced in the State Assembly in 1992 to make it harder for the courts to overturn death sentence convictions. In January of 2006 New Jersey passed a one year moratorium on executions. Finally in December of 2007 a New Jersey General Assembly bill passed by a margin of 44-36 to abolish capital punishment in the state making it the 14th state without a death penalty and the first state to abolish it by legislative action rather than by judicial decision.

Nathan confessed to all of the murders. He was proud that he had 'gotten away' with so many. He never made the connection that he had not 'gotten away' because he would spend the rest of his life in prison. His confession was deemed admissible as evidence in his trial. He was sentenced to life in prison without the possibility of parole and is currently housed in maximum security at the New Jersey State Prison in Trenton, New Jersey.

# Detective Cornell Bush

When Detective Bush left East Jersey Prison after seeing the security tapes and identifying the images of The Professor's daughter and grandson as being Cassandra and Nathan he immediately returned to Camden. He called Dr. Ingrid Rolfheiser on his way back and she told him her interpretation of the last note they received. She told him the words engraved on William Shakespeare's grave were a warning. She took all of the quotes and deduced that the killer was pointing to Gil as being Shakespeare and the last note meaning his death. When Cornell told the profiler that Cassandra was The Professor's daughter and Nathan was her son, she explained what The Professor meant by 'the antagonist and the executioner are related'. She told him that Nathan could be the actual serial killer.

She also informed Cornell that she thought it meant Your Epitaph and said it more than likely meant that there was only one epitaph which corresponded to the month of January and the death of 'Shakespeare' would be on the eleventh because of the eleven letters in the words, *your epitaph*. She summarized that Detective Gil would be the next victim on this very date.

Cornell was shaken and called Captain McCadry. He quickly explained his theory to the captain when they met outside of Cassandra's home. Although the captain was skeptical of Cornell's reasoning because of what Gil had told him earlier of his suspicions, the captain, Cornell and the officer went and looked into the front window of the Cassandra's house and saw what was about to happen. They stormed the house through the front door and Cornell just missed being shot by Cassandra and he returned fire. His bullet lodged in her chest where she died at the scene.

His partner was devastated by the events that took place that night but understood that Cornell did not have a choice. Cornell was subsequently exonerated by Internal Affairs in a follow-up investigation into the shooting. He still continues his career in the homicide division.

## Detective Gil Clifton

Detective Gil was traumatized when his girlfriend of three and a half years turned out to be his mortal enemy. A police psychiatrist was assigned his case for emotional distress and for the next year Gil saw him on a weekly basis. Gil was changed by the events and his work as a detective became more of a job rather than a career. During this time his partner and Captain McCadry were very supportive of Gil and even though Gil's work was not up to standard, the captain never questioned Gil's abilities.

After his election, Sheriff McCadry had a meeting with Gil at Gil's request and it was the detective who ultimately decided to finally retire in 2014 after serving in law enforcement for 35 years. Sheriff McCadry officiated at Gil's retirement ceremony and praised the detective as one of the best the department ever had and challenged others to strive for the effectiveness of such a distinguished and dedicated detective. Gil was most appreciative of the kind words.

## William Shakespeare

One of the world's most widely regarded writers of English literature was born on April 26, 1564. His extensive works include 154 sonnets, 2 long narrative poems and 38 plays. The plays were written between 1589 and 1613 although exact verification is difficult to substantiate He was often called the Bard of Avon.

Translations of his plays have been made into every major living language and are performed more often than any other playwright. His works have been analyzed by many scholars from different cultures throughout the ages and very often with controversial interpretations.

Although Shakespeare declared himself in perfect health in March of 1616 during the signing of his will, he died a month later on April 23, 1616.

\*\*\*

*'The fault, dear Brutus, is not in our stars*
*But in ourselves'*

Julius Caesar Act 1 Scene 2

# ABOUT THE AUTHOR

Randy L. Hilmer, an Austin, Minnesota native who recently retired from the corporate business world in Las Vegas, Nevada and has written his third novel, <u>Murder Is An Education</u>. His previous works include <u>Murder Amongst Friends</u> and <u>BFF Spells Murder</u>. He is currently residing in Texas.

Made in the USA
Las Vegas, NV
29 March 2025